[handwritten inscription]

PENGUIN MODERN CLASSICS

ULTRAMARINE

Malcolm Lowry was born in 1909 at New Brighton and died in England in 1957. He was educated at the Leys School, Cambridge, and St Catharine's College. Between school and university he went to sea, working as deck-hand and trimmer for about eighteen months. His first novel, *Ultramarine*, was accepted for publication in 1932, but the typescript was stolen and the whole thing had to be rewritten from the penultimate version. It was finally published in 1933. He went to Paris that autumn, married his first wife in 1934, and wrote several short stories in Paris and Chartres before going to New York. Here he started a new novel, *In Ballast to the White Sea*, which he completed in 1936. He then left for Mexico. His first marriage broke up in 1938 and in 1939 he remarried and settled in British Columbia. During 1941–4, when he was living at Dollarton, he worked on the final version of *Under the Volcano*. In 1954 he finally returned to England. During half his writing life he lived in a squatter's shack, largely built by himself, near Vancouver. His *Selected Letters*, edited by H. Breit and Margerie Bonner Lowry, was published in 1967, and *Lunar Caustic*, part of a larger, uncompleted work, appeared in 1968. Margerie Bonner Lowry and Douglas Day completed, from Lowry's notes, the novel *Dark as the Grave wherein my Friend is Laid*, which is in Penguins. *Under the Volcano* and *Hear us O Lord from Thy Dwelling Place*, a volume of short stories, have also been published in Penguins.

'The style, the method, the verbal magic – the hallucinatory, drunken, nightmare world which only Lowry could evoke – are all here' – *The Times Literary Supplement*

'This young man's sea story is tight as a ripe seed-pod with all the towering, extravagant talent that was to flower' – Kenneth Allsop in the *Daily Mail*

'The author had himself made several such voyages, and his habit of keeping notes no doubt explains the realism of the crew's talk' – *The Times*

'. . . it is vivid and sensitive and the dialogue is very good' – *Sunday Telegraph*

MALCOLM LOWRY

ULTRAMARINE

a novel

PENGUIN BOOKS

Penguin Books Ltd, Harmondsworth, Middlesex, England
Penguin Books Australia Ltd, Ringwood, Victoria, Australia
Penguin Books Canada Ltd, 41 Steelcase Road West, Markham, Ontario, Canada
Penguin Books (N.Z.) Ltd, 182–190 Wairau Road, Auckland 10, New Zealand

—

First published by Jonathan Cape Ltd 1933
This new and revised edition first published by Jonathan Cape Ltd 1963
Published in Penguin Books 1974
Reprinted 1975
Copyright © Margerie Bonner Lowry, 1962

Made and printed in Great Britain by
Hazell Watson & Viney Ltd, Aylesbury, Bucks
Set in Linotype Times

INTRODUCTORY NOTE

Ultramarine was written following a sea voyage Malcolm Lowry made at eighteen, as a deck hand, cabin boy and ultimately a fireman's helper on a tramp steamer. The voyage provided him with the background for the novel, but its real theme is the necessity of the boy, Dana Hilliot, to prove himself as a man among other men.

Malcolm was graduated from The Leys, a public school in Cambridge, England, in 1927 and had been entered for Christ's College, Cambridge. But the sea was in his blood; he had read O'Neill and Joseph Conrad, and his home in Caldy, Cheshire, was near the great seaport of Liverpool. He finally persuaded his father to allow him to go to sea for a year before going to the University. His father, in what proved to be nearly a disastrous excess of good will, not only procured him the job on a freighter out of Liverpool, bound for the Far East, but even had him driven to the dock in the family limousine. This obviously did nothing to help Malcolm's standing among the crew, to whom he was already a green Outsider.

When he returned from this voyage, which had taken him through the Suez Canal to Shanghai, Hong Kong, Yokohama, Singapore and Vladivostock, he went up to St Catharine's College, Cambridge, in the fall of 1929. He had kept notes during the voyage (as he always did: I have his notes made on our walking tour of the Lake District in 1957, just prior to his death); from these notes he wrote first two short stories which were printed in the Cambridge magazine *Experiment*, edited by Gerald Noxon. This was Malcolm's first published work. One of the stories, 'Seductio Ad Absurdum', was chosen by E. J. O'Brien for the *Best British Short Stories of 1931*, and the second was given honourable mention for 1933. These stories were later incorporated in part into *Ultramarine*.

While he was working on the novel, he read *Blue Voyage*, by Conrad Aiken, and *The Ship Sails On*, by Nordahl Grieg. Both

7

of these made a deep impression on him and their influence can be seen plainly in *Ultramarine*. Malcolm was very young; but while there are certainly traces of imitativeness in the novel, it is also highly original and, for its time, experimental. Malcolm had sought out Aiken in Boston, in 1929, working his way over on a freighter; they returned to England and, at Malcolm's request, Aiken took him for a time as a pupil. They became fast friends and after Malcolm went up to Cambridge, he spent nearly all of his vacations with Aiken at Jeake's House, Rye, Sussex. In the long vacation of 1930, however, he made another sea voyage, working his way as a coal trimmer on a Norwegian freighter to Norway, to meet Nordahl Grieg, with whom he also established a friendship that lasted until Grieg's death.

Ultramarine was finished, I believe, during Malcolm's last term at Cambridge, and was accepted by a London publisher. Then followed the first of a long series of calamities which pursued his work relentlessly. (*In Ballast to the White Sea*, a novel, was completely destroyed when our house burned down in 1944; the manuscript of *Under the Volcano* was lost, and recovered.) One of the directors of the publishing firm had his briefcase stolen from his car: he was apparently away only a few moments, but when he returned, the briefcase was gone and with it the only typescript of *Ultramarine*.

There seem to be conflicting versions of what followed, and I can only report what has been said. Malcolm had written much of *Ultramarine* at Aiken's home, but he had completed the final draft at the home of a friend, Martin Case. Malcolm later told me he had thought the novel completely lost, since he had destroyed or thrown away all previous drafts and had not kept a copy of the final version, or even his notes taken on the voyage. But Martin Case, he said, had retrieved the cast-aside material and now came forward with it. When I met Case in London many years later, almost his first words to me were, 'Did you know I was the man who saved *Ultramarine* from my wastebasket?' Conrad Aiken, however, says that he had a version of the novel in his house in Rye, and that Malcolm knew it. But who can sort out what actually happened, after thirty years?

In any case, the novel was rewritten and first published by Jonathan Cape Ltd, London, in 1933. Readers of *Under the Volcano* and *Hear Us O Lord From Heaven Thy Dwelling Place* will find in *Ultramarine* many of the themes which were developed and deepened in the later books. The most important thing about this book, to me, is not its partially autobiographical content, but the fact that at this early period Malcolm was already so completely the self-conscious artist, in control of his material and his style.

This new edition of *Ultramarine* reproduces the changes Malcolm had made, over the years since 1933, in his own copy of the original edition. During the years we spent together he was always working on two or three projects simultaneously, and there was, too, a spasmodic running commentary on *Ultramarine*. I would come upon him with the battered copy in his hands staring at it angrily and making notes on the pages, or sometimes just holding it and gazing out of the window; he would turn to me and say, 'You know I must rewrite this someday.' I cannot remember exactly when he decided it was to be, in its rewritten form, the first volume in a group of six or seven novels, to be called collectively *The Voyage That Never Ends*. But it was at this time that he changed the name of the ship from *Nawab* to *Oedipus Tyrannus*, to conform with Hugh's ship in *Under the Volcano*. He had also intended changing the viewpoint in Chapter 3 from first person to third person, and had projected a much more extensive revision than that contained in the marginal notations I later transcribed.

One of his additions, the recurrent joke about Pat Murphy's goat, came about in this way: while we were living on the beach at Dollarton, British Columbia, we had as a neighbour and very dear friend an old man from the Isle of Man, Jimmy, a boat-builder. One stormy late afternoon in autumn, when Malcolm had stopped work and was having his tea, Jimmy dropped in. I have no recollection of what brought this to his mind, but at some point he began to chuckle and in his lilting Celtic voice came forth with this expression. Malcolm was simply delighted by it, he had the old man repeat it and he wrote it down. Then he jumped up from the table, took *Ultramarine* from the bookcase, and immediately made notations as to where he would use it, laughing all the while.

MARGERIE LOWRY

Los Angeles, California
June 1962

ULTRAMARINE

Take any brid and put it in a cage
And do al thyn entente and thy corage
To fostre it tenderly with mete and drinke
Of alle deyntees that thou canst bithinke
And keep it al-so clenly as thou may
And be his cage of gold never so gay
Yet hath this brid by twenty thousand fold
Lever in a forest that is rude and cold
Gon ete wormes and swich wrecchedness.

GEOFFREY CHAUCER, *Maunciples Tale*

Let who will speak against Sailors; they are the Glory and
Safeguard of the Land. And what would have become of Old
England long ago but for them?

SAMUEL RICHARDSON

1

'What is your name?'

'Dana Hilliot, ordinary seaman.'

'Where were you born?'

'Oslo.'

'How old are you?'

'Nineteen.'

'Where do you live?'

'Sea Road, Port Sunlight.'

'Any advance?'

'Yes –'

'Next please! What is your name?'

'Andersen Marthon Bredahl, cook.'

'Where were you born?'

'Tvedestrand.'

'How old are you?'

'Thirty-nine.'

'Where do you live?'

'Great Homer Street, Liverpool.'

'Any advance?'

'Yes –'

'Next please. What is your name?'

'Norman Leif, galley boy.'

'Where were you born?'

'Tvedestrand.'

'How old are you?'

'Twenty-nine.'

'Where do you live?'

'Great Homer Street, Liverpool.'

'Any advance?'

'Yes.'

'Next please –'

... Had he arrived anywhere, having been blown through this six weeks' engulfing darkness of interminable ritual spelt out by bells and jobs, a six weeks' whirlwind of suffering? I am on a ship, I am on a ship, and I am going to Japan, Hilliot repeated over and over again. Why? Perhaps the answers were too copious and melancholy anyway, and even if he had once evolved reasons, probably by now they had long ceased to be true.

Two bells sharply interrupted his thoughts. Five o'clock. He had been knocked off an hour. In another hour they would be alongside. Then he would turn to with the lamptrimmer and the port watch on the poop when the *Oedipus Tyrannus* would be made fast fore and aft. After that he was free.

Below him on the well deck some able seamen were under the bosun, working at the derricks. He watched them thoughtfully. At Tsjang-Tsjang, he supposed, the same interminable performance would be gone through as before; the usual stream of hawkers would surge on to the ship; the stevedores would clamber up the side from the lighters, or swing in on the derricks; the winchmen would soon be seated on their straw mats, and a shore serang, having been given a cigar by the first mate, would be watching an opportunity to steal his watch –

'... Hilliot! Come and lend a hand here.'

'Blast the bloody bosun,' said Hilliot, but slid down the poop ladder to the well deck, and set to with the others. A thick rope roared and ripped on the drum end of a winch, and the yellow derrick slowly rose toward the sky.

'... All right! That's enough! Take in the slack!' shouted the bosun. 'Square off them guys. Hilliot, you there! Take in the slack, take in the slack, I said! Somebody here, you, Horsey, show him how to do it, for Christ sake ... Hilliot, get out of that! Come here. Over here. Spell-oh, you others.'

'Now Hilliot,' he smiled, 'you can go back and dream to your heart's content. What are you standing there for like that? Go on. Now men,' he said, turning to the others immediately, 'now for the standing derricks on the fo'c'sle head!'

As Hilliot was going he met Andy the cook coming down the poop ladder. Oh Christ, he thought. But perhaps today would be an exception. He smiled. 'Hullo.' Andy scowled darkly at him, blocking the companion ladder. He was rolling up his sleeves, his enormous arms were tattooed all over; a Norwegian

16

flag, a barque in full sail, a heart, presumably, and God knows what. This was the sort of man to be, all right. But there was something weak about him, he had such a weak chin. Andy made no move to let Hilliot pass. He spat deliberately. 'Now look here,' he said, 'I've been twenty years at sea. And that bosun's been about the same time at sea. I've sailed with him twice, and he knows bloody well same as myself it doesn't pay to shout and be unkind to youngsters, not if you want them to do well, and he told me that he thought at first you would be one of his star turns. Well, I didn't say anything – I know your type – see? You would be one of his star turns ... And now you've turned out nothing but a goddam nuisance. And he can't help it. He can't help shouting at you – see? He doesn't like it, and you don't like it. And Christ knows I don't blame him – he can't help it if you're just a bloody senseless twat –'

'Look there,' Andy pointed over the side, 'that's where you want to be. See that?'

'?'

'It's a shark that's been following the ship. They always say they do that when someone's going to kick the bucket on board. Well, I'm sure I don't know, but I've heard fellows say sharks like little boys –'

Hilliot went past him up the ladder. He had found out it was no good doing anything about this sort of abuse; but it was worst of all coming from Andy, who could never get over toffs who came to sea. Perhaps they reminded him too much of those days twelve years before, when he had lost his ticket as a second mate on a tramp steamer out of Christiania. Matt told them that he had struck the new skipper, a Stavanger man, for calling him a Bergener.

Oh, well, he had heard all of it before in the forecastle. Useless, we don't know what sort of bloody man you are at all. Just a nancy. Not all of it had been unkind, but he knew that they thought he wasn't one of them. He had offered to fight, but the men had pulled out combs, or drummed their knives on the table. They didn't much care about his making a hero of himself in that way. 'We'll see you bloody well logged,' they had laughed. He watched the shark again, for which he felt now almost a sort of affection: it reminded him just now strangely of a swift in flight, then of a boomerang he had once had in Frognarsaeteren. Now it had disappeared.

On the poop Hilliot found a coil of rope. Lighting his pipe he tried to think clearly about the situation. Looking round him as if for enlightenment, he suddenly discovered that he was staring aloft, where a bird – a kind of gull or dunghawk, was it? – perched like a finial on the swaying mainmasthead, was preening its feathers. But the sun hurt his eyes. Lowering his head, he tried to calculate how long it had been there. Today, or was it yesterday? Two days ago. All the days were the same. The engine hammered out the same stroke, same beat, as yesterday. The forecastle was no lighter, no darker, than yesterday. Today, or is it yesterday? Yes, two days it must be. Two days – two months – two years. Six weeks. How remote, how incredibly remote it all seemed. It was ridiculous, but he could not get a clearer vision of anyone or anything at this moment than of the clerk in the Board of Trade office, and of the desk at which the signing on had taken place. And really he felt that he might not have been questioned there within the space of time at all, but in some dreamed other life ... I am on a ship, I am going to Japan – or aren't I? I have been to a certain number of ports – Port Said, Perim, Penang, Port Swettenham, Singapore, Kowloon, Shanghai. This evening we reach Tsjang-Tsjang ... No, there was precious little meaning left now in this life which so surprisingly had opened out before him. Nor could he see why he had ever been fool enough to set this seal upon such a wild self-dedication. No meaning at all, he thought, as he shook out some ash from his pipe. Not, at any rate, to himself, a man who believed himself to live in inverted, or introverted, commas; to a man who saw the whole damned business in a kind of benign stupor. His recollections were suddenly enlivened and illuminated, and he remembered how he had almost at once picked out Norman, the galley boy, with his fair hair falling over his eyes, and Andersen, the tattooed cook, him whom they called Andy, whose weakness of chin was complemented by his extraordinary dignified forehead, as those among the crew who would be his friends; he remembered just where he had stood, just what he had said, and how he said it, just how the silver compasses of the Liver Building clock had indicated half-past eleven. Norman and Andy – Norsemen (were they?). And once more his thoughts turned tenderly to Janet. She it was he apprehended in their voices, she, and no other. And he thought of that time when their families, for ten years neighbours in Port Sunlight, had met in Christiania when he was a boy, and how their love for each other had never changed. That winter they had seen an elk in the street, driven down from the mountains by starvation – everyone was on skis – all was white –

Then the ship's articles, meaningless to him, had been intoned by another sort of clerk – 'Seamen and firemen mutually to assist each other,' he had said, as though Britons and Norwegians, a Spaniard, an American, and a Greek would spend their watch below in a brotherly communion! A pale-faced fireman told him where he could get his clothes, and the two of them whiled away an hour lounging against the swimming bar of the Anchor.

'Nearly all of us are Norwegian our side of the fo'c'sle,' he said, 'but the two cooks are Norse too – the sailors are nearly all English on yours. I am the one they call Nikolai, but my real name is Wallae.' And the little fireman wrote down his name, 'Nikolai Wallae,' on an envelope for Hilliot –

'I was born in Norway too,' Hilliot had said when Nikolai had finished.

'I tink you are very much English all the same,' the other smiled. 'Our two cooks have been very long time in England, and now you don't tell them from Liverpool men. But Bredahl is the best cook I ever sailed with, I will say that,' he added magnanimously. 'Andy, they call him. Well, the ship is like that too, you knaw. She was built in Norway, but she has been under the English flag for years. Some of the notices are in Norwegian, nowadays –'

'It gives me such a queer feeling to think of that,' Hilliot had said.

'Oh, I don't knaw,' said Nikolai, 'English or Norwegian all the same. In Falmouth I make a fire to my pipe, you knaw, and I stood listening to the children playing – laughing over the same troubles as Norwegian children, you knaw. But Falmouth left me a souvenir of my wisit,' he added laughingly, 'the third time I have had a souvenir in England.'

'Did anything exciting happen last voyage?' Hilliot asked after a silence.

'Oh, well,' smiled Nikolai, 'the first mate got a dose. Going round the land in Finland we make a small wisit this trip to Helsingfors. The men they was all drunky – all the time, oh, there was much dispeace. They all had knives, you knaw, and they made a great fiest. But two mens and three womens they was all killed. By coffee time it is all forgotten. So this voyage we go to Japan again – long voyage. Oh, it will be a long voyage on our rotten ship.'

After agreeing to meet Nikolai on the *Oedipus Tyrannus*, he had gone with some of the sailors to a 'Mutual Aid Society Booth' in Cathcart Street, near the berth of the ship, a street dreary in the grainy rain, and loud with the clatter of shunting dockside engines and the shouts of floury stevedores; large drops had fallen in his eyes and down his neck, and he had felt desolate and miserable, wishing that he could have stayed in England with Janet forever. He had bought – good God, what had he bought? – a sea jersey, two singlets, a shanghai jacket and dungaree trousers, and a pair of sea boots. Norman, who bought a pair of Blücher boots, had advised him to get all those, as it was his first voyage. The boatswain, who was in the booth himself, crackling a huge yellow oilskin, had smiled at him kindly. 'You always want to hang up an oilskin, son, when it gets wet. Don't throw it around anywhere, like.'

But Andy, the chinless cook, yet with such a queer, gentle look in his eyes, from whom above all he would have liked a kind word, was unsympathetic and morose. 'Well, I don't want to say anything at all. I suppose you think it's pretty good coming to sea. Well, you'll find out pretty soon what it's like; it's just a question of working as hell – one port's the same as another. Yes, you'll find out pretty soon too. The bosun won't give you all the tiddley jobs to do by a long chalk –'

But the boatswain had given Hilliot a sly wink. 'You always want to keep in with the cook when you're in a ship.'

Later that day, before he returned home to say good-bye to Janet, he had heard Andy remark to the boatswain, 'I hate those bloody toffs who come to sea for experience ...' And indeed, after his guardian had driven him up to the wharf where the *Oedipus Tyrannus* was berthed, and after he had clambered out of the car and slung his seabag (from which the drum of his taropatch protruded) over his shoulder, the misery of parting with Janet overwhelmed him.

He saw it all again vividly, imagined himself wearing his blue suit, saw again his guardian wave good-bye to him, for Janet would not come to the ship, saw the two detectives on the *Oedipus Tyrannus*, the night watchman and the dirty firemen carrying wrenches; saw himself enter the forecastle and put his seabag in a bottom bunk before looking into the sailors' mess-room; saw the light burning, and the shadows which galloped over the long cedarwood table with forms round it, riveted to bulkheads, saw the stove with a twisted chimney on which a dishcloth and a pair of dungarees were drying. A skylight opened out on the poop. A crew list on a notice board contained his own name, spelt wrong – D. Heliot. There were some notices in English and others in Norwegian. It was all very strange, like a nightmare, but also exciting. At length one of the detectives came into the forecastle and invited him to the pantry for a cup of tea. The tea had condensed milk in it. The ship was not to sail till six o'clock the next morning –

After that he had continued, in the bitter watches when he knew the mind must be fixed on something or give way, to puzzle about Andy's attitude towards him. The way he reasoned to himself was as follows: unless he justified his presence on the ship in some way with the crew, Andy not only would never allow him into his companionship or turn to Hilliot's own, but also would resent his acceptance by Norman: he would remain a 'toff', a someone who didn't belong: and until he shone in some particular way in his work, or performed some act of heroism, they would never be the contented trio whose formation alone would render life tolerable on the *Oedipus Tyrannus* ... After they had knocked off they would have met, and talked or sung wild songs, together they would have gone ashore for a deaf, blind debauch; or in the eyes of the other members of the crew enjoyed a sort of collective status, some distinguishing name for their trio.

21

For to be accepted by Andy, who seemed to rule amidships as he did the forecastle, was not that to be accepted by the crew? And to be accepted by the crew, was not that also to justify himself to Janet? Certainly he was willing to do anything, cost what it might, to show that he was one of them, that he did belong. How often, for instance, as now, he had looked up at that mast with extraordinary desire! Some day, he felt, someone would be up there and lose his nerve: he, Dana Hilliot, would bring him down. The captain would call for him and congratulate him. 'My boy, I'm proud of you; you're a credit to the ship –' Actually on the ship they had taken very little notice of him except to put him in his place: as he was a first voyager he must go through the mill like any other bloody man on his first voyage, a man who went to sea for fun would go to hell for a pastime, that was the way of things. While Andy, pursuing logically his conduct in the Mutual Aid Society Booth, usually went out of his way to be cruel. He had called him 'Miss Hilliot'. 'Hurry up there, Miss Hilliot, seven bells gone half an hour ago, your ladyship.' And the stewards laughed. Yet he knew himself to be jealous of those splendid adventures ashore Andy boasted of so magnificently, adventures in which he himself would have dearly liked to have been included, and of which any first voyager might be truly envious: or was it, he asked himself, that he wished to boast of them merely, rather than to be included in them, to be part of them? Or was it that he really hated Andy, the 'chinless wonder,' that his interpretations of his attitude as friendly or jealous were both equally false? Anyway, it would be admirable to score off Andy sometime, about that particular physical defect. 'You chinless wonder,' he would snarl it out, with portentous contempt –

Hilliot suddenly lifted the skylight by which he was standing, and looked down into the messroom of the sailors' forecastle: tobacco smoke curled up towards him, and there was a fresh smell of soap and water. It was as if he had lifted the lid of a box of toys. There they all were: Ted opening a tin of condensed milk with a marline-spike; Horsey making an oilskin; and old Matt the riveter, who lived in Cheapside, and Cock – and the eternal card-players ... On the other side of the alley-way the twelve-to-four firemen's watch were having their supper, and the rest of the seamen had wandered over there for company. The others he saw in a mist, no figure stood out. The steering gear creaked: below, the engines were pounding: cloom – cloom – cloom – cloom. Andy must be in the galley, then. He dropped the skylight with a bang, and Matt's shout of 'Hey, what do you think you're doing?' was suddenly muffled.

Hilliot went to the rails, which vibrated as though they would uproot themselves from the deck. Fourteen men in a forecastle. How swiftly, how incredibly swiftly they had become a community; almost, he thought, a world ... World within world, sea within sea, void within void, the ultimate, the inescapable, the ninth circle. Great circle ... From his place there on the poop – for the fo'c'sle was 'aft' – Hilliot allowed himself to examine the visible structure of the ship, the deep red-leaded well deck, the companion ladders, the winch deck, and beneath it the white-painted galley with its geniculated, blackened smoke-stack splayed at the top like (he had said in a letter to Janet) a devastated cigar; the quartermasters' rooms and roundhouse amidships, up to the bridge, which the officer on watch paced ceaselessly with a slow rhythm, a rhythm sometimes ridiculously hastened by the swing of the sea. Once he saw him level his binoculars at the coast of Manchuria, a mile or so to port, sighted at five bells that morning, whose brutal mountains strode into the blazing sky. The brasswork burnt and flickered in the heat. Two firemen slept under an awning. Beyond, the bow did whatever a bow did, lolled back, then did it again ... It was getting late, they would be in port before night; in another half-hour –

But now it was absurd, he reflected, absurd to be preoccupied with anything besides this, this world so peculiarly his own. Why bother with Andy or anybody else? 'Yes, but if you had a chin I'd hit you on it.' That was what he would say when the time came, that was the way to treat him, the bastard toad –

He was walking, stimulated by his thoughts to angry energy, along the throbbing alleyway past the quartermasters' rooms. He walked briskly over the tarred seams, occasionally being forced into a side-step. The slight head wind blew coolly and clearly in his face, rumpling his chafing dungarees, stained with red lead, round his ankles. Cloom – cloom – cloom – cloom. The

23

Oedipus Tyrannus was making about eight knots, and her engines throbbed away cheerfully somewhere down below: a shovel clanged, and an endless spout of water and refuse was splashing from her rusty side into the Yellow Sea. And there, and there, the joyous derangement of the boundless waste must be their harbour. It was impossible to believe that so soon the sad sea horizons could melt into another land line, another climate, another people, and another port which would emerge, inevitably, out of such nothingness! The ship rose slowly to the slow blue combers, a ton of spray was flung to leeward, and that other sea, the sky, smiled happily down on her, on seamen and firemen alike, while a small Japanese fishing boat glimmered white against the black coast – oh, in spite of all, it was grand to be alive!

But the *Oedipus Tyrannus* poured out black smoke, mephitic and angry, from her one enormous funnel; its broad shadow slanted blackly along the sea to the horizon; it was the one smudge on all that glad serenity.

Hilliot poked his head in through an iron engine-room entrance, and watched the engines, a maelstrom of noise which crashed on his brain; it was humiliating to watch the nicety with which lever weight and fulcrum worked, opening and closing their hidden mechanisms and functioning with such an incomprehensible exactness! He thought of the whirling clanks holding horribly in their nerveless grip the penetrating shaft that turned the screws, that internal dynamic thing, the life of the ship. He walked round the fiddley, and looked down to the stokehold where Nikolai, who had scarcely noticed him once they were aboard the ship, seen through a shower of sparks, like red blossoms, was leaning heavily on his slice bar. He threw the slice away, and hastily shovelled more coal into the furnace, then he returned to his slice. The furnace blazed and roared, the flying clinkers were driving him further and further back into his corner, the fire was beating him. He dropped the slice with a curse, and mopped his face with his sweat rag. 'Plenty hard work!' he shouted grinning up at Hilliot, a firebright fiend. 'Like hell you say,' Hilliot muttered. As they spoke a trimmer emptied a bucket of water on the ashes, a tremendous cloud of steam hissed up with an awful sound, all was dark.

24

It was a pity that Nikolai always seemed to be down below, or skylarking with the other firemen: he could never see him. But despite their work the firemen seemed to get more fun out of life than the seamen, and seemed somehow to be better, in some queer way to be nearer God –

Suddenly three bells rang out, *tin tin tin,* and were echoed by the lookout man, and from far below, down in the engine room, three submarine notes floated up and were followed by the jangling of the telegraph, while the engine changed key.

What sorrow was it, stirring in his mind behind the screen of time? A note of memory merely, growing fainter, drowning in the yellow sea of his consciousness? Ah, but no, he had it, and following it, he suddenly saw a small boy, himself three years ago, inkstains on his fingers, sitting upon the steps of the swimming baths at school, his eyes burning . . . Forlorn! The very word is like a bell. To toll me back from thee to my sad self. What could it have been that reminded him? The engine, possibly, of the steam heater, that pounded there all day to warm the baths. Green water. It had been like plunging into moss . . . Left out of the swimming team, the important match against Uppingham. He had stolen out of last period to have a look on the notice board. A smell of peat smoke from the fens. He had got up when he saw two prefects coming down past the Hall, early from the Doctor's Greek Testament class:
εἰσί δὲ νῆες πολλαὶ ἐν ἀμφιάλῳ Ἰθακῆ– how did it go?

Later, in the dock, at Kowloon it was, he had been able to show that at least he was the fastest and most skilful swimmer on board the *Oedipus Tyrannus* – not that anyone cared. Norman had merely floundered about near the steps, and Andy, who couldn't swim at all, had come down stripped to the waist to show off his extraordinary tattoo marks and to laugh at Norman . . . Now the engine pounded on smoothly at its lower speed.

A moment later, Hilliot was walking again in the direction of the well deck. He was thinking of the first time he had seen Andy in the booth, where he had been talking about a girl at Tsintao, on the bathing beach there. How on earth, how, he asked himself, could a woman like a man with no chin? Yet Hilliot knew nothing about women, not in Andy's sense, although there was Janet of course; yes, perhaps that was precisely what was wrong with him ... His thoughts came to a sudden check. There was a commotion down on the well deck.

He descended the galley companion quickly, his hand slipping on the greasy leather of the hand rail as he did so. Before him, on the number six hatch, seamen and firemen – and Norman! – were gathered. They were staring up serenely at the long tapering mainmast aft, which swayed gently with the vibration and motion of the ship. Andy, outside the galley, a dishcloth under his arm, was staring heavenward impassively, his chin impudently *retrogressive,* thought Hilliot, as he joined a group of firemen. They had been interrupted in the middle of supper, and they stood on the hatch with cups of coffee in their fists watching in their shuddering dungarees. 'Wot's to do there?' one of them said, 'it's only a bloody dunghawk.' 'Well, I'm going up to get it anyhow,' replied Norman, 'it's been there for three bloody days and it will be bloody starving.' 'That's all right, I'll go,' said Hilliot, and made for the mast, but a big stoker in a chain-breaker singlet soon put a stop to that idea. 'Aw you, you'd pass out before you bloody got to that bloody table, you would,' he blustered, his tattooed arms (where had they been tattooed, Iloilo, Zamboanga?) folded on his heaving chest. And Norman, the Norwegian galley boy, who had been taking a spell, added, 'You want to mind your own bloody business, you do,' and when Hilliot raised his head again was already halfway up the mast. 'That's the boy, Norman,' they shouted. ''Urry up or it'll fly away.' 'That's the stuff, Sculls,' shouted the Englishmen. 'Good–good–fine! There now, come to Daddy.' 'Shut up or you'll scare the damn thing away,' put in Hilliot, who had to say something to justify his defeat. But they took no notice of him now that both seamen and firemen were so immensely pleased with their new hero.

It was a tricky job at the top, too, for as Hilliot could well see, Norman had to leave the topmost ladder, in itself a flimsy enough thing and scarcely ever used, to scramble as best he might up the great mast, which was so thick it was impossible for him to get his arms round it properly. Somehow he did it, returning to the deck with the bird securely captured under his dungaree jacket. He was quite covered with soot and grime,

26

which now was blowing directly on to the mast from the funnel. The bird was a grey carrier pigeon, tired and hungry. It had round its leg a message which no one could understand, for the one word decipherable was 'Swansea'. But it seemed to be, or Hilliot felt it to be, a message of reprieve.

'It can't have come from Swansea though, that's plain enough,' chattered Norman. 'It's on the other side of the world.'

'It's probably just some Englishman sending a message from one of the ports along the coast or something of that,' said one.

'A code –'

'A bloody dispatch,' mumbled one and all.

But there was a queer elation in the eyes of the Liverpool men as they shuffled into the forecastle. Something had happened, at any rate, a tender voice from home had whispered for a moment to those in exile, a mystery had shown its face among the solitudes. Hilliot stood apart from the others, leaning over the rail. After all . . .

What was the good of understanding? The pigeon might be the very messenger of love itself, but nothing would alter the fact that he had failed. He would hide his face from Janet forever, and walk in darkness for the rest of his days. Yet if he could only see her at this moment, she would give him another chance, she would be so gentle and companionable and tender. Her hands would be like sun gently brushing away the pain. His whole being was drowning in memories, the smells of Birkenhead and of Liverpool were again heavily about him, there was a coarse glitter in the cinema fronts, children stared at him strangely from the porches of public-houses. Janet would be waiting for him at the Crosville bus stop, with her red mackintosh and her umbrella, while silver straws of rain gently pattered on the green roof . . . 'Where shall we go? The Hippodrome or the Argyle? . . . I've heard there's a good show on at the Scala –'

Oh, his love for her was not surely the fool of time like the ship: it was the star to the wandering ship herself: even labour, the noble accomplishment of many years, could be turned into an hourglass, but his love was eternal.

Had he not sought her in the town and meadow and in the

sky? Had he not prayed to Jesus to give him rest, and found none until the hour he met her? . . . Again they seemed to be sitting together on the sand dunes, staring at the sky; great wings had whirred above them, stooping, dreaming, comforting, while the sand, imprinted like snow, had been whistled up about them by the wind. Beyond, a freighter carried their dreams with it, over the horizon. And there had been nothing that mattered, save only themselves and the blue day as they scampered like two children past the Hall Line shed to the harbour wall just in time to see the Norwegian tramp steamer *Oxenstjerna* pass through the gate of the inner dock, while a scratch four paused on their oars watching her entrance steadfastly, their striped singlets dancing in the afternoon sunlight.

It was strange that it should have been the *Oxenstjerna,* for they had seen her first in Norway, in Oslo Fjord. And he remembered later – three weeks later it was, the day before he joined the *Oedipus Tyrannus* – seeing her again sailing out mildly for Tromsö on the last stage of her journey and in the Liscard bus afterwards telling Janet the story (which did not impress her) of the Swedish minister after whom the ship was named who once took his small son to a Cabinet meeting, saying afterwards, 'My boy, now you see with how little wisdom the world is governed!'

And in Norway itself, where they had first fallen in love, over beyond Sandvika, the goat bells going tinkle tonkle tankle tunk –

Tin-tin: tin-tin: four bells rang sharply on the bridge, were echoed in the engine room, and then, far away, on the forecastle head. *Tin-tin: tin-tin* . . . Then Norman went away with the pigeon. They were under the lee of land now, and it grew calmer. The sky darkened, but almost imperceptibly, and the little waves danced and galloped, putting up their lips for the last kisses of the sun. A white motor boat came curtsying out of the harbour, rolling nearer and nearer: as she rounded the stern of the *Oedipus Tyrannus* her name was visible, *Mabel–Tsintao,* and all at once the order came for all hands to muster for a short-arm inspection while a fat doctor hauled himself up the Jacob's ladder.

The sailors were lined up amidships, and taken in order of

rating: Chips, the bosun, Lamps, Andy, Matt, Horsey, Ted, Norman, Pedro, Pardalo, Jules, and finally Hilliot himself. But Norman was not passed immediately; he had to go away for an interview, and came back hanging his head but smiling; the bosun and Andy laughed softly to themselves, but with all the good will in the world. '. . . Just fair wear and tear . . .' '. . . Borrow some of yours . . .' The doctor gave Hilliot a pat on the back. But it was soon over. The doctor descended the ladder cautiously – oh, how slowly; would he never get down it, the old sinner? – and the *Mabel* was away again in a minute, before the *Oedipus Tyrannus* started to warp into the river entrance which formed the port.

They were now sailing into Tsjang-Tsjang harbour, but the *Oedipus Tyrannus* did not feel the swell at all. A wild delight leapt in Hilliot's heart, there was gladness in his soul for a moment, but then the old despair came back, rending him with its claws. If Janet could only see this with him! The white roofs sparkled and flashed as if with rubies, sea gulls screamed and mewed over the funnel, blowing in the fresh wind that swept round the headland. And already he could see trams, streetcars, the crowds in the market: he could make out the letters on the Standard Oil Company wharf, SOCONY, while high up the mountain a train was climbing infinitely slowly. The sun bled away behind chalk-white fields. A bugle blew sharply from ashore. There was a war raging behind that headland too. He found himself laughing with excitement, but checked himself suddenly. What did another port mean to him now? Only another test of his steadfastness. Would he break his faith with Janet this time, after keeping it so long?

'It's all right, eh?' said Norman, beside him.

'Yes, it's all right,' nodded Hilliot. 'Grand.'

'You ought to see Rio.'

'Could it be better than this?'

'What! Better than this! You bet your life, boy. Well, ta-ta, I'm going to get some clean gear on . . . Watch your step, sonny, we may be in for a storm: the glass is dropping.' But the lamptrimmer suddenly appeared, uneasy and bellowing. 'Didn't you hear the bosun say all hands fore and aft?' he shouted to Hilliot. 'Get up on the poop, man, and stand by!'

29

'Horsey, you go and get steam up on them winches, will you, for Christ sake! I don't know what you think you're doing idling round the sodding ship.'

On the poop Hilliot caught his breath with joy. Tsjang-Tsjang was by now all around and over the *Oedipus Tyrannus*, with what he took to be rice fields, formed in steps, sloping perilously down to the sea: and the port itself, grouped at the bottom of the cliffs, was every moment growing larger. He heard – or was this in his mind? – the beating and crashing of gongs, ponderous, crepuscular, and slow. There was an endless procession of rickshaws going down the streets, threading the wildernesses.

The bugle blew again, a long call; and from ashore came the honk of motor horns. Then the *Oedipus Tyrannus'* siren roared, and the mountains and rice fields and the town roared back thunderously at the *Oedipus Tyrannus*. They were right inside the harbour now, gliding smoothly towards their berth past ships of many nations, and Hilliot's being thrilled to a dream of strange trafficking and curious merchandise.

'There we go, boys, there's the old Sapporo –'

'There's the Miki Bar!'

It seemed to Hilliot that a new, vague delight now possessed those standing on the poop before the second mate should give them the signal; half-joyous, half-tired faces gathered round the crowded bulwarks, eager yet humiliated eyes hailed with gladness this new port: tonight meant perhaps to a young scared face the marvels of an unknown land; to others the renewal of an old passion, long mutilated, drowned in sad sea horizons, clouded by the smoke of far cities and snoring volcanoes; to others a familiar seat in a low bar, a familiar rail at a counter, a stevedore they remembered, but always there must be girls in their thoughts, girls in bars, in dance halls, girls that crouched in dark hallways, in the shadows on the pavement, girls laughing up to them in linked quintets in the lamplight –

'There we go, boys. Is that old Mother Kulisorka standing outside, the old bitch? . . . Very sweet, jig-a-jig, eh.'

Soon the wharf loomed up, shutting out the town, which dropped away behind the sheds. The winches were set in motion: the wire runners were unwound from the hand winches, and as the command drifted aft to get a line ashore the *Oedipus*

Tyrannus quivered through her length under him, and her bow swung in towards the number seven wharf where the stevedores awaited her. Fenders were thrown overside. Hilliot picked up a heaving line, and also waited for an order. All at once the order came. He cast the line, which fell short. He cast again, and the stevedore trapped it by the monkey-knot: the bight of the hawser followed. The hawsers dropped and groaned and were hauled ashore. The *Oedipus Tyrannus,* travelling very slowly, straightened out until at last, going dead slow, she was parallel to the wharf. As he had witnessed half a dozen times before the derrick booms were swung overside, guys were slackened and tautened, and the stevedores and coolies tumbled aboard, swarming and cursing. Soon the lamptrimmer said, 'All right, men, that'll do for now,' and Hilliot got the seamen's supper from the galley, dodging swinging cargo. Then he washed up, hung his dishcloth to dry on the docking bridge, and changed into a clean singlet and clean dungarees. As was his custom in port he sat on the iron step of the forecastle entrance, watching number six hatch unload, and smoking a pipe. The winches continued their familiar rattle . . . That day it was, on the Saughall Massie Road, with Janet, when they had found the white campion on the windy hill, it was the only sound to break the stillness, the traction engine, and the sleep-shattering fall of white stones. Afterwards they had had tea at Hubbard and Martin's, in Grange Road . . . Now it must be the noise of winches that hissed and spluttered through the silence.

He rose and moved to one side to let a sailor, an American, out of the forecastle.

'Going ashore?' he asked the sailor.

'You bet your boots,' he replied. 'Going to give the girls a treat. You coming along to the shanties too?'

'No. No girls for me.'

'Well, I must be getting along. So long.'

'So long.'

He watched him dodging along the deck. With an absurd reflex ducking of the head he barely managed to escape ten crates of Pilsener which were swinging perilously past.

Well, why not? he asked himself as the sailor stepped off the gangway. Who was to prevent him going ashore anyway? Surely he was free, knocked off. Moreover had he not earned the right to his pleasures ashore? What stupid inner check prevented him, had prevented him at the last half-dozen ports, from having a woman? Janet need never know. Yes – why should he, of all people, prefer to remain aboard, dreaming sadly of he knew not what while the others roared in the bars of brothels, and tavern doors were on the swing?

The stevedores paused at their work, the winches were silent for a moment, and Hilliot, his mind confused and fluctuating, took his opportunity to escape amidships, making for the galley companion from which the handrails had been temporarily removed. At the top he turned to pause outside the galley, looking down into the well deck. No: he would stop aboard, leave the evil to the blind and the dumb – let them return to their own vomit.

But in his heart he knew himself to be afraid; afraid of living, afraid of manhood, and now he muttered something that was very like a prayer: 'Please God, I love Janet so. O Lord, show me the way.'

From where he stood Hilliot looking down could see the word SEAMEN on the worn brass plate of the forecastle entrance, and on the starboard side a similar dark and cavernous entrance was surmounted by a similar plate – FIREMEN . . . Seamen! That had been his home for two months, and would continue to be for another ten months. Whenever he recalled his first few weeks on the job he recalled the skipper's first inspection of the boatswain's messroom, which he had had to scrub out by five bells that first awful Monday: the struggle to weld brain and muscle into something like union: the bells spelling out those first wingless and most crawling hours. His hands, stinging from caustic soda. The Pyrene extinguisher upon whose gangrened surface no amount of what the skipper was pleased to call 'elbow grease' could produce the ghost of a semblance of a shine: and finally at five bells the skipper's entrance with the words, 'Well, this place isn't as clean as it used to be – all right, you can go out on deck now.' His utter fury and disappointment all the morning. And then, when at one bell he had to fetch the watch's chow from the galley, all had been made infinitely more bitter by Andy, who cried, 'Why, here's Miss Bloody Hilliot coming for the watch's chow, but seven bells is the time to come for that, not half-past bloody eleven, you poor twat.' Good God, after all this, after all the blood and agony and the sweat, didn't he deserve it?

Had he no right, as others, to seek the 'star that shines above the lives of men'?

As he brooded Norman came up beside him, changed and washed, carrying a cage.

'What've you got there?' asked Hilliot, and suddenly felt foolish at the obviousness of the question.

'Bosun's old canary cage,' said Norman. 'He just lent it to me. I don't think it's big enough, but still, it'll have to do for the time being.'

Norman settled the cage on top of the breadlocker. 'I'll make another one tomorrow, and clip the little bastard's wings.'

'I say, Norman,' said Hilliot, who now had to go on talking, 'I wonder why it had a message from Swansea round its leg. It makes you think, that, doesn't it? In the Yellow Sea.'

'Maybe some fellow had it on a Welsh boat round here, as a pet. One of those bloody St Mary Axe boats, the *Leeway*, is knocking round here. Only its wings aren't clipped.'

'I had the time of my life in Swansea once. I was playing football down there,' smiled Hilliot reminiscently, 'and afterwards we all went round the town, well, you know how it goes.'

'I suppose you sheiked them all right,' Norman said curiously.

Hilliot flushed.

'Yes – well, a crowd of us all picked up tarts, if that's what you mean. But we just took them to the cinema, there was nothing more to it than that . . . But look here, Norman, we're not talking about that. What I really meant to say to you is that you know I was just damned well afraid to go up that mast.'

'Oh no,' laughed Norman. 'What would you want to go climbing up topmasts for, anyway, for Jesus sake. They weren't made to climb . . . Safer on deck, eh? No, it's a twat's game to go climbing topmasts for no reason at all.'

'No, there *was* a reason,' insisted Hilliot, 'but I just didn't like to risk that topmast . . . I think I'll go ashore and just get the hell out of it. Are you coming, Norman?'

'Yes, I'm going when Andy's finished dressing. But what is it – are you going running after women, or what?'

'Yes,' replied Hilliot, with determination, but feeling a queer pang of terror.

But Norman's voice suddenly grew grave and distressed.

'Steer clear of the Janes here, I should. You know what v.d. is, don't you?' Norman looked round guiltily as he spoke. 'Now I don't mind telling you this because you're a young fellow that ought to know. Now, I've been unlucky! Voyage before last, in Muji, it was, I picked it up, the finest dose you ever saw, voyage before last in the *Maharajah* – she's lying in this port now . . . And I wasn't quite right when I got home. And then next time I got home the missus is having a kid, see. Wind up! Well, who wouldn't, eh? I was in the hell of a state. Still, it all came all right in the end, you know . . . It's all the same in the harbour too. See what I mean? Trip before last I went bathing in this bloody place, down off a pilot ladder, never been down a pilot ladder before and all, it's bloody worse coming up too and all. Then I see our QM standing on the winch deck, you know, shouting and waving his arms like a pair of bloody scissors. Well, every damn fool knows what that means – a shark, eh? – God, I swam like hell. Just got on the pilot ladder in time, too. Dunno if it's the same now, heard a rumour there aren't any now, but I don't bloody well believe it. It's not worth taking the risk, is it? Of course I can't swim like you, you know. Just do it for the fun of the thing like. But I'll tell you I swam that time and I was up that bloody ladder as fast as hell, you know. No more bathing for me in this bloody place. And it's the same in the bloody port. The old shark gets you. Then it eats you, bit by bit.'

'She didn't have the kid.'

'No – she didn't . . . But look here, you take my advice. Steer clear of the Janes in this dump.'

'I see what you mean all right, Norman, but it's not so easy when the crowd do nothing but rag me from morning to night. I can't make them understand that I love one girl at home more than anything else in the world, and mean to be faithful to her.'

'They'd understand all right,' said Norman stiffly, 'if they believed you. But you don't act up to it. You've been oiled in every port all the way up the bloody coast. You've got a girl, haven't you? Well, it's a funny thing that everybody knows you haven't had any letters this voyage. And it's a funny thing you don't buy her some nice curios instead of trying to wrap the deck round you for a blanket in every port.'

Hilliot stared for a moment down into the depths of his own contemptibleness, and searched vainly there for a truth. Then he found words.

'I *am* trying to be faithful to her, all the same,' he said at last very slowly. 'As for letters, I didn't give her any posting dates till we got to Shanghai. After all, it's only a tramp, and we don't know where we're going and she wouldn't want the sort of letter she wrote me to go astray.'

'Well, it's nothing to do with me,' said Norman. 'But still, what I said before goes – you never know what sort of thing you may pick up in these ports. Of course there's no need to get anything.'

'No. I've heard that too. That there's no *need* to get anything –'

When Andy came up beside Norman he said nothing, but started to roll a cigarette. He had exchanged his white cap and singlet and soup-stained check trousers of the working day for a trilby hat, a blue reefer jacket, and blue trousers, freshly pressed. Blue trousers and brown shoes, that was the way with the *Oedipus Tyrannus* push when they went ashore! This was a new Andy, Andy with his go-ashore suit, all dolled up to go ashore, Andy the chinless wonder, going to give the girls a treat . . . Yet Hilliot felt he could not ask to join them. No, a second cook and a galley boy would not like to be seen drinking in the company of a deck boy who got only fifty shillings a month. Why, even Pong, the Chinese galley boy of the firemen's forecastle, got more than that: and, for that matter, so did Ginger, the pantry boy, who had confessed to Hilliot one night in the Red Sea that his ambition was to become a butcher on a mail boat. Fifty shillings a month! Norman's salary was nearly three times that amount, and Andy's was something quite beyond his ken . . . Andy was puffing at the newly rolled cigarette, and now he looked with contempt at Hilliot.

'I've heard the skipper's going to give you an AB's job,' he sneered. 'That's as a reward for climbing the mainmast, eh? Rescuing a dunghawk. Well, I'm glad to hear of your promotion. It certainly is about time you did something. You've been nothing but a bloody nuisance on this ship since you came on it . . . Coming, Norm?'

'Well. Good night,' said Norman, for decency's sake, and gave a condescending nod to Hilliot. 'Come on, Andy, let's go!' Hilliot looked after them as they shambled down the alleyway, a patch on Andy's trousers giving him from behind, curiously, a rather shabby look after all, and watched them descend the gangway cautiously . . . Now they were gone.

Soon he stole after them.

Behind the numbered sheds the town roared. A jet of steam shot up behind the sheds, there was the stuttering crash of assimilating buffers, and an unseen dockside train started on its way, ringing its desolate bell of warning. A rickshaw wallah, leaning on the shafts of his jinrickshaw, looked up at the ship: aloft giant cranes dipped and beckoned. Dodging bales and boxes he crossed the wharf and continued through an open shed until he came to a square. Behind the sheds he heard the noise of the *Oedipus Tyrannus* loading.

He was standing by a sign: *Seamen's Temperance Restaurant – all welcome*. Then he remembered that he would get no money from the purser until the next day – he was penniless. Still, what was there to see? Nothing: nothing at all. It was the same in any seaport town at night. He might as well be back in Liverpool – or Swansea!

Looking from the square down a long street he could see tram lines, and far away, two dim figures crossing them. Could they be Norman and Andy?

Oh, it was no good persuading himself to the contrary; to be left out on a night like this was worse than death itself. At home, perhaps, it would be daytime, and the same commonplace faces passed down the street; they were those who carried the whole horizon of their lives in their pocket. And so they would be buried in the commonplace, everyday grave.

But here there was a low whisper from the harbour taverns, there was the smell of the East, lovers were met with a call, a

36

glance, a smile; a seething phosphorescent gleaming rolled along the cold coast of the houses; it was the eternal vortex of youth itself. Thou shalt not –

But don't be a fool, Dana, it's not so much the vengeance of the Lord as the lack of a little chemical knowledge.

All at once Hilliot started. Near him were the skipper and the mate, and judging by their voices, they were starting an argument. Hilliot crept into the shadow of a godown and waited for the fun to begin.

'Well, what the bloody hell has that got to do with you? Surely a mate of a ship's got a right the same as any other bloody man to have his –'

'– Look here, who are you talking to? If you weren't a friend of mine I'd see to it you never came back in this company, now I'm telling you straight –'

'– Oh, for Christ sake, Billy, we're ashore now –'

'That doesn't make any bloody difference.'

'– Trocadero! –'

'– Oh, have your –'

'– What's that –?'

'– up your ear –'

It won't do to be seen skulking about by the skipper, thought Hilliot, and he cautiously re-entered the shed. The *Oedipus Tyrannus,* sea-weary, leant up against the wharf. Beyond were the black ghosts of ships in the harbour.

His evening had not been absolutely wasted after all, he told himself; he had heard something nobody was meant to hear. Who'd have thought it, the skipper and the mate! And a laconic joy possessed him as he climbed the gangway.

'Well,' said the gangway quartermaster, 'you haven't been ashore very long.'

'No, I didn't want to be seen hanging about by the skipper. I never got permission to go ashore, you see, and there were the skipper and the mate quarrelling on the wharf. Besides, I don't get any money till tomorrow.'

'I could lend you a Hong Kong dollar,' said the quarter-master, 'but I'm afraid that wouldn't be much good to you here. But I'll tell you what – I'm just coming off watch. Come along to my room and have a slice of old squareface.'

The quartermaster had one green eye, and one brown one, and Hilliot knew he came from King's Lynn, the decaying port in the wilds of Norfolk.

They walked along the alleyway, past a bunker hatch, and an engine-room entrance, towards the quartermaster's room. The quartermaster squeezed his arm, feeling the thickness of the muscle, and Hilliot recoiled. However, he said, 'It's good of you to ask me in, QM, thanks.' The door was on the hook, the electric light was on, and the brass sill burned brightly. They went in, and Hilliot sat down while the quartermaster reached the gin bottle from a cupboard.

'Now you wouldn't think it,' began the quartermaster, 'but I'm an educated man, respectable. Well, I know you are. Now you don't need to tell me anything. I'm a very blunt man, plain speaking, I say what I think. Now the very first time I see you on this whore ship – you come in a car, didn't you? – Christ knows what he's going on this packet for, I says to myself, eh? But let me tell you something. I've got a car myself at home. Yes, and I drive it at sixty miles an hour – with myself at the wheel! Yes. Don't wear no coat. No. Never wear no coat. But, anyhow, that doesn't matter . . . Have some water. No – don't though. This damned water glass's full of mozzies: that's a sure way to get malaria. The second steward nearly croaked himself doing that, last voyage. And it's never really left him since . . . Well, here's a go. What made you come to sea, anyway?'

'Search me,' said Hilliot. 'To amuse myself, I suppose.'

'Well, a man who'd go to sea for fun'd go to hell for a pastime,' said the quartermaster, drinking his gin.

'That's what Andy said to me first time I saw him.'

'It's an old sailor expression, like more days more dollars . . . Got any cigarette papers, eh?'

'No: I smoke a pipe.'

'Yes – you know, my first voyage in sail, if I'd dared to smoke a pipe, I'd have had it knocked out of my mouth. Still, they're all different now. They say there's not much sailors can do now that the firemen can't. But the old bosun's knocking hell out of you, isn't he?'

'He kept me under winches right through the Red Sea, he sent me up the funnel before I'd learnt how to knot a bosun's chair properly. And he turned me to, this afternoon when I was knocked off, God damn his eyes.'

The quartermaster winked his green eye, solemnly. 'What were daddy and the chief officer quarrelling about, eh?' he asked mysteriously.

'It appears that the mate wanted to go to the Trocadero, and the skipper thought it was a bore.'

'Aw: they're always quarrelling, those two. Never mind them. Andy and Norman've gone ashore together, eh? Andy's a good sort, eh? So's Norman. Norman oughtn't to be a sailor at all: what he really wants to do is to grow another inch and be a policeman . . . He's always telling me that. He's got a nerve on him, that boy has. What do you think about him getting that mickey down today, eh? Good, eh? No bloody ladder – right up there!'

'Sure,' said Hilliot. 'I was watching.'

'Sure it was good, eh. But you wouldn't believe me if I was to tell you that that boy got all poxed up to the eyeballs, voyage before last – I was with him – it was a shame – you'd never believe me. Married, too. Yes, he was poxed all the way to hell.'

Hilliot was silent.

Eight bells were struck on a ship out in the harbour. *Tin-tin: tin-tin: tin-tin: tin-tin*. The bells of hell, ringing for Norman.

'But I don't see what those fellows want to go ashore for at all. Straight I don't. A young chap like you doesn't want to go getting mixed up with any of the tail here . . . Have another drink . . .'

'Well, why not, why not, why not?' said Hilliot. 'I don't go running after women, because I'm trying to be faithful to one at home. Otherwise I see no reason – provided you take proper precautions.'

'Now I'm going to be frank with you, eh?' said the quartermaster. 'I don't believe in going ashore when you can get all you want right here aboard. Now I've had it on every ship I've been in, and I'm not going to be disappointed on this one. Come on now: what do you say, eh?'

'Nothing of that,' said Hilliot, although long before anything was said he was already apprehending the trend of the

39

quartermaster's remarks, and was already composing an excuse before he had been in there a minute.

'No offence meant.'

'All right: I've been drinking your gin anyway . . . ,' replied Hilliot. 'But as a matter of fact, I'm going to have another.' He poured himself out about three-quarters of a tumbler, finishing the bottle, and drank it immediately, watching the quartermaster. The quartermaster was silent. Hilliot put down his glass. Then he went out, closing the door with deliberation.

Outside he laughed, so crazily that he wondered suddenly: shall I die laughing like this? He put one hand on the deck rail, and looked at his hand. Was he laughing, then, for a misery that was so great that all he could see was that his fingernails were incredibly dilapidated; or was he drunk? But he was still laughing when again he came to the engine-room entrance, and, on an impulse, stepped over the iron sill. Starting to walk round the fiddley, he paused a moment by the board where the carpenter had chalked up the tank soundings. From the fiddley he could now see down the narrow sheer ladders to the engine room, whose upper labyrinths were all about him. How easy, how desperately easy, it would be to put an end to everything. A sudden impetus of mind, the relaxing of a muscle, and it would all be over. He seated himself on one of the top rungs . . . Buried at sea. With firebars at his feet. For Thine is the kingdom, the power, and the glory, forever and ever, Amen. God. Gawd. Good. Good Gordon Highlanders . . . Janet's favourite oath. Yes; he might well look down at the engine room, as he was doing, with such bewilderment, yes indeed! He should contemplate it! He should worry. For here as nowhere else he could understand precisely what was so all-poisoning in him, this incapacity to position things and see them in their places . . . A murmur of voices passing the entrance dwindled into the polyphony of the screeching coolies, and the acceleration of winches, whose rattle was becoming more and more infrequent, was resumed. Somebody else going ashore? Would they meet Norman and Andy? Andy, the Dutchman's breeches, ha ha! Merry laughter. On the board, also, at school, Pythagoras. The small child liked Pythagoras, or it might have been Euclid, because he drew upon the sand (how delightful!) such nice pictures of the moon. But at school geometry had puzzled Hilliot and frightened him, had become to him eventually a sort of monster. It had resolved itself into a human and dreadful shape of perpendicularly arranged concentric circles with a long tangent of arms, with huge hands throttling and triangular. Also, he remembered, he was forever losing his instruments and making a fool of himself in class, the mathematics teacher having once actually given permission for the whole form to crowd around to watch his pathetic attempts (with his clumsy spatular hands he had always hated) to create a regular hexagon. To make it worse his compasses, which he said he had lent to Milhench of the Fifth (who anyway was in the Sanatorium), were discovered by the master himself in the chalk box . . . This was it, this was always it, this lack of order in his life which even now permitted him only vaguely to be aware of the ship as a sort of Moloch, as a warehouse. Nor was it enough to know that she also visited lands where the grape vines came down to the water, or where the sun bled away behind chalk-white fields. No economic, no related perception of the ship was possible to him. He felt he would never be able to understand the mysteries and tortuousnesses of tangled derrick guys and winch levers: this stilled engine, which nevertheless groaned and panted after its long journey in a way all its own, and into which he was now peering with despair, was equally meaningless and imponderable at sea, when it was teeming chaos. And now, in this very chaos of a motionless engine, those rods – were they not waiting, longing perhaps, for the time they should grasp other rods in rhythmical and revolting confusion? The desire of the link for the pivot; of the lever weight for the fulcrum ... Yet in the engine of the *Oedipus Tyrannus*, with whose disunion, as perceived by him, he felt his sympathy to be perfect, existed also that revolution from complex he so desired: and it was precisely this order, more particularly regarding Janet, but also in regard to Andy and Norman – and the quartermaster! – that his consciousness lacked – was it lacking in intensity too? – and would, so far as he could see, always lack. Order, do you hear? Listening, Janet? Would you really believe that Dana Hilliot, who loves you, stood here with gin-laden breath in a ship's engine room in China thinking these

41

things . . . But perhaps, he reflected, what he didn't see, what he might never know, were just those few instants, those few white flowers of memory which were so precious to Janet. Ah, what could they be? That walk they had in the country, over the fields from Upton, 'Public footpath to Thingwall'. Some stupid boy (or was he, on the contrary, being profound) had turned the red signpost in the opposite direction, towards Wallasey, towards Leasowe, towards the sea. Warm fresh bread and butter with their tea. It was in Greasby they saw the horse in the stable – 'dreaming and warm', she had read of someone calling a stable – and in Upton the slate-paved dairy, cold and clear: the primroses in Marples field under the yellow gorse. 'And those flowres white and redde swich as men callen daisies in our town.' Over the grey familiar fields to happy go. How could she ever tell him of it? How, for that matter, could he ever tell her of it? Extraordinary, he thought, slowly fingering his pipe, that those moments that had brought them most happiness should sound like a recital, an inventory, of the lyrist's stock-in-trade . . . Coming along to the shanties tonight? the sailor had asked him. Selah. Over the grey, familiar Masefield to happy go. Forgive him, for he knows not what he does . . . Yet it was John, who started his career writing sea shanties, and John, ship's carpenter, who sent the last wedge spinning out of the cleat, *crack, crack, crack,* while the tall ship sailed on, merrily plunging and creaking, the grey-faced quartermaster, amorphous, fixing his swimming green eye (the other one was brown) upon a singing star. Matthew, Mark, Luke and John, went to bed with their trousers on. The carpenter's hammer swinging – swinging –

A vague memory of something learnt in childhood raised its pale face from the mists, whispering, Go on, little Jesus, play on with your nails in Nazareth: Set them out in rows on the shaving-strewn floor! You have asked what your father Joseph is working with, and he has replied, 'A hammer.' But don't ask him any further questions, don't ask him what the hammer is for, he must get his work finished. No – for a hammer is to drive nails in with, and it is by the eight nails and the great hammer that you shall die.

No, forgive me, you can save yourself if you will, save yourself, ah, for my sake. Your life will hold no terror, there will be no carnage, no smouldering cities and starving children, everything will be as kind and as good as the first night in the manger, with the straw crackling like harsh rain at the window, while outside is the deep winter, dark and cold. Oh save me, Jesus, save me, don't let me be like this always, don't let me die like this.

Save yourself. The ship will get you if you deserve it.

He shivered. Without his noticing it, the noise of the loading had stopped. All was quiet as he walked again along the deck: the stevedores had gone. Somewhere, on another ship perhaps, a violin was being played, the music was blown about him – a sailor or a fireman rehearsing his pride. Do you see the garden at home with its snow of blooms?

The eight-to-twelve gangway quartermaster, stoking the galley fires, peered round at him.

'Good night.'

'Good night.'

The light burning in the forecastle was the lamp of sanctuary; it seemed to Hilliot now that the *Oedipus Tyrannus* had a manifold security: she was his harbour; he would lie in the arms of the ship, the derricks would fold about him like wings, sleep would bring with it a tender dream of home, of suns and fields and barns: tonight, perhaps, he would talk to Janet again. He jumped the perforated steam piping, passed the carpenter's shop, the clusterlocker and the lamplocker and ducked into the blackness of the forecastle alleyway opening. He found his bunk and sat on it, gently stroking the hairy mattress, the donkey's breakfast'. Then he lay down flat on his back. He began slowly to go to sleep, gliding, as it were, down a steep incline. Thousands of children at New Brighton, on a Bank Holiday, making for the sands with their pails and shovels, glided with him: suddenly a man glared at him in a public convenience. Please drop used towels in hopper below. What was a hopper? He had never found out. Then he was walking again with Janet, slowly, through the crowd. Electric lights swam past. Gas jets, crocus-coloured, steadily flared and whirred. The shouts and cries of the market rose and fell about them like the breathing of a monster. Above, the moon soared and

43

galloped through a dark, tempestuous sky. All at once, every lamp in the street exploded, their globes flew out, darted into the sky, and the street became alive with eyes; eyes greatly dilated, dripping dry scurf, or glued with viscid gum: eyes which held eternity in the fixedness of their stare: eyes which wavered, and spread, and, diminishing rapidly, were catapulted east and west; eyes that were the gutted windows of a cathedral, blackened, emptiness of the brain, through which bats and ravens wheeled enormously, leathern foulnesses, heeling over in the dry winds: but one eye plunged up at him from the morass, stared at him unwinkingly. It was the eye of a pigeon, moist and alone, crying. Where would he die? At sea! His body buoyed by slow sustained suspension, pushed at by sea strawberries and sea sponges and fiddler crabs. Coiling and heaving, buzzing and falling. Humus for the sea polyps, for the ocean-storming behemoth. But where are your instruments, Hilliot? I lent them, sir, yesterday, to Milhench. But life was like that. Come and see the regular hexagon of Dana Hilliot, observing particularly his Promethean liver, chewed by the eagle (by special request) – week-end prices! Step up, ladies and gents, step up, ladies and gents: the Campbells are coming, yo ho, yo ho: the Campbells are coming along the grey familiar fields to happy go: πολλὰ δ᾽ ἄναντα κάταντα πάραντά τε δόχμιά τ᾽ ἦλθον; good Gordon Highlanders, eh. Lost without a compass. I am on a ship. I am on a ship, and I am going to Japan. Lost. Lost. Lost.

2

'Arise and shine. The men'll be wanting their coffee, Hilliot. Hey, I'm not going on shaking you all day, gawd blimey – wake up and make the coffee!'

'What's the time?'

'Nearly 'arf-past five. Hurry up! The men'll be having your life.'

'Well, it's your business to get me up, quarter. How many bells is it?'

'There aren't any, you poor twit. We're tied up to the wharf –'

'Well, they were going last night ... anyhow you know what I mean. You can hear them on the ships out in the harbour, can't you? All right, I'll get up.'

'Don't forget to call the petty officers.'

'Oh shut up!'

'Don't say shut up to me, you lousy deck boy! Going ashore tonight? ... Aw, kick my bloody arse –'

Lamplocker. Clusterlocker. Carpenter's Shop.

Firemen. Oedipus Tyrannus – Liverpool. Tin-tin: tin.

'Good morning, Norman. Had a good night, eh?'

'Oh yes! Yes! Fine, boy, fine!'

'Andy in a good temper this morning?'

' 'E's all right, you know. Wot's to do about Andy?'

'Nothing. I just wondered, that's all.'

'I should be careful of him if I were you, my son. He's a nasty man to get the wrong side of – especially for you – I mean your always being in and out of the galley, like.'

'What doesn't he like about me?'

'He thinks you're doing a good lad out of his job, you know.'

'Good God! It's surely up to the lad to get the job himself, isn't it?'

'You bet your boots on that, sonny. But he says you had influence at the office.'

'Well, so I had! I told you that myself.'

'Don't you bother yourself about it, son. Ten months from now we'll all be docked in Liverpool, anyhow!'

'You bet! Ten long months. But it'll be all right then, eh?'

'Yes, all right, eh?'

Certified for the Use of Six Apprentices. Oedipus Tyrannus, Liverpool. Galley. Lamptrimmer. Carpenter. Bosun.

'Oh, so it's you. Well, I've been up ten minutes and I've seen the mate and got the orders for the day while you've been messing around doing sweet Fanny Adams!'

'I'm sorry, bosun.'

'Sorry bosun! *Sorry, bosun!* It's always sorry, bosun! I'll sorry bloody bosun you!'

'Yes.'

'I thought at first you was doing well. I though you might turn out one of my star turns. Highton, he's one of the quartermasters on this ship now, he was one of my boys once; one of my star turns! They called him the King of the Derricks. But you're nothing but a goddam nuisance. Have you made the coffee yet?'

'No.'

'No. No. No. No. It's always bloody no, and sorry bosun. And I get hell for what you don't do. Oh well, I'll have to put up with you. Run away and play. Both Lamps and Chips have been up for ten minutes.'

Carpenter. Lamptrimmer.

Galley.

'Good morning, Andy. Morning, Mcgoff – after you with the dipper.'

'Hey, don't you forget to get the crew some butter this morning. I don't know what sort of bloody man you are at all, letting the crew run short of butter.'

'That's all right, I won't. But I haven't made the coffee yet.'

'– ruddy saloon –'

'– that's what the bastard sez, takin' a spell, I was –'

'– brasswork –'

'– ruddy saloon –'

Seamen. Certified as Sailors' Messroom ...

'Morning, Matt! Morning, Lofty!'

'How go? You've been a perishing long time with that coffee!'

'Sorry, the bosun's been giving me a heave.'

'Morning, son.'

'Morning, Ted. Morning, Horsey. Morning, Cock!'

'How are you doing, there?'

'Is this coffee, then, for Christ sake?'

'Why don't you give us some beer, man?'

'The hair of the dog –'

'Last night, I tell you, Hilliot, I had the hell of a time: you should have been there – there was this girl, you see, and she got up on to the table –'

'Well, I'm going to take my coffee out on the hatch.'

'I'll come with you.'

'Reminds me of the time in Miki when –'

'Well, he'd got eyes like a poached egg – ha ha – in a bucket of blood.'

(*Puella mea* ... No, not you, not even my supervisor would recognize me as I sit here upon the number six hatch drinking ship's coffee. Driven out and compelled to be chaste. The whole deep blue day is before me. The breakfast dishes must be washed up: the forecastle and the latrines must be cleaned and scrubbed – the alleyway too – the brasswork must be polished. For this is what sea life is like now – a domestic servant on a treadmill in hell! Labourers, navvies, scalers rather than sailors. The firemen are the real boys, and I've heard it said there's not much they can't do that the seamen can. The sea! God, what it may suggest to you! Perhaps you think of a deep grey sailing ship lying over in the seas, with the hail hurling over her: or a bluenose skipper who chewed glass so that he could spit blood, who could sew a man up alive in a sack and throw him overboard, still groaning! Well, those were the ancient violences, the old heroic days of holystones; and they have gone, you say. But the sea is none the less the sea. Man scatters ever farther and farther the footsteps of exile. It is ever the path to some strange land, some magic land of faery, which has its extraordinary and unearthly reward for us after the storms of ocean. But it is not only the nature of our work which has changed, Janet. Instead of being called out on deck at all hours to shorten sail, we have to rig derricks, or to paint the smokestack: the only things we have in common with Dauber, besides dungarees, is that we still 'mix red lead in many a bouilli tin'. We batter the rusty scales of the deck with a carpenter's maul until the skin peels off our hands like the rust of the deck ... Ah well, but this life has compensations, the days of joy even when the work is most brutalizing. At sea, at this time, when the forecastle doesn't need scrubbing, there is a drowsy calm there during the time we may spend between being roused from our bunks and turning out on deck. Someone throws himself on the floor, another munches a rasher; here how Horsey's limbs crack in a last sleepy stretch! But when bells have gone on the bridge and we stand by the paintlocker, the blood streams red and cheerful in the fresh morning breeze, and I feel almost joyful with my chipping hammer and scraper. They will follow me like friends, through the endless day. Cleats are knocked out, booms, hatches, and tarpaulins pulled away by brisk hands, and we go down the ladder deep into the hold's night, clamber up along the boat's side, where plank ends bristle, then we sit down and turn to wildly! Hammers clap nimbly against the iron, the hold quivers, howls, crashes, the speed increases: our scrapers flash and become lightning in our hands. The rust spurts out from the side in a hail of sharp flakes, always right in front of our eyes, and we rave, but on on! Then all at once the pace slackens, and the avalanche of hewing becomes a firm, measured beat, of an even deliberate force, the arm swings like a rocking machine, and our fist loosens its grip on the slim haft –

And so I sit, chipping, dreaming of you, Janet, until the iron facing shows, or until eight bells go, or until the bosun comes and knocks us off. Oh, Janet, I do love you so. But let us have no nonsense about it. The memory of your virginity fills me with disgust. Disgust and contempt! You are like Arabella, you would let Claudio die rather than sacrifice it – Claudio – Hilliot – die ... with no bride to fix his swimming eye.

And this poor Claudio you would invest with shy, abstemious promises. Claudio, continent in his prison! The story of the Scots professor on the ship who had never been able to make up his mind whether to marry or travel! You are suffering from forrced celibacy! ... Good God, I loathe you, abwhore you,

Janet! Forgive me for having thought that, it is not true. Let's make it up. Do you remember the time you wore your white sweater, which gave you a kind of woolly smell, and I put my hand on your heart to feel it beat? It was like feeling a lamb's heart beating, your sweater was so innocent and soft. I love you . . .)

'Lor lumme bloody days, here comes the bosun, and me not finished my coffee.'

'Where are we, men? Turn to. Get your brooms!'

Tin-tin.

'Why, there's no wash-down today, for Jesus sake.'

'No wash-down in port!'

'Hold your jaw, Horsey. You're going to turn on all those stiff salt water taps today, so there's a tiddley job for a strong man.'

'I'll turn the hose on you, bosun.'

'Shut up; come on, men, get a move on. It's six o'clock already. I never saw such a crowd for Christ sake.'

'Hilliot.'

'Yes, bosun.'

'Get a move on you. You're the same like this every morning, every morning. It's not like as though you were a bloody man that mucked in like the rest of us, not like as though you were a bloody man who been having a bit of tail. I don't know what sort of bloody man you are at all. You ought to be getting your soda from the lamptrimmer by now. I can just see the same old thing happening. Half-past ten and you not out on deck yet. And then, Sorry bosun! Go on, man! Jump to it, for Jesus sake.'

Lamplocker. Carpenter's Shop. Clusterlocker.
Certified for Use as a Sailors' Messroom.
Seamen.

'Hullo, Taff! Taking a spell? How's the work?'

'Oh, that damn chief steward gives us a dog's life in the pantry. That bloody fellow Joe Ward too – always grumbling.'

'Never mind: ten months and we'll be docked in Liverpool again. Ten little months . . . By gosh, that's the hell of a biceps you've got on you, Taff. How did you do it?'

'Oh that! That's fair enough, ain't it? I used to be a black-smith's assistant.'

'What? Under the spreading chestnut tree?'

'Amlwch I lived. I used to work in a forge near Bull Bay. I was a caddy on the links there for a time –'

'You don't know Swansea, by any chance –'

'Hey, Jimmie!'

'Yes?'

'Oh, I don't mean you, Taff. It's Hilliot I want. Do you want some soda for the scrub-out?'

'Yes, I do.'

'Got your bucket there?'

'Yes.'

'Here you are then. If you put some Board of Trade lime juice in that it'll come as white as a lamb's arse. What about your brass work? Going ashore tonight?'

'They all ask me that. Well – so long, Taff. I've got some paste all right, thanks, Lamps. See you in the pantry sometime, Taff. This morning, in fact.'

'Well, take some of this as well. With that the brass'll shine like a sixpence on a nigger's arse, or I'll call the King my uncle.'

'Thank you, Lamps. Thanks very much indeed.'

'That'll be all right, Jimmie, that'll be all right.'

(*Seaman*, with bucket on his arm, with singlet on his back, with sweat rag round his neck, Dana Hilliot, nineteen, enters the messroom. In the bucket is a mixture of soda and hot water. To this he adds three drops of lime juice, Board of Trade bottle, price 15s. He then gets his scrubber – Star Brush Company – and his wad – one of the second steward's cast-off singlets – and goes down upon his knees under the messroom table. In this hieratic position he scrubs so energetically that sweat trickles down him and drops now on to the deck, now into the bucket; sweat appears in beads on the metacarpi of Eugene Dana Hilliot. While he scrubs he thinks of Janet... He thinks of her while he scrubs the messroom table itself; he thinks of her while he scrubs the washhouses, and the alleyways, and cleans the scuppers with a bamboo pole ... Yes, Janet, it is I, although you would scarcely recognize me. Here, on the other hand – let me introduce you to her – is the tramp steamer *Oedipus Tyrannus*, outward bound for hell. When you come to think of it – an ideal match. Both of us born of Viking blood, both robbed of our countries and left to make out as best we can; both, finally, with the same wandering, harbourless, dispossessed characteristics. Her very history is enough to fill me with a narcissistic compassion! First she was registered in Tvedestrand, then bought by an English firm, who re-registered her, altering her derrick plan; then she was bought back by Norway; after which she was rebought by England and, after her reconditioning was completed, received a charter. She sailed out an exile, an expatriate; with *Seamen* scarcely substituted for *Matroser*, or *Firemen* for *Fyrbötere* ... Considering myself, my brief education in Oslo, my meeting of you, my father's tutorial appointment in Harvard, my being taken away, before I was five, on interminable voyages all over the world, and seeing none of it; considering also how every country from which I have been forced to emigrate has left a gaping hole in my heart, considering the fomenting heterogeneity of the crew, the minute Greek and Spanish and French firmament as well as the Norse, English, and American – is it any wonder that I feel humiliated by it all, and as homeless, as exiled as the ship itself? Cambridge, Mass., or Cambridge, Eng.? Booze racket in Cambridge, Eng., say beer barons. Forgetting depresh. of departing semester. Difficult to say where I was most at home ... Strolling with my father through the Harvard Yard, passing the Widener Library, so absurdly like our Bibliotheket, and Amy Lowell's house. How gay we were, happy enough then with our sausage and buckwheat and root beer: with our oysters and swordfish and quahaugs and clams; and the hermit crab, that pirate of crabs, seeking its shelly cave, and those, what's their name? – like animated hairs. Weaving fearful vision ... 'What shall we talk of, Gene – Santayana? Or Cambridge, Eng.?' If we only knew, if we only had known that we were happy at the time there would have been no need, as if against our wills, to have forced out of the present some opportunity for immortalizing the past; or wouldn't it make any difference? 'Yes, Gene, you must go to Cambridge. I had a rotten time in Oslo. Nothing but working as hell, a lot of us in stuffy rooms. And then – my scholarship to Oxford, for one year. That was very funny. It was nothing but 'have another gin' all the time, balancing tea cups and talking;

my God, you know how damnable it is. As a matter of fact, Cambridge will be much better for you. Wonderful friendships, freedom, youth ... Everything. But still I was glad when my book on American literature was published, and, largely owing to Spingarn's friendly review, got me this job here ...' Misericorde. Verily the ways of man are dark, beloved. He cometh up as a shadow, and is cast down. He fleeth – and continueth not. Under the *Aftenpostens Lysavis*, standing in the *Drammersveien* with you; I thought that – after we had dined at Jacques' Bagatelle in the Bygdö Allé, that day we saw the Viking ship – 'he cometh up as a flower and is cut down; he fleeth as a shadow and continueth not.' Standing there the news of the whole world flowed above us, an opium dream of electric light, Finland, Reykjavik, Berlin, Tokio, Kjöbenhavn, Finland, Reykjavik, Berlin, Tokio, Kjöbenhavn, London, Singapore, London, Singapore – Viking Kalosjer verdens beste – Viking Kalosjer verdens beste ... Your lamb's heart was beating under your white woollen sweater. A sheep in sheep's clothing ... a tiger's heart wrapped in a sailor's hide.)

Signaliseringsreglerne maa nöie efterkommes.
Kvinder, barn, passagerer og hjaelpelöse.
Personer skal sendes iland för skibets.
Besetning Kristiania April 1901 ...
Fordeling til Livbaatene ...

Batt nr 3 of 5	*Baat nr 4 of 6*
Baadsmand	*Styrmand*
Donkeymand	*2 den Maskinist*
1ste Kok	*Telegrafist*
1 Matros	*1 Matros*
1 Letmatros	*2 Letmatros*
2 Fyrbötere	*2 Fyrbötere*

Galley. Oedipus Tyrannus – Liverpool.
Certified for Use of Six Apprentices.
Certified for Use of Four Quartermasters.
No Admission except on Business.
Saloon. Pantry.
Tin-tin: tin-tin.
'How are yer doin' there?'
'How are yer doin' there?'

'O.K. Good morning again, Taff. I've come for some butter and a tin of condensed milk.'

'Butter! For Jesus sake ... Ginger'll look after you, son. It's in the ice chest. You ought to have got the condensed milk from the storeroom on Saturday. We can't give you any.'

'Why not?'

'Because there ain't none to give.'

'Whew, I'll have your sweet young life one of these days, comin' in here at all hours. This damned ice chest won't open anyway. Give us a hand, Taff, will you? That's a boy, that's a boy ... here we are! My, I'm tired. Taff and I had a night's drift all right last night.'

'Was she nice?'

'You can bet your boots on it.'

'Well, be careful, Ginger my son, or you'll find yourself in the lock instead of being a butcher on a mail boat.'

'Touch wood. But what else is there to do, for heaven's sake?'

'By Jimminy Christmas, yes, what else? How would you like our job? Up at five o'clock, make coffee for officers. Make officers' beds. Clean out the pantry, scrub out the engineers' saloon, polish the fans, empty the slops, clean all those bloody gratings outside the officers' bathrooms, beat the mats – and never a moment to ourselves all day, except when we eat, and we have to do that sitting on bloody biscuit tins. Yis.'

'Yes – Taffy's right, and wot with the chief steward bawling at us and Joe Ward grousing –'

'Where is Joe now?'

'In the engineers' bathroom, I think.'

'It's a dog's life.'

'Still, ten weeks more and we'll be docked in Liverpool.'

'Ten little weeks.'

'It's ten *months*, not ten weeks, Taff.'

'Let's pretend it's weeks.'

'All right. I've got to go. So long.'

'So long –'

Saloon.

Purser.

Third Engineer – Oedipus Tyrannus – Liverpool.

Certified as Engineers' Bathroom.

No Admission except on Business.

Cammel Laird Shipbuilding Company, Birkenhead.

Bosun. Carpenter. Cooks.

Seamen.

Tin-tin: tin-tin: tin-tin.

'So you've got some butter at last. Muck it is, too.'

'Fresh butter, Mcgoff. I don't know what you're always grumbling about. We get better food on this packet than I've ever had at home.'

'Gawd blimey, the meat's all tainted, for one thing. The chief cook doesn't know what he's bloody doing. He ought to be on a tug boat. And the chief steward? I bet *he* gets his bloody bonus all right.'

'Oh well. What are you doing? Taking a spell?'

'Yes. And look here, son. See you get the breakfast on the *table* by eight bells today, and the coffee made an' all. We don't want any waiting about when we've finished work. And see you turn out on deck at half-past ten, not a quarter to ruddy eleven. Because that bosun says to me, if that ruddy boy's not out of the fo'c'sle by 'arf-past ten I'll put 'im underneath the winches again scraping the paint off. And what with the winches being red hot that'll be bad, that I'm telling you. That bosun says to me, 'e says, I'm going to break that boy's back with work this voyage even if I get the No. 1 to make 'im trim coal on 'is bloody watch below. Casual bastard, 'e says –'

'But that's not true, Mcgoff. I've done all right, haven't I? I'm doing my best.'

'Well, that's what Horsey and me says. We stood up for you, and says, well, can't you leave the boy alone, we think the kid's not too bad. After all, we says, it's his first voyage, and we all make mistakes our first voyages. That put the bose on his ear, and he said, Well, first of all he forgets to call me in the morning, wot with first one thing and then the other, then I get complaints from Andy –'

'Bugger Andy!'

'What! I don't know what sort of bloody man you are at all.'

'Well, there you are, you see! Well, I must be getting. Coming along ashore tonight?'

'I'll say not. Cheerio.'
'_'

Tin.
Galley.

'Hullo, here's a sailors' ruddy peggy! Ship ahoy there! Goin' ashore tonight?'

'Oh Christ, I dunno. Hi there, Ginger!'

'Norman, has Andy got the sailors' chow ready yet?'

'Oh, you're too early, you are! It's a hard job, a cook's is ... no, there's Andy bawling for you now.'

'I know it. All sailors' jobs are too hard for my liking.'

'Hey, come on there, 'Illiot! Cooks ain't got no time to waste talkin' to boys. Come and take the sailors' breakfast away. Here you are, kippers: you wait till September when there's bergoo and you've got to take that down when she's rolling like hell! Made your coffee? ... Gawd strewth, you're some fellow, you are! *I* dunno how you got this job on this packet, and I reckon no other fellow does either!'

'You speak for yourself, Andy.'

'Why, you couldn't get a job as assistant pantry boy on a Chinese bloody junk. Nor a firemen's sodding peggy either.'

'You go and take a running jump at yourself.'

'Eh? Wot did you say? You put down that breakfast and let me get at you.'

'I'm not going to put down the breakfast for you.'

'Put down that breakfast.'

'Get the hell out of it, Andy. Go and dump yourself down the ash shoot.'

'Ha ha ha!'

'Ha ha, that's one on *you*, Andy.'

'You're a damned yellow coward, running away from me! A dirty rat: a Port Mahon son of a whore. You know you daren't stand up like a man and fight.'

'I'm afraid of hurting you.'

'I'll complain to the mate. By Christ I'll complain to the mate! Doin' a good lad out of his job. Little bastard.'
'_'

Tin-tin: tin-tin: tin-tin: tin-tin.
Seamen. Certified as Sailors' Messroom.

'Chow up, you birds ... Ted, could you tell 'em in the wash-house while I go and get the coffee?'

'That's better, Hilliot. Punctual – right on the very tick. Things should go like clockwork on a ship, I always say.'

'Thanks, I'll do my best. Now I've got to go and get the coffee ... Oh, I say, thanks awfully, Megoff, that is really good of you.'

'I thought I better bring it down for you, son. The atmosphere in the galley is electric – that's what they say, isn't it? – electric. Yes, that's the only word for it, electric. Andy'd dump you down the ash shoot if you went there again, coffee and all: then we wouldn't have nothink to drink. Why do you always put Andy on his ear? I get on with him all right.'

'I dunno.'

'Aw Christ – kippers again.'

'Can I have yours then, Ted?'

'You bet. Do you like 'em?'

'You bet, Ted.'

'Well, you're ruddy welcome ... Dear Muvver. I 'ope you are quite well. I 'ave three meals a day – one goes up and two goes down. Your lovin' son – Ted.'

'Hooray! Good old Ted.'

'Hey. Hilliot, you ought to rinse this teapot out with some soda. Get some soda from Lamps. He'll give you some.'

'It's not the teapot – it's the coffee pot. Oh Jesus!'

'Yes, but we told you about this before. This isn't good enough. If the skipper saw the teapot like that, gawd blimey, he'd chase you round the ship at the end of a broomstick.'

'You could bet your boots on that, sonny.'

'All Lombard Street to a Tahiti orange on it.'

'Well, he has seen it like that, and, what's more, he's asked me to come back next voyage. And, anyway, you'll have to drink the coffee because I've used all the soda on the scrub-out.'

'Yes, that's what you say all the time. And then you don't clean out the teapot.'

'And you 'aven't washed that dishcloth yet. It fair stinks, I can tell you.'

'Stinks to hell. Yis.'

'Wot's for dinner, Hilliot?'

'I don't know. I haven't asked. Why, man, this is breakfast.'

'I don't know – is it breakfast?'

'He's mad – we've got a crazy deck boy.'

'Who don't know what sort of bloody man you are at all.'

'Why not, what was it you said, you afraid of Andy?'

'No . . . no.'

'You don't like him, though.'

'No.'

'Aw, you're afraid of 'im – didn't you 'ear 'im call you a bastard this morning?'

'Yes, but did you hear what I said to *him?*'

'You said sweet f.a. to him.'

'You're a liar!'

'Look here, son. You can call a table a bastard. Or a chair. Or a job of work. But not a man.'

'No, but at the same time, Matt, you can't *hit* a superior officer, or what amounts to a superior officer.'

'*Certainly* you can. A cook ain't a superior officer any more than *I* am.'

'Well, the cook has almost as much hold over me as the bosun.'

'You can hit a bosun for that matter. We had an apprentice, Taylor was his name, and 'e was one of those slow, slow chaps, and one day the bosun come along –'

'Hey, Hilliot, where's the new tin of milk you were going to get us?'

'– bang slap in the scuppers –'

'Yes?'

'Yes?'

'They wouldn't give me any in the pantry.'

'Anyway –'

'Anyway, we all like Andy. 'E's a good old scout.'

'Yes, we all like Andy. We don't like 'is food, but Andy's all right.'

'Well, I suppose that I'm the other way round: I can't see anything wrong with the food, and I don't like Andy, or I *do* like him.'

'Aw, you're all away to hell, Dungy.'

'*That's* a good name for you. Dungy!'

'Ha ha ha!'
'– full of prunes.'
'–'
'Yes, that's a very good one.'

$$\text{(ἐπὶ δὲ τῷ τεθυμένῳ} \\ \text{τόδε μέλος, παρακοπά,} \\ \text{παραφορὰ φρενοδαλῦς,} \\ \text{ἥμνος ἐξ Ἐρινύων.)}$$

(The Furies, singing over their victim, sending him mad. Janet, enjoying it in a white sweater, gloating in a thin, ululating treble.)

'Going ashore tonight?'

'I don't know.'

'You 'aven't been ashore all the voyage – have you? I don't know what the devil made you come to sea, if you don't make some use of it.'

'Well, I didn't get a draw till we got to Shanghai – but I have been ashore. I went ashore in Shanghai – that time we played cricket against all those swaddies, with the firemen from H.M.S. *Danae* looking on. Don't look at me like that, you know I did. And I went ashore with Joe in Penang.'

'Yes, you're a damned good cricketer, I must say. You go in first and run out the chief steward.'

'And make one run.'

'One little run. Still – that's better than nothing.'

'Certainly it is – but that's not going ashore all the ruddy same, not what you might call having a real night's drift.'

'Why! I went ashore in Penang. And in Singapore and Kowloon and in Port Swettenham too!'

'All right, all right – there's no need to wink like that.'

'Here, you mind who you're speaking to.'

'I played billiards in Penang with Joe Ward, in the Chinese quarter. I haven't been much further than the first bar I've seen at any port. Anyway, you wouldn't let me go ashore with you.'

'Why do you always go ashore with stewards? Ain't you a sailor? Why don't you have a woman? You'd perhaps get our chow prompt if you had a woman.'

'You've said it yourself, no need for us to say it. We don't think you're a man. You're a kid should be home with its mammy.'

'Aw, don't always be getting at the boy – the chows was prompt enough today, for Jesus sake.'

'I don't know why I haven't. I haven't anyway. I promised my girl at home.'

'Well, I say the boy's quite right if 'e's promised 'is Jane ... Gawd blimey, I 'aven't got any use for running after women in port. It's too easy.'

'Oh, hell's bells – what's the good of talking to him? – haven't we done nothing else all the voyage –?'

'Oh well, this Jane I've got, she's funny that way. You know what I mean. Jesus Christ, you must know what I mean.'

'You use the language all right –'

'No, we don't want to persuade you to do anything wrong. We're not telling you. You've got a trim of a bloody man. We want you to act for your bloody self. Now them houses are no good – haven't got any use for them my bloody self.'

'I was third mate, son, once; lost my ticket through the booze – on an old Chambers tramp out of Liverpool S.S. *Bowes Castle*, and a young fellow was signed on for experience, he said, same as you. Son of an old skipper of mine, retired – lives in Greenwich. Asks me to look after this chap. Well, he was worse than wot you are, a good deal he was: he was a proper bumscrew. He was thrown out of the bosun's mess because he couldn't keep it clean: then out of the O.S.'s mess, and in the end the Able Seamen threw him out of theirs for being scruffy – they had three different messes on this packet. We had a ten-month voyage, with six weeks in York –'

'What is she, Hilliot? A nice little typist, I'll bet. You toffs get all the luck.'

'You weren't calling me a toff a moment ago –'

'In New York, when we docked in –'

'No, but what I mean to say is, you know, you've got the position, like. We all know that you got eddication and we ain't.'

'We're just –'

'– When we docked in London I went home with him to see

his daddy, and of course I spilled a lot of bull to him; told him he'd done well, but he'd had enough, and all that eyewash. The only thing the twot had learnt to do was to *swear!*'

'– Wot you might call plain working men, like. We makes no claims to being nothing else, just plain working –'

'Couldn't climb a standing derrick: didn't know the difference between an eye splice and a handy billy, and he thought a wire runner was a sailor's rating. Couldn't and bloody well didn't wash his dungarees. Seamen chucked his dirty gear overside, and all he had when he docked was a dirty pair of check trousers I give him, a sweat rag, and a shanghai jacket the Chinese No. 1 give him, and, by Jesus, his mother was glad to see him. Oh boy! Gave him a hot bath, put a decent suit of clothes on his back, good soul his mother were, worth three on him. And no sooner had he sat down than he started to show 'em all he'd learnt at sea ... Pass the bloody salt, Ma, he says, *hee hee*, this voyage was a proper *bar*stard, he tells his old man –'

'Hilliot, when you made this tea, did you rinse the coffee out of the pot?'

'Yes.'

'Well, next time use a little water to do it.'

'This ain't coffee.'

'No, and it ain't bloody ditchwater neither!'

'Good idea is to wash a singlet every day before you turn in: then you don't have so much to do on Sunday –'

'This first mate's a bloody man: he's got me weighed up like that.'

'What did you do in Singapore, then? I'll bet you fooled around that old Malay bar all right.'

'Got drunk?'

'Yes, I don't know where. I didn't run after women. Oh Jesus!'

'Oh Jesus, eh? What would your mother think if she heard you say that?'

'No, and let me tell you you're right, sonny: half of these fellows here don't know what they *have* got.'

'Ha ha! Ha ha!'

'Ha ha! Do you remember *Smithy*?'

(ἐπὶ δὲ τῷ τεθυμένῳ
τόδε μέλος, παρακοπά,
παραφορὰ φρενοδαλής,
ὕμνος ἐξ Ἐρινύων.)

'– And the next day he comes to me with tears in his eyes and shows me them. Caw – they were as big as your fist. And 'e'd let it rip – got it in Muji he had, and never said damn all to anybody – kept it to himself for thirteen months. Well, the doc sends him up to the skipper, and the skipper says, "Get off my bridge, you *stinking* beast." '

'Gawd blimey!'

'So they 'ad to keep 'im on brasswork after that.'

'Like a fellow I knew in Belawan –'

'Well then, Hilliot, you say all this dope about cutting out things for her sake. Why not cut out the bottle too? You're one of the most regular booze artists I ever struck.'

'You don't need to be old to drink.'

'No, and you don't to have women neither, sonny: anyway, what is all this love business? What is love, for heaven's sake?'

'Exactly what?'

'Christ – any bloody man on the ship'll tell you the same. You drink enough to put out the bloody fires of the ship. It's not natural not at your age – that's what we all says.'

'You take my advice and steer clear of getting tied up to a Jane. You're only a kid – a bloomin' innocent, a diddy!'

'That sounds all right, Matt – but I'm not.'

'Well, you know that funny little place in Java. What's its name? They don't have rickshaws there – do they? Little wot you might call drays – horse drays. Caw, we 'ad a chief steward, a hell of a great fellow he was, and he got into one of these 'ere horse drays and he put his foot right through.'

'– Yes?'

'Yes –'

'– *Sure* 'e 'ad it – that bloody chief steward – 'e had a dose. But wot's to do about it for Christ sake? If you get it here the chances are you'll get cured before you get home, and your folks won't hear of it. If you don't get it here you'll get it at home, and your folks *will* hear about it.'

'Yes, that's right. Matt's right.'

'When I was about your age, son, I thought I'd got it, and I went to a doc, and said, "Doc," I says, "I've got it." "You got wot?" 'e says. "A vile disease," says I. "Let me see then," he says, *seriously* though 'e says, "Have you ever been with a woman or anything of that sort?" "Yes," I says, "Well – how many?" asks the doc, smiling. "Well, that I can't tell," I replied. "I been with so many I lost count." "Well, *why* you ain't got it," he says, "at least not from what I could see then, but we'll put down the blinds, 'darken ship' like I believe you sailors call it, and I'll put on the jolly old spyglass . . . He he no," he says, "you ain't got it. You are a one," he says, "coming in here all for nothing. Say aah," he says, "and ninety-nine." So I says aah and ninety-nine. Then he says, "If I was you I'd take a glass of hot water every night before you turns in – "'

'Ha ha ha! For gosh sake –'

'– for gosh sake –'

'– so drunk that he tried to wrap the deck round him for a blanket.'

('– a selection of the real language of men –' '– the language of these men –' '– I propose to myself to imitate and as far as possible to adopt the very language of these men –' '– but between the language of prose and that of metrical composition there neither is nor can be any essential difference –' *Lingua communis*. Once aboard the Hooker! *Oxenstjerna*. What was it about the docks that had always attracted us? Often they were empty save for a few fishing smacks and a trawler or two, but we loved the smell of the place and its sound. The swinging bridge, the dock gatesman's whistle and the deliberation with which he made fast and loose the chains, all meant something very particular in our lives. We stood there often on our way to Bidston, or returning to New Brighton, and watched the sea gulls dipping and diving in the Great Float: or listened to the rattle of a steam winch tightening a hawser. The crane that dived its long arm into the darkness of the hold and brought up the cargo! . . . But when the *Oxenstjerna* came in, just as we arrived, Janet suddenly squeezed my hand. It was curious that we had seen her twice before: first in Oslo fjord, where she was tied stern-on to the stump of a tree, among bluebells and foxgloves: then we had seen her in Birkenhead, unloading nitrate from Iquique: and now, surprisingly, here she was again, in Birkenhead, homeward bound from Batavia. It was as though she had become an iron bond between us, but also she was a secret in our hearts as light as the summer air . . . A small crowd stood on either side of the wall, and a procession of cars and cycles waited there for the bridge to close. A tug pulled the big vessel towards her berth. She glided through slowly, the mate, with the starboard watch, stood on the forecastle head, firemen with sweat rags craned over the rail at us, *Oxenstjerna – Tromsö* we spelt out from the enormous letters painted along her side, and *Oxenstjerna – Tromsö* we read on her receding stern. As the giant flat gates clanked to behind her, the dock gatesman blew his whistle, while the cars and cycles – on the far side was the big yellow Liscard bus we should have caught, but we both pretended not to notice it, that could take care of itself! – streamed over as with sudden relief. The *Oxenstjerna* moored alongside the wharf. A gangway was lowered. Men crossed to and fro from the ship to the dock. What would the cargo be? Tea from India? Sugar from Malay? Or was it Chimborazo, Popocatepetl –? Strange to think that coolies, under a tropical sun, had last handled it. A sailor standing by said she was a dirty squarehead, but after all she'd done a lot of sailing. Rio and the Plata: Cuba and Colon: Pernambuco, Rangoon – she'd been everywhere! But there was no need to tell us that, for we knew well that a wanderer of all the seas like the *Oxenstjerna* came back always with rich and romantic cargoes . . .

Janet – Janet – do you remember, an aeroplane was going over very high, we heard its engine fitfully, and it was such a small dot in the glare of the sunlight? And the wind that day? Those whistling draughts that fairly blew us laughing out of the Goree Piazzas, where they used to chain the slaves: Father showed me a bill of lading for one before he went mad – and old Ropery? Alas – those melancholy horses' heads that nodded and wavered along the dock road, with their clattering carts behind. The sea gulls were blowing and screaming over the *Oxenstjerna,* the air felt as though it were streaming in at every pore, shadows of clouds whirled on walls and towers –

But one day another ship came into harbour, and that ship was called the *Oedipus Tyrannus*.)

'Come on, Paddy, boy, give us a song.'

'Yes, Paddy – good old Paddy –'

'Paddy – give us Paddy McGulligan's daughter, Mary Ann.'

'Oh shag off!'

'I tell you –'

'Seraphina's got no drawers, I been down and seen her, Ser-a-phina!'

'No, that's no good as a song; we want one of them old sea shanties, one of the real old timers.'

'*Shenandoah.*'

' 'Illiot – you give us a song, give us a song on your ukebloody-lele. The Chinese cook was telling me you was a dab 'and at it.'

'It isn't a ukelele. It's a taropatch.'

'The Chinese cook, 'Illiot – your old shipmate, he he.'

'I bet you like the Chinese cook better than Andy, eh?'

'Better than Andy, yes. We all know you don't love Andy.'

'The Chinese cook was telling me 'e was thinking of getting 'Illiot a job as firemen's peggy.'

'Firemen's peggy. Ha, ha, ha, ha!'

'Firemen's peggy, now you're well in 'Illiot, you mustn't let an opportunity like *that* slip away from you. Think of all the little children you've got to support in Shanghai.'

'I haven't got any children in Shanghai, God damn your mucking eyes.'

'Ah – but you will have, we saw you.'

'You didn't.'

'Well, why didn't you go ashore here? Behave like a sailor, for God sake: why, you're a disgrace to the ship . . . This time at the Board of Trade Office Hilliot was just behind me signing on – old chap behind counter says, "Hey, do you wish to make an allotment?" "Wot's an allotment?" asks Hilliot. "An allotment? Why of course I see this *must* be your first voyage!" He he!'

'Never mind, you thought it was a cabbage patch, didn't you? Never mind, dearie, you live and learn. You live and learn. We'll go ashore tonight and have a little drink together.'

'You've promised to give me your oilskins and sea boots, eh Hilliot, when we dock in London?'

'No, he's promised to give them to me.'

'You get the hell out of it. He promised them to me.'

'I didn't promise them to anybody. I'm going to keep them myself.'

'Hurray! Hurray!'

'– proletariat –'

'Come on, go and get your ukelele an' sing us a song.'

'Aw, I could make a better noise myself on a cigar box.'

'Plunk plunk plunk, crooning to the Chinese cook.'

(Between the Tarot and the cabbage, the systole and diastole, between the pleuritic friction, the intercostal spaces and the wild west; between the paroxysm and dyspnoea our child, Janet – this has occurred to me; to what extent may it not be subject to the pre-natal influences? Supposing we ever had one. Heredity. Tee-hee! Or perhaps the humour of the *thing* escapes you. That in the original unity of the first thing lies the secondary cause of all things with the germ of their inevitable annihilation? . . . Will it be a son? Then we must buy toys, a perambulator with pneumatic tyres, books that will be useful when the little Hilliot gets older; *Peter Rabbit, The Adventures of Jeremy Fisher,* and *The Tailor of Gloucester,* in fifteen variorum volumes. And after the little Hilliot is born we shall read to him each night one of those innocent stories. Yes! When he is fresh from his evening bath, his cheeks red, and his hair rubbed up the wrong way to make it curl! And as he lies there with his dream-bright face, how excited he will become over Peter Rabbit's escape from the wicked gardener MacGregor, who wished to use his skin for tobacco and (what was worse) actually threw at Peter Rabbit a prize marrow. Actually! as he was escaping round the potting sheds. Proud parents, Janet, proud parents when we give him, as reward for good conduct, his digestive biscuit . . . His pyjamas, blue with a white stripe. Sliding into slumber down the smooth snow of sheets. The soft white curtains bellying inward, blown softly by the summer breeze. The clock on the wall saying – what? Tick tock? Tock tick? Time? Peace? Peace, peace, peace, peace, says the clock. The child sleeps, we draw back the curtains, and look out over the drowsy garden; from the fields comes the murmur of falling dew; we look out over the dunes and out to sea where the *Oxenstjerna* is going with the high tide, is passing out, out, beyond our dreams, our knowledge, but always living in our hearts, always kind to us – farewell! farewell! farewell! If we only knew, all hands were rigid with gazing at the sky. It is sundown. The galley boy has stopped peeling potatoes, rising from his little stool, and watches, leaning on the ash chute; the cook has come out of the galley, cleaning a steam cover; a seaman joins them. The other hands have stopped their song, and crowd, craning over the bulwarks, the shorter ones standing on the saltwater piping. A stoker, blackened and fire-scarred, just up from the stokehold, watches too, supping the wind. The wind! The wind! The cold clean scourge of the ocean. Yes, they are all saying, yes, that's the last of England. You remember the history books, William the Conqueror 1066. Not much fun there. A week and we'll be docked in Tromsö –

O le pauvre amoureux des pays chimériques! Death. Outside time drips its rain for our son, who lifts to be kissed, a twisted, witless mask, grinning sightlessly at us, two holes in the bridgeless nose, the sightless eyes like leaden bullets sunk into the face . . . Myself, also, the man without a soul. It died, suddenly, at the age of eight. I felt it die a little every day . . . A little, little grave, an obscure grave –)

'When we signed on it was –'

'When we signed on it was at the Board of Trade Office in Birkenhead, the fellow behind the counter says, "Do you wish to make an allotment?" . . . I was just in front of him. "An allotment?" he says, surprised like. "Why, oh, I see this *must* be your first voyage." '

'– She's in the water –'

''Oo's in the water? –'

'Old Bill's daughter.'

'And 'oo's going to get her out?'

'I'm going to get her out.'

'And who the bloody hell are you?'

'Hilliot the sailor! Hilliot the sailor!'

'Aw, that fellow.'

66

'Going! Going!'

'You're going to give us your sea boots, aren't you, when we dock in Liverpool?'

'And yer oilskin?'

'No. 'Aven't you 'eard? 'E's going to give them to me.'

' – back in Eskdalemuir, boy – I wish I was there again. A shepherd I was, breeking the hoggs, we used to do it. Ever seen them stells? Enclosures like, where we put the sheep when the storms came on . . . And the clipping. The fiddles playin' at night in the kitchen and perhaps a pig's bladder hanging up there, like a balloon, eh? Christ, aye. Knew a sweet lass, best little woman you could wish to meet . . . Twenty miles it was to Langholm, and twenty to Lockerbie – there was a picture show at Lockerbie, once a week; me and my lass used to go down there in the boss's car –'

'Mr Hilliot come aboard in a car, right up to the wharf, never mind talking of going to a picture show, didn't you, Mr Hilliot?'

'Well, so would you perhaps, if you'd got one.'

'What say? Well, let me tell you this much, I *have* got one. Yes, Mr bleeding Hilliot, and what's more, I drive it at sixty miles an hour with *myself* at the wheel –!'

'Ahum. Ahum, James. Home, James. Tell us, where is Heton, Oxford or Cambridge?'

'Well, what's a quartermaster think he's doing in the fo'c'sle anyway, a fairy one at that –'

'Sapporo Bar's the place to go, down the Yamagat Dori.'

'Yes, the Sapporo Bar, Hilliot. Follow the tramlines, it's just past the Customs House. Meet you there tonight.'

'Yes, you know the style. Wrap up nicely: yoku sutsunde Frankyon, arigato. This way: kochira. Slowly: sorosoro. Left: nidari. Stop: tomare. Right: migi. Go on: yuko. Bath: furo. Fine: kirei. Bill: kanjo . . . You know the style, Hilliot, you're the boss!'

'Go to hell, you people; stop talking to me.'

'*Hullo,* second. No stewards in here.'

'What's the matter with you? You look as if you'd swallowed Pat Murphy's goat and the horns were sticking out of your arse.'

'I'm going to take a spell – down in the storeroom. I'm giving all the firemen their rations in a minute.'

'Well, you might give Hilliot a tin of condensed milk and a clean dishcloth.'

(Where shall we have mittag, Janet? And when? In the Röde Mölle? At half-past two? Admirable. The geraniums are out: Ibsen, the author of *Ghosts,* looks sternly down the Storlingsgaten, past the gutted Casino restaurant, past where Ramon Novarro is playing in *Sangeren fra Sevilla,* past the Hotel Plaza restaurant and the Gamle Heidelberg, always forward, while Björnson watches the park attendant gather up the autumn leaves. Tonight dinner, modestly, at the Tostrupkjaelderen! And afterwards, what shall it be – for we must make the most of our emancipation from our parents – the Nationaltheatret or the Circus or the Chat Noir? What about finishing up once more at the Röde Mölle? No. For the moment we give little attention to these plans. Instead, let me show you the grave of my little uncles and aunts, all buried so neatly in a row, all my father's little brothers and sisters, all my mother's little brothers-in-law and sisters-in-law. The gods hugged my forebears to death. Come, take my hand; let us read: so: Harald Wiers Hilliot, född 29 desember 1866, död 2 mars 1867. Brigit Eva Hilliot, född 16 november 1867, död 13 desember 1867. Edvard Nikolai Hilliot, född 8 april 1869, död 6 mai 1870. Mary Sarah Hilliot, född 22 june 1874, död 23 june 1874; without a country. Like myself, like Herman Bang, like the ship, like my excellent father, the only surviving son, who is now in a home eating the buttons off the chair at clairaudient intervals, and composing a sonnet sequence, *Songs of Second Childhood* . . . While my mother, who occasionally writes me, is going blind. A queer family, Janet, a queer family. As for myself, I am the only sane member of it, the only one who has escaped the taint. Aren't you delighted, Janet? Come; come; delighted that I am as I am, pleased to see me back? No? Not pleased that the sailor is home from the sea and spitting brown once more? The huntsman home from the hill with a hare on his chest? Yes, Janet, home from the sea, but with a difference, a grave and far-reaching difference, a difference you will discover to your cost, and all because, all because he broke all the shy, abstemious promises with which you invested him. Woe, woe, woe! Nevermore may they stroll arm in arm over the grey fields of Wirral, over the sand dunes of Wallasey, or past the lighted shops of Liverpool. Nevermore sit in a lunar park in Aalesund, holding hands or eating smorbrod. Nevermore stand in the gallery at Revy Circus Globus. Do you remember? Vi nar nu program for alle og enhvers smak. Hand balances from a Springboart and Tumpling act! Morsomme Klovner! Akrobater! Balansekunstuere! Slangemennesker! Luftakrobater Obs! Populaere billetpriser: Galleri kr. 1. No more. Never, never, never, never, never. Pay attention to your trouser button and see him if you will for yourself, Dana Hilliot, the syphilitic, as he strolls aimfully down Great Homer Street. Look! How everyone he touches is smitten with the dire disease. It is just one little word, the word that kills. Now everything is wasted. *Dies Irae.* They have fallen from ash and are grey. This is he, the human husk, the leaf of ash, ashes to ashes and dust to dust. As he passes down Church Street the wind rushes round him with a cold, monstrous, final insistency. He walks without thinking where he is going. Tramlines run in front of the offices; mothers with warm-smelling furs are fussing with their school-capped sons into the Bon Marché; further away secret tunnels bore through the gloomy buildings, and the overhead railway and a number of sloping bridges leading to the landing stage spread round in bleak and bare confusion. Tram bells clang. Brutal buildings stride into the air above Dana Hilliot . . . But the wind has enveloped and overarched all these masses of iron and concrete, all this little humanity, and is sweeping these sparkling buildings with rushing, tremendous shadows. '*Yacko,*' shout the newsboys, wearing, like aprons, the announcement: 'Norwegian liner aground in Mersey!' 'Last *Echo Exprey!*' He retreats up Church Street, Castle Street, down old Ropery again. The wind blows up from the road an old copy of the *Liverpool Express,* rumples and whisks it down the Goree Piazzas. It clings finally to a lamppost, like some ugly, cringing wraith. The lamppost was an erect viper, poised in climax of anger, to bite . . . Crowds drift to and from the ferries, battling with the wind, their coats whipping round their knees, or blowing over their heads. A drove of black cattle clatter past, herded by a hooligan with a twisted stick.

A dockside train with its diminutive engine is rumbling along cautiously beneath the Overhead Railway bridges in the direction of Mann Island and the Canning Dock, the sinister bell of warning singing out its desolate nostalgic phrase, *y'lang y'lang y'lang y'lang*. The voice of the chiming bell buoy, chiming and wallowing and rolling. The voice of the leper tolling, enforcing his sad solitude. 'Ware Shoal! A woman passes. *Y'lang y'lang*. Norwegian liner aground in Mersey!

It is the *Oxenstjerna* they are talking about, the *Oxenstjerna* that has gone aground. It is the *Oxenstjerna* which now turns over and sinks into the sand, while the oil spreads a mucous film over the Mersey; and now the white sea gulls, which knew once the dark, smoking rocks, the white sea gulls known by name to the dockers, are dying by the score –

When the door of Dana Hilliot, old age pensioner, was forced, the police found him lying on the mattress in an emaciated and verminous condition. Death from exhaustion and self-neglect –)

'Letters for Firemen Wallae, Erikson, Knudson; for Seamen Mcgoff and Bredahl. Anybody seen Andy?'

'None for me?'

'None for you, Hilliot.'

'– Yes. In Persia it was, Macasser the Sultan came aboard with all his harem under bloody umbrellas. Get anything there for a few old tins, you could, yis. Flogged a dozen singlets for some empties the chief steward give me –'

'Bombay! That's the place for me, mate. Gawd blimey, I've never seen anything like the *birds* there, the air was thick with 'em –'

'Now then Hilliot, that's the place for you.'

'– Bombay duck –'

'Aw, I don't mean them sort of birds.'

'Talking of birds, how's your mickey, Norman?'

'Andy's got a fine place he goes to nearly every night: a fine girl. He knows something, that Andy.'

'A fine cook, eh? Chief cook on a mail boat he was once.'

'Whew, Christ it's hot . . . Reminds me of Cebu in the Philippines. Last voyage we tied up nose-on to the maternity

70

hospital. They say they dump the miscarriages into the ditch. None of the crowd would go bathing, anyway.'

'How many people can swim on this ship?'

'Hilliot, you're the boy, ain't you? You're the Captain Webb of this party, ain't you?'

'Ain't you seen it either? You must come and see it. I've been making a cage an' all, and I've clipped its wings. I've put him on top of the breadlocker. When he gets used to things a bit I'll let him out on an old heaving line on the number four hatch. You give me a hand to paint it Sunday afternoon –'

'What is tomorrow? Saturday?'

'Sure.'

'You love that bloody thing like a brother, eh?'

'Never got a chance to let my bloody brother out on a string –'

'Andy lost his job through the booze?'

'I don't bloody think.'

'But he's a real good scout, he is. Last Christmas it was, in Singapore. Andy was making a Christmas cake for the old man. We'd warped in to the wharf on Christmas morning, and we had all the rest of the day off. Well, what a bloody job, eh, on Christmas morning? Andy was proper stupefied drunk, too. But he made this cake all right, because the skipper, you know, had company and all –'

'Everybody boozed too, eh?'

'Yes, except one of the apprentices . . . Well, Andy made this cake, a good meal for the crowd too, turkey and all, and then afterwards Daddy got tight in the saloon, with all his fine tarts in there, and sent me – I was QM at the time – to find Andy so that they could all thank him like. Well, Andy wasn't in the galley or in the round house or nowheres, and me and my mate, we searched everywhere, yis. Up on the winch deck, down the quartermasters' alleyways, everywhere, yis.'

'Well?'

'Yes, where was he? Now I ain't telling you the word of a lie. We found him on the boat deck under the Union Jack, fast asleep with one of the tarts –'

'– for Jesus sake –'

'– for Jesus sake –'

'I sailed with Andy before as a cook. On an old Greek bastard of a tramp steamer – they piled her up on Lundy in the end – called, what do you think? I remember the name because I had to paint it on the lifebelts: the *Dimitrios N. Bogliazides* . . . We had a hell of a time, back in 1923, this was. We were bringing a cargo of timber from Archangel to Garston, you know. Cold, gosh it was like a milk van . . . The galley and the engine room were the only places you could go to keep warm. We lost the sailors' peggy that trip – frozen stiff he was – that's where you ought to have been, Hilliot – a sailors' peggy that trip, eh? Yes, and he was so cold that next morning at eight bells when we buried him, Chips said that he had an icicle where 'is –'

'Where are we, men?'

'Hullo, bose.'

'How go, bosun?'

'I want two Able Seamen for the mail. Lofty, you come, will you? Pateman, you too.'

'Can't you let a man have a sit on this whore ship, for Christ sake?'

'Who put you up to this little game, bosun?'

'Never mind, men. You must come on. It's the mate's orders –'

'Aw, this mate's all away to hell.'

'This mate's a bloody man. He's got me weighed up, like *that*. This bosun, 'e's too cocky for my liking. 'E was only a lamptrimmer last voyage.'

'Yes, and he'll be a bloody *coal*trimmer soon if he doesn't look out how he treats the chief.'

'I don't know where they come from, but Leicester Square's full of them.'

(Oh Lord God, look down on your unworthy and unwashed servant, Hilliot, the seaman, the Liverpool-Norwegian, whose knees knock together at thunder, whose filthy hands tremble always in impotent prayer; Oh Thou who createst my eyes from the green mantle of the standing pool, who createst everything, the weak and the strong, the tender with the cruel, the just and the unjust, pity his small impulses of lust, and see that little beauty in his life, which so soon shall be among the green

72

undertow of the tides; and as he stands alone, naked, weapon-less, deliver him from his bondage and bring him out of the darkness and the grief and the pain into sunlight.)

'I went ashore with Joe in Penang.'

3

The *Oedipus Tyrannus* was still asleep, lying against the wharf; all the ships in the harbour were asleep. The stevedores had not yet come to work; the winches lay idle; the dew was not yet dry on the derricks. And it was then, as I prepared the coffee for the crew at five-thirty, that I made up my mind. It was as if I had made up my mind to commit a murder. Passing between the galley and the forecastle in the long cool grey of the morning, I thought about it calmly –

The captain stood on the bridge, cleaning his teeth in a draw bucket. The mate, his forehead pearling with sweat as the morning drew on, yawned beside me, pulled out his watch. But I turned away from all with a grim look, which meant: let them go down below and argue about the Trocadero. That night I was to go ashore myself, to have a night's drift.

Now the tropical sun rose high above the *Oedipus Tyrannus*. Loading resumed, coaling began; she was taking in bulk oil and water. The derricks swung ceaselessly to and fro, like dinosaurs at play. The fiendish heat of the day seemed to make the rattle of the winches more monotonous, and the heavy stink of molasses and urine hanging about the ship made my thoughts darker and more fearful. To hell with Janet. She could take care of herself, and let whoever wanted shed tears of blood about it.

I gave Norman's pigeon a drink of water: Andy still had a taunt for me, and Norman said again that the Janes weren't any good. But I would have to find all that out for myself.

Surely Janet wouldn't mind that; she would *want* me to be a man, a hell of a fellow like Andy. Besides, I felt with a renewal of intensity my failure to be a shipmate among shipmates. My breaking faith with Janet in this simple fashion meant, I argued to myself, my acceptance by the community in a matter of hours; then, surely, it was worth while. Moreover, the crew itself would at once be unified. Plainly, every one on the *Oedipus Tyrannus*, even the fairy quartermaster and those few who were either too old or too dumb to do anything save sit around and sew, had, at any rate, tried it!

Meantime, I had a lot of lousy jobs to do. I began by chipping a stanchion on the port side by the galley. From where I worked I could see Norman's mickey, in its cage of unpainted white wood. It was so innocent there, it seemed to me. When Norman had dumped his last mess down the ash chute, hung up his dishcloths, and made up the galley fires, he would share his own supper with it, then turn in himself. He gave it as much freedom as he could during the daytime by letting it out on to the number four hatch forward of the galley. When it wandered about there Norman always had it tied by the leg on a long heaving line to a cleat. And as I chipped, long, unco-ordinated thoughts of home blossomed out of this inno-cence. It would be summer at home now, and the turf crisp with the summer heat; again the lazy tennis players lay below me, on the bank; blue speedwells suddenly started up from under a hedge. That time Janet and I had crossed Marples field together. Milk-white stitchworts . . . No! To hell with that – to hell with it! Gritting my teeth I chipped the more furiously. Tonight all that would be stamped out. It was neces-sary to work hard, for the mate was watching, and the sweat, which made my eyes tingle, poured off me like water off a dog: all round people were sweating, and the stevedores working numbers five and six hatches had taken off their dirty rags, placed them under the tap on the well deck, and were piling cargo naked. Some women were among the coal-humpers, and I remembered with horror having seen one of them in the luncheon hour lying with a stevedore down a coal bunker. Hawkers had spread out their goods – lacquerware, postcards, rings, and toothpaste – on the tarpaulined bunker hatches and on the hatches that were not being worked; a barber on the poop cut hair and shaved for a few sen, or whatever the cur-rency was; sow-sow women invaded the forecastle with their 'changey for changey'; all day naked boys moaned for chow, and once a native appeared on the wharf and shouted in English for newspapers. Andy threw down an old copy of the *Mukden Daily News*; the native tore it into strips, set fire to them, swal-lowed them one by one, and produced the newspapers whole

75

again, and folded, from his right ear. One of the officers threw money to him. Andy, white-aproned, dishcloth on his arm, hung over the rail watching. Jesus, I muttered, how I hate that bastard. And I remembered with remorse letting Norman get the pigeon from the topmast, and how Andy had taunted me for my fear.

But tonight things would all be changed, tonight I should be the hero, the monster –

The day rang with shouting and confusion; the sky was a blue wall which reverberated and echoed with din. Cockroaches and steam flies crawled in the messroom. Flies were crying 'like bleeding babies', the bosun said, as they died, heaving, on the yellow flypapers. Sweating rust and coal dust, I made my bunk, which was full of chippings shaken from my dungarees. Then I had to chip the bed of a winch . . . 'See those bloody great chunks of paint; pull them off with your fingers,' said the bosun. 'Like that, see . . .' 'Oh Christ, I can't do any more,' I moaned. The sack I was lying on seemed to be searing my stomach; there was no room to work with my wrists, which were bruised every time they came into contact with the sprocket of the reverse gear. Paint and burning oil dropped off the winch on to my face, mingling with my sweat. I longed for the open sea, to be able to wash myself, to be able to wash my clothes – to be clean! Tomorrow would be Sunday, but how would I be feeling then? Ah, Sunday's little idylls which the week's toil had earned! That Sunday, bound for Hong Kong, we had come up on deck. We paused; God brought a wind, a wind! And the sun and wind danced through our clothes, strung on the line. All around us was the morning's blue crystal; the sun sparkled with a thousand flashes on the waves' gentle fall. The sun shone on deck as I washed and scrubbed my coal-black dungarees, stiff from dust and ashes, red lead and rust and grease; I stole a heaving line from the poop, and my washing dangled along the line, so that the forecastle was quite dark. But the sun spun round in its might towards the evening land of clouds, the atmosphere turned to evening with the burning of pale red stars – that night the *Oedipus Tyrannus* had reached another port, Hong Kong. She glided in silently at four bells in the evening. Lanterns were swinging at the water's edge, an army of lights marched with torches up the slope to the barracks, a few natives came aboard wearing enormous cymbal-shaped hats. Behind the ship the Peninsula Hotel at Kowloon loomed darkly, but on the ship was dead silence, save for the hiss of water that was part of the silence, falling from her side into the darkness. Oh God, oh God, if sea life were only always like that! If it were only the open sea, and the wind racing through the blood, the sea, and the stars forever!

But although that was not the way of things, the thought of it gave me courage, and soon I had finished the winch, only to be called forward to shift hundred-weight barrels of oil and paint in the lamplocker with the lamptrimmer. My right arm ached terribly with sea boils, and I had bound it with a sweat rag belonging to a fireman. Gritty coal dust was everywhere, and flies heaved and sizzled and bred on the bulkheads. Coal dust got into my eyes and blackened my nostrils, while the sweat rag round my arm was covered with a black film. The heavy-smelling lamplocker lay right forward by the chainlocker in what was really the forecastle, and I had wondered at first why it was not used as the men's quarters. Later I had discovered that five Chinese deportees were berthed there, and they had remained there as far as Shanghai. Some of the drums of oil were so inaccessible that we had to shift them with a block and tackle, others we carried, piling them neatly in corners. With only three of the former shifted I caught four fingers in the snatch block. The drum of oil fell on a bag of lime, which it opened, then on to my feet. The lamptrimmer took three minutes to free me. 'Now get to hell out of this,' said the lamptrimmer.

In the fore-cabin three sea apprentices, painting the name of the ship on lifebelts, laughed. 'What you want is a good strong woman!' I staggered aft, covered with lime, my temples beating, my fingers bent back, dazed, and trembling in every limb. In the forecastle there was a smell of damp straw from the winch mats left overnight by the stevedores and thrown down the forecastle skylight. On the table there were two letters for me, one from my mother, and one from Janet. My bowels melted, all my strength flowed out of me like water, as I saw her boyish handwriting. And then I made a queer grimace. How bloody funny! You can't fool me, you little bitch. What was the use now? My mind was made up. And suddenly I hated her for the letter!

So now she would try and console me, would she, just at the right moment; try and warn me what was coming to me if I wasn't faithful to her; but this time she'd be disappointed. I'd show her, by God, that nothing was so homeless as that letter! And I forgot all my pain as I stood there stupidly reading and re-reading the address. So the letter had been forwarded from Singapore? Why, she hadn't even troubled to consult the posting date I had given her. She might at least have taken the trouble to look the ship up in the *Journal of Commerce* –

Flinging myself down on the bunk, I groaned and cursed. Then I looked at my hand. The blood had run out of the fingers of my right hand, and they were all twisted together anyhow, like strands of a heaving line in an unfinished eye splice. I separated them one from one with the left hand. Soon the blood was coming back; there was no serious damage. Pull your bloody self together. There was a heavy step outside ... The bosun entered the forecastle. 'Well! ...' he drew a long breath. 'Well, you're the strangest bird I ever met and I've seen some. What in hell do you think you're doing?'

'A drum of oil dropped on my foot,' I said.

'Why, can't you walk?'

'Certainly I can walk.'

'All right. Come on, then. Turn to.'

The bosun said no more but went immediately out of the forecastle, so there was nothing for it but for me to follow him. Outside, the iron well deck was so hot I felt it burning through the soles of my shoes.

'You could fry an egg on this deck,' said the bosun. 'Now then, son,' – he pointed to the stevedores' rags that had been left behind under the tap at the well – 'shovel these overside – on the wharf. If they fall in the ditch so much the better. They're not likely to go in swimming after them.'

'Are there sharks here, then?'

'Yes, you can bet your boots on that ... Well, get that squared off,' the bosun said magnanimously, 'then when you've finished them dishes you can put on some clean gear and go ashore.' The bosun winked evilly. 'Well, there's no need to do that,' he added. 'I forgot for the moment you were one of those who preferred your right hand –'

As I shovelled, flies rose in a cloud of steam from the clothes and something that looked like a flying walnut glanced in my face. The garments, sweaty and obscene, fluttered in a cloud of flies down to the wharf, some falling in the gap of water between. Those that fell on the wharf were pounced on by naked boys who fought for them. When they had decided who was to have them, they went on shouting for chow, so Andy threw them a dirty crust that had fallen in oil and coal dust and water, and they fought for that too.

I squared up and went to the washhouse for my bucket. There was no room in there. A trickle of blue water ran down the dirty tiles and over the step from where someone was scrubbing his dungarees. I looked into the steward's room, bucket on my arm. Taff and Ginger were sound asleep. From the alley I could see out on the well deck and up the galley companion. The lamp-trimmer leaned over the galley rail, pausing with the anchor light in his hand. Andy was hanging a singlet on a line. Outside, I found the crowd watching a ship come into harbour.

'P. & O. boat over there.'

'Garn, that's not a P. & O. boat. That's a bloody B.I. boat, for Jesus sake.'

'That's a bloody P. & O. boat.'

'And I say it's a bloody B.I. boat.'

'Then you're bloody wrong, you bloody twat. Can't you see her house flag?'

'That's no ruddy house flag. That's the Chinese No. 1's ruddy dungarees hanging out to dry.'

'Aw, shag off with you all,' said the lamptrimmer, coming down with the anchor light. 'I've just been putting in some overtime. What's all this about? ... Aw, it's a P. & O. boat.'

'It's a British India boat, I'm telling you. For Christ sake shut up, let a fellow have a nap, can't you –'

'Ay, you're right, Lamps. It is a P. & O. boat.'

When I had washed I saw that there were crenellations of light in the sky, against which the latticed cranes dipped and beckoned. Come. Come. Come. Night glided down on the *Oedipus Tyrannus*, and the dishes strapped up at last, I re-entered the forecastle to dress. There I took my blue suit out of my sea box. While dressing I remembered how the first night aboard the ship I had creased these self-same blue trousers, holding them under my chin, folding them over and over and then, with such remorse, dropping them into my sea box, a part of my life gone. The end of a chapter. Clean, blue dungarees, drained of most of their original colour, and brown shoes, were the general rule when the *Oedipus Tyrannus* push went ashore. But now it was the right time to wear my blue suit again. I put my two letters in my inside pocket – I would read them ashore, that was all they were worth! Then I struggled my arms into the sleeves, and went out on deck, where wire runners and derrick blocks and wedges lay in all directions, and all was noisy confusion. For a minute I peered down into the deep rectangular well of number six hatch, where a cluster of lamps glared on six stevedores, a new shift, their backs as glossy as moles, and watched them rolling boxes into place. One of the sea apprentices who had laughed at me in the fore-cabin was on watch down there, huddled half asleep on a bundle of cured goatskins. I made a rude gesture at him. Good-bye to the ship for a time. Beside me a great derrick slowly reared its long neck into the dark sky.

I arrived amidships among the screeching coolies with their bandy legs, who tipped coal from their baskets into the bunkers. They ran in a never-ending procession up the swaying planks. I splashed through coal dust and oil and water. The dust was whirling everywhere from the clattering buckets of coal thrown into the bunkers, sticking to the white paint that was damp with the tropical dew. The loneliness struck up from the wharf, never before so painfully new, and footsteps, shadows, arc lamps, the hum from the dark town. There man was met by man with a call, a glance, a smile –

Never before had my heart loved in that solitude!

It was as if the air quivered with an electric tension, with hesitating, anxious desire, with derision and petrified delight. My yearnings sailed over sea and evening and dawn; and for the first time I felt I knew the meaning of the city, where all nights could intoxicate and torment, and where all hearts spin towards the light and burn themselves in its fire, whose nerves are played to death and sing like violins in defiance and painful exultation, because we still exist –

Standing at the gangway head a moment, I looked along the wharf, and then I went down. The quartermaster, who had just arrived on the gangway, shouted amiably at me, 'Don't come back so bad we have to haul you up in the coal mast.'

I shouted over my shoulder to the quartermaster swaying down the last few steps of the crazy gangway, 'Well, if you don't drop the gangway down enough for the tide I'll be in the dock anyhow.'

I sprang to the wharf, the unyielding solidity of which felt strange to my feet. Close by the coal-humpers wailed as they ran up the planks to the bunkers. Near them, standing by a coal heap, was the first mate. He was rolling a cigarette, and looking at the rusty, fouled side of the ship. 'Dirty old cow, isn't she,' he remarked cheerily to me as I passed.

'Well, you can't expect anything else, with this coaling, sir.' I paused, embarrassed.

'We'll have her all cleaned up before we dock in Liverpool. We've got a winter in New York before that. But we can't get any coolies to paint her here, though. No sir,' said the mate. 'We ain't got time. Well, I see you're all titivated up to go ashore. Going to give the girls a treat, eh?'

I compromised. 'I want a walk more than anything else.'

'Don't you get enough exercise on this ship then, for Christ sake? Chipping that samson post, eh? I wish your mother could have seen you yesterday.'

I thought, but said nothing, remembering the letter.

'Well, go along ashore and have a good time,' chattered the mate, and added expansively, 'The Trocadero's a good place. And the Miki or the Baikine; you'll find plenty of bobbed head tigers in this dump.'

'Well, I hope so. Good night, sir.'

'Good luck!'

I moved off quickly. Let the mate do his chattering to the skipper!

Seamen's Temperance Restaurant ... The harbour was lit up like a town. The dock was a coffin of molten iron, with long white candles burning. A hooting siren called from a ship

81

coming in, Hoo! ah hoo! and in answer the tenuous stutter of winches in different stages of acceleration, like a number of sewing machines, was borne over the water from the roadstead. Row on row of angular sheds frowned at me as I walked along, and in a gap between them I saw the wide scarlet tracery cast in bars of riding lights on the water. No. 1 quay. No. 2 quay. No. 3 quay. No. 4 quay. I passed a priest, who might have been a Russian Jew, in long black robes, his beard reaching well down his chest. He had a seraphic smile on his face as he paced the quay, and I thought he looked like Our Saviour. Above him distorted giant skeletons of cranes waved their steel and bronze arms. There was the sound of hammers banging in a rhythmic thunder, harshly reverberant steel. Native night shift. The song of iron accompanied my footsteps infuriatingly until I realized I had gone the wrong side of the restaurant and was keeping too much to the line of the docks for the town. It became gloomy and smelly, round behind a godown, and I was just making up my mind to retrace my steps when a voice hailed me, 'Abend.'

'Hullo!'

The man was sitting on a bollard smoking a pipe, and rose to meet me. Near him, a row of natives squatted on their haunches, fishing in the dock.

'What can I do for you?' I asked politely.

'You are an Englishman?'

'Yes.'

'I am a German. I was wondering if you could tell me where I could get a bumboat back to my ship. I am more or less stranded here. The last boat, surely, it appears, has gone anyway, otherwise.'

'I see,' I said. 'You're moored out in the harbour, and you can't get a boat. Too bad. Ich bin auf ein Englisch Schiff *Oedipus Tyrannus*. Luckily we're alongside. No. I don't think you will get a bumboat now,' I added.

'Nein?' The German shook his head.

'So spät –'

The German looked tough in the light of the fishermen's dim kerosene lamp, and rather dirty. Whatever his rating, he wore mufti – a blue suit similar to my own.

'Ich bin ein Matrose,' I said. 'Und Sie sind ein – Heizer, nicht wahr.'

The German roared with laughter. 'I shall tell the bloody skipper your story,' he choked. 'Ein Heizer, a stoker, you say? Nein, nein, I am der – zum Beispiel – I am the you say *Sparks*, nicht? Ein Heizer! Gut! Gut! Fabelhaft! ... I am on the *Wölfsburg*.'

'Well, I *am* sorry! Entschuldigen Sie, mein Herr. Es tut mir leid.'

'Es tut *mir* leid.'

We laughed happily, and for a moment all the harbour noises stopped at once, so that we heard the sough and lap of the green water against the quay steps. Eight bells struck from somewhere out in the harbour, and then another, but suddenly the titanic thunder of the native night shift started again. There was a smell of fish and seaweed and strong tobacco.

'That is the *Wölfsburg*.' The German pointed.

'So.' I looked out at a silhouette, with a dancing reflection of mast lights in the water.

'Well, what do you say you let the *Wölfsburg* look after herself for the time being and come into the town?'

'Wie?'

'Kommen Sie mit, zu trinken,' I said.

'Nur habe ich zu viel, verstehen Sie! On the ship!'

'Oh,' I said laughing. 'But Pilsner, Münchener; we will have the hell of a time. Let us enjoy ourselves.'

'All right,' said the German. 'Come on then. It's no good staying here ... This way, then, past all the tramps. Liners, ja, Atlantic service. Aber, nach dem Krieg, we have no mercantile marine service. The *Wölfsburg* is a tramp ship, though.'

'Schrecklich, es ist schrecklich.' I nodded.

We started to walk together. A miasmic stench rose from the docks. A stern rose up before us: *Matsuye Maru – Osaka*. It was an old passenger steamer with raking masts and one black smokestack with an O on it in white. The boatswain and his men, under dim ceiling lights, were washing down her decks, and the hose was splashing water on the quay. That was the sort of thing Japanese did at night. A fireman with a sweat rag round his neck, off watch, grinned over the bulwarks at us. Forward, under a lamp as yellow as his face, another of the crew washed singlets in a bucket.

A second receding stern loomed up before us. *Jefferson – Seattle*. An obscene monster, with ashes pouring out of her side.

Seattle – where was Seattle? But the Stars and Stripes floated and furled listlessly over her stern.

'Amerikanisch,' said the German.

White-capped sailors, smoking, craned over her rail. Three men aft were rigging an awning. The German and I were spelling out together *Maharajah – Liverpool*, and I explained gaily, even proudly, that she was a sister ship to the *Oedipus Tyrannus*, and that those two standing by the roundhouse talking must be the cook and the galley boy. There was a light in the galley, and I said then, 'Somebody must be making coffee.' The last ship on that wharf was the *Martensen*, from Oslo. But the *Martensen* was as silent as a graveyard on a dead planet.

'I was born in Norway,' I said, 'and our cook and galley boy are both Norwegian. I was born in Oslo when it was Christiania, so I can always say if anyone asks me, that I am a Christiania boy –'

'So.'

'Is this a little like Hamburg?' I asked.

'Ja. Oder London. Oder Liverpool.'

'Or Saigon. Or Trebizond. Or Samarkand.' I said.

We came to another wharf, passing slowly other great ships: *Petropalovsk, Erzherzog, Franz Ferdinand –*

We reached the tram lines, and soon three trams, crowded to overflowing, passed, wailing as they swayed down the lines in rapid succession . . .

As we walked on in silence I thought of New Brighton trams – other trams in other places: strolling with Janet over beyond Sandvika. The cowbells had tinkled faintly up the forest road. The woman was picking berries – red currants. Crickets chirped. Dandelions – wild sweet peas – cornflowers – oats. Tinkle tonkle tankle tunk. Spinkle sponkle spankle. The pig chased the dog round the lawn. There was a snake in the grass . . . You see, that is Orion. And that . . . Cassiopeia . . . And that? We call it the Milky Way . . . And we call it Wintergarten. Well, where's Saturn then? . . . A goat bell had shaken its measure of notes from the terror of the woods, and we ran hand in hand through the forest to look for Saturn –

'Es ist gut so,' I said to the German.

Rickshaws whirled by, a native clerk pedalled by on a shiny new bicycle, a sikh – would it be a sikh? – policeman looked disdainfully at us at a crossroads. We passed the south station of the town, an anatomical museum, and a Scandinavian sailors' home.

A poster of the *Free Press* in English, said: MURDER OF BROTHER-IN-LAW'S CONCUBINE ... *Bar. Boston Bar. Café Baikine. Bar and Cabaret. Trocadero. Satsuma Wares. Grand Revival – Richard Barthelmess in 'The Amateur Gentleman'. Miki Bar. Dancing. Norddeutscher Lloyd Steamships.*

'There,' I said, 'your great line, Norddeutscher Lloyd –'

We paused before the brilliantly lighted windows in which were two models of the company's ships; there were also time-tables and a garish poster.

'Ja,' said the German.

'Ja,' I smiled.

'That might be our ship or your ship.'

'Ours have only one funnel each; that has two.'

'Well, let's shoot a few whiskies down the hatch, and you'll see three.'

'I see you want to make me drunk,' he laughed.

'No, it's not that. It's simply that I'm damned lonely.'

'Lonely,' the German sighed, 'I also.'

'Ich auch.'

Cabaret Pompeia ...

We entered a little bar and sat down. We were the only two in the place. A native came from behind the counter like a spider from under his leaf.

'What'll you drink?' I asked. 'Pilsener, Münchener; I don't know what they've got.'

'Nay, nay, Gin.'

'Gin. All right. Waiter, three triple gins, please.'

'Triple –?'

'Bring six glasses of gin. Our friends are coming.'

The waiter brought six glasses of gin on a tray, and the card of the house. I handed him a ten-yen note, and some coins with holes in them, which the purser had given me as part of the port's draw.

'Prosit.'

'Prosit,' said the German. 'This mixes well. Es ist gut so.'

We drank the first one straight, no heeltaps.

'Drei?' said the German. 'All these – für mich?'

'Ja, ja,' I said. 'You will be drunk.'

'I am never drunk,' said the German.

'Let us get really drunk,' I said.

'I was drunk when you met me.'

'You will be drunker still.'

'All right, let's drink them both this time.'

'Alles gutes.'

'Alles gutes.'

'Come on now, what are you going to have now?'

'Beer. Let us get really drunk.'

The waiter brought Pilsener and some change. There were some coins with holes and a five-yen note. The beer creamed deliciously in the glass.

'Salt air makes thirsty men,' I said. 'Where have you been this trip?'

'Oh, we have been away a long time, over a year,' he replied. 'This time we made a trip to Sudamerika – Santos and Paraguay, San Francisco, Florianopolis – Port Allegre. We have been rolling all around the world, you know. Ach! But everywhere is the same – Prosit.'

I drank deeply, tilting the rim of the glass and pressing it on my nose. I had not heard of many of the ports, and it seemed to me that some of them were not ports, but countries. But what did it matter? We were ashore! And I felt suddenly comfortable and happy. I would dismiss Janet from my mind. I *could* drink, anyway; there were no complications about that. While here – and what could be more delightful? – was a representative of another community, another world, drinking; the wireless operator of a world such as my own, with a stokehold, a galley, and a forecastle. It was like being in Homer and drinking with an Ethiopian. Or 'Ben Jonson entertains a man from Stratford.'

'You know English pretty well,' I said.

'Yes, not bad. I knew many Englishmen when I was in Bonn.'

'You were in Bonn?'

'Ja. Vor dem Krieg.'

'I was at Cambridge. Nach dem Krieg.'

'What is your name, may I ask?'

'Hilliot. Dana Hilliot. And yours?'

'Hans Popplereuter.'

'Well, hooray!'

'Hooray!'

'This is a one-eyed hole,' I said. 'Let's see what it says on their card. *Cabaret Pompeia and first-class Restaurant,*' I read. '*Meals served at all hours and all kinds of best liquors. Best dancers on the stage. The best Jazz Orchestra Pompeia. Dancing. Please show this card to the rickshaw coolie. A block from Yamato Hotel, 45 Naniwa-cho 2-chome. Proprietor and Manager: A. J. Fourmanento.*' I called the waiter. 'Hi Confucius! What about this dancing?'

'Behind,' said the waiter. 'We used to. We shut up that last night. Miki Bar is your place. All same firm, sir.'

The waiter returned to the counter.

'We'll go to the Miki Bar some time tonight,' I said.

'Ja, you don't like this.'

'Well, nicht so besonderes schlecht!'

We ordered more drinks.

'Have you been in Bonn then?' asked Popplereuter.

'No. As a matter of fact I didn't learn German at school or at Cambridge. But I took a course once in the holidays at a local school of commerce. Not that I learnt anything. You see, I was in love, and was always late –'

Suddenly I remembered imitating the Herr Professor for Janet.

'The Herr Professor used to say, "Ah, Herr Hilliot ist spät,"' I continued. ' "I was expecting you. Ein Vater, Herr Hilliot, und ein *Sohn* dienten bei demselben Regiment-Corporal, nicht wahr? In French, n'est-ce pas? Pronunciations of both exactly the same ... Can the man not answer because of the colonel I will open his mouth for him. No. Ein Vater, Mr Echtwarts ... I am waiting, Mr Echtwarts. The father of the *Unteroffizier?*

Nein. Too bad, too bad . . . you might please all write down the following – all, you too, Mr Hilliot. Sie robt ihn. No, no. Sich weden. I am going to gif you a number of worts and sentences of my own! You know the style!" I never learned a bloody thing.'

'Wie geht's?' said Popplereuter. 'You are in love.'

'I was in love.'

'Nicht so besonderes schlecht.'

We rose and shook hands solemnly.

'Salt air makes thirsty men.'

'Salt air makes thirsty men,' assented Popplereuter. 'Are you,' he smiled, 'as the English say, an old sea dog?'

'No. This is my first voyage to sea.'

'So. I am interested. What makes you come to sea?'

'Ah, well. There you have me. I don't know.'

'You have been to Cambridge?'

'Yes. But I was sent down.'

'You were –?'

'Sent down. Expelled. Fired. Sacked. Herausgeschmissen!'

'Mein Gott, you are like me. Vor dem Krieg I go to Bonn Universität as a student. I belong to a good corps, too. But at this Cologne Carnival I threw a man into the Rhine. Also . . . all my life I have been fond of wireless. I became a wireless operator in the navy. When the war is over I fall in love, and then more trouble.'

'That's where the trouble begins.'

'Then more and more trouble.'

'Oh hell! It's the same with me. I didn't come to sea entirely because I was sent down.'

'Your father, then, what did he say to you?'

'My guardian? He was good to me. You see, I had only one year at Cambridge. He took me to the pictures, the Lichtspiels, the very first night home. He said you better settle down now and do some work. . .'

'Why were you sent down, as you say?'

'It was nothing, nothing at all. I failed my first-year examinations, verstehen Sie, what we call "Mays". And I was had up once for leaving a pub after ten – what you call a Weinlust. And I was arrested on November the fifth for knocking off a policeman's hat. Silly, silly, silly things. The Master of the College sent for me and said, "You neither ride, row, nor read –" '

'Schrecklich,' nodded Popplereuter. 'Schrecklich.'

'But that was not really why I came to sea.'

'Nor I.'

'It's hell.'

'Were there nice women in Cambridge? Not for business, eh? Ha ha!'

'I don't know. Since I was sixteen I've been faithful to one girl.'

'Faithful, ah,' said Popplereuter. 'What is that?'

'Virgo intacta.'

'Gesundheit.' Popplereuter raised his glass.

'Chimborazo, Popocatepetl . . .' I toasted.

We sang. We sang *Drei Segelmann*, which I don't know, but I joined in the chorus. We sang *Mademoiselle from Armentières*, *Deutschland über Alles*, and *Lisa*; *For He's a Jolly Good Fellow*, and *God Save the King*; *Lisa* again, and *The Bastard King of England*, with which Popplereuter was unfamiliar, but he waved his glass and sang, 'Back to the Bastard King of England,' again and again, to the inscrutable pleasure of Confucius.

'England good country. Wunderbar,' hiccoughed Popplereuter.

'Germany bloody good country,' I hiccoughed.

'We fought because we had to,' Popplereuter went on, 'for the "balance of power", you call it.'

I forgot to mention there was a war on about half a mashie shot away, it being June 1927, but that has not part in the story.

'War is a bloody good thing,' I said. 'I'd like to fight against Belgium. I don't blame you marching on the bastards.'

'War is schrecklich, schrecklich. You have to fight to know that.'

'Yes, war is schrecklich.'

'Perhaps you will write a book of your experiences.'

'Ja, perhaps,' I said. 'That is certainly a point. But the desire to write is a disease like any other disease; and what one writes, if one is to be any good, must be rooted firmly in some sort of autochthony. And there I abdicate. I can no more create than fly. What I could achieve would be that usual self-conscious first novel, to be reviewed in the mortuary of *The Times Literary Supplement,* a "crude and unpleasant work", something of that nature, of which the principal character would be no more and no less, whether in liquor or in love, than the abominable author himself. I fear, also, that the disease is a childish one, diarrhoea scribendi simply. But I don't expect you to follow me. I'm sorry; I always speak like this when I'm tight.'

'No. I don't understand you.'

'I was bitterly hurt when my supervisor in his last interview with me before I left the college said, "You are not nearly so unusual a type as you think you are!"'

'So.'

'That was a bitter thing to say, eh?'

'Ich weiss nicht . . . Herr Ober!'

'Hail, Confucius!'

'Noch ein – zwei –'

'Two more –'

'Nein –'

'No; come back – let's have two starboard lights. Savee starboard lights?'

'Me savee.'

The drinks were brought, and I had to explain to Popplereuter the difference between a starboard light and a *crème de menthe.* When he had tasted it, he asked how my mother liked my going away.

I made no reply, remembering the letter.

Then I remembered Janet's letter. 'Forget it, you son of a bitch,' I said aloud.

'Wie?' said Popplereuter.

I felt in my inside pocket and brought out the letters. My heart seemed to be beating in the pulses of my body and in my mouth.

'I can't read it,' I said to Popplereuter. 'You read it.' I handed him the two letters.

'Read the top one first,' I said. 'It's from my mother.'

He opened it and read: 'My Dearest Son – Just a little note to say may God bless you and keep you in the right path. I do hope you are comfortable and keeping *clean,* because I don't want my son coarsened by a lot of hooligans. I've no time for more because as you know, my eyes are so bad these days. Very much love from your own Mother.'

'Does she really say that – "I don't want my son coarsened by a lot of hooligans"?'

'Yes. The other letter is from your girl. Don't you want me to read that?'

'Not yet, no.'

I made my mother's letter into a funnel, and filtered the starboard light through it into an unfinished glass of beer.

'She doesn't love me,' I said. 'I wish she did. What's the use of anything.'

'Who – your mother?'

'Yes – and now I feel somehow that I daren't hear my girl's letter – six weeks is a long time, you know, and she hasn't written before.' I began to feel sorry for myself, and rather drunk.

'Well, I don't know.' Popplereuter took a long breath. 'I think you are very lucky and young. I must tell you that I am trying to forget. I got news here, my little girl, my little love, daughter of the house, of the Hotel Rheinischer Hof. She has just got married. Oh, Hans is very unhappy, very, very unhappy.'

'Well, we're a pair of them, that's all,' I said. 'I've got a girl on my mind too – I've been trying to explain –'

'Yes, but you are too young for such a big worry.'

'Oh hell.' I sighed. 'What I might have explained was this. Your calling, your profession, is the sea, whereas mine simply is not. I'm not going to stick around chipping winches, don't you think it. I simply can't imagine why I'm here so many miles away in this god-awful place. At least, I'll try to explain –'

'Prosit.'

'Prosit.'

I felt my eyes dim, my eyes grow placid. I didn't want to try and explain. I gazed at a thousand bubbles on top of my beer. I had thought of explaining to Popplereuter just why I had gone to sea, but surely that was not possible. Were it possible to explain he would not understand any more than I would understand why Popplereuter had gone to sea. I could not for that matter explain to myself. I had already been sufficiently difficult, as always, for one evening. One bubble makes a grain of sand. Sixty stars to each man. I put down my glass noisily then picked it up again, and gazed mournfully at my reflection. Narcissus. Bollocky Bill the Sailor. Bollocky Bill, aspiring writer, drawn magically from the groves of the Muses by Poseidon. But had it been so much Poseidon? I looked more deeply in the glass. Christ, was this me? What was there? Sadness! Misery! Self-disgust! Terror! No getting away from it, no getting away from the unfortunate Hilliot, this strong creature with a head of filthy, infected hair, and a maggoty brain and a rotting consciousness, who dreams of archetypal images; this sad dish, Eugene Dana Hilliot! Thy hand, great Anarch, evil ghost who must follow me wherever I go! Hear chaos! Hear me, stinking cod fulfilled of donge and of corrupcioun! Tinfoil Jesus, crucified homunculus (who is also the cross), spitted on the hook of an imaginary Galilee! Who is the crown of thorns dripping red blossoms and the red-blue nails, the flails and the bloody wounds. The tears, but also the lips cupped to embrace them as they fall; the whips, but also the flesh crawling to them. The net and the silver writhing in the mesh, and all the fish that swim in the sea. – The centre of the Charing Cross, ABCD, the Cambridge Circle, the Cambridge Circus, is Hilliot – but every night, unseen, he climbs down and returns to his hotel – while the two great shafts, the propeller shafts, the shafts of wit, laced with blood, AB, CD are the diameters.

Now with his navel as centre and half CD as radius, describe a vicious circle! An order imperiously given! Hear me, Janet, maker of all these thoughts and words, these finite stupidities and speculations, an incantation for yourself, our unborn son, and me. Repeat them slowly and fondly to yourself as though you loved them ... Did you know I was liable to stigmata? Yes, the blood flows from my feet, from the upper surface as well as the soles, and from the palms and backs of my hands. My forehead becomes moist with blood, and blood flows there also. I lie on my back, my bleeding hands enveloped in cloths on my knees. And at the same time blood oozes out of the stigmata of my side and feet, and it trickles down my temples, cheek, and neck. My head drops to one side, my nose, as in a mescal trance, feels like wax; my hands are icicles ... A clammy sweat breaks out over my whole body. And that is only *one* thing! There are a thousand other more significant disclosures I could make of myself! After which, could you still believe in me, still believe in the notion that my voyage is something Columbian and magnificent? Still believe in my taking a self-inflicted penance; in this business of placing myself within impenetrable and terrible boundaries in order that a slow process of justification to yourself may go on. Very well, then, prepare to be disillusioned, for, like Melville, I shall strip my motive like an onion down to the innermost bulb of degradation; listen, if you value my love, to the story of my obfuscated ignorance, of my bespattered idealism; of my flawless insincerity ...

'I don't know, Hans,' I said. 'I don't know what I could tell you about my life that would interest you, or if it did interest you, what you would understand. First, I am a strange man, or I would like to be a strange man, which is nearer the truth – you will have seen that: some might say, almost, the fool. I was born in Christiania, in the Christian den 4 des gade, dangerous names for me! My youth was ruined by a curious passion for collecting, among other things, universities. For instance, I played baseball in Harvard and set fire to Brattle Square. In Princeton I nearly drank myself to death. In Moscow I was a camera man under Pudovkin. In Oxford, Missouri, I wrote a song. In Yokohama I taught botany. When Christiania became Oslo I sold, in my desperation, the *Dagbladet*, and lectured on the Greenland occupation. Cambridge, Eng., where I remained ten years as a fellow of Westcott House – playing the mandolin on Armistice Days – gave me an honorary degree. At Cape Cod I held office simultaneously as the town constable, the ticket collector at the cinema, and the local bootlegger; it was there, also, I committed my first murder, in a windmill. In Barbados, in Bridgetown, I remained a week, playing the taropatch in a brothel. While accepting the offer of the fifteen-year-old daughter of the house, I sold her to the Negro doorkeeper for a bottle of gin. This, however, I was in too feeble a condition to drink. In Tsintao I defrauded a Chinaman of a bottle of Batavian arak, weeping afterwards, when he refused, publicly, to shake hands with me. In Stamboul, I played chess with the Sultan's sister. I pursue women from street to street, from lamp to lamp, from Petty Cury to old Chesterton, always remaining a virgin. When they speak to me I run away. But why go on? I have lived. I have bathed in blood at Saigon and Singapore. I have, like Masefield, worn my jackknife in my cap to catch the lightning at Cape Horn – what my shipmates called being on the horn of a Demelia. Once, for a week, adrift in an open boat, I kept up the spirits of the crew by playing the taropatch. In the end we had to eat the strings. But no, please do not interpret my conduct as unconventional or schizophrenic. No, a thousand times no. I have always been popular with officials. Yes. Men in authority, many hundreds, have seen me home when drunk. At Honolulu it was the harbourmaster. At Yokohama it was the assistant harbourmaster. At Bombay it was the deputy conservator of the Port Trust. At Naples it was the capitano del porto. At Constantinople it was the captein port. In Turkey the newspapers described my arrest for the little matter of the Sultan's sister as "une fantaisie bien américaine". I had given my name to the police as Whitman . . .

'In Batavia no one saw me, but at Calcutta hundreds of people wondered why I took the sacred water of the Ganges. Barcelona I knew as well as Rangoon. Piraeus as Gibraltar. Manila or Surabaya? They are all the same to me. You know what they say in the Bible . . . "And they removed from Ezron-Gaber and pitched in the wilderness of Zion which is Kadesh. And they removed from Kadesh and pitched in Hor in the edge of the land of Edom . . . And they departed from Zalmonesh and pitched in Punon. And they departed from Punon and pitched in Oboth . . . And they departed from Almon-diblathaim and pitched in the mountains of Abarim, before Nebo."

'Well, that's me. The almanac. And in all these places I have wept; wept for my lost opportunities and my found opportunities, my profoundly lost and my profound opportunities, for my lack of wit and my overflux of power, for my tenderness, my super-sensual cruelty, for my lost childhood and my extramundane intelligence; and then, as the roar of a million cities has closed over my mind, I have wept for them altogether because I was always very drunk. Yes, Hans, yes, and in Literature my name is scarcely less momentous. The *Honolulu Star Bulletin* says, "A name to conjure with". You see, unemolumented but monumental. When I was fourteen I was under the delusion for a year I was Thomas Chatterton ... mad? No ... not even that. But a kind of semi-madman, pernicious and irritating and apathetic in the extreme, for whom in madness, as in death to the impotent, exists the only dignified escape. No, no, no, no. Yes, yes – still, after all, who am I to care if nobody believes me?

'Read my collected works first, several thousand volumes, including the much-discussed *Othello*, all tightly bound, paying special attention to my masterpiece, *How to Be Happy Though Dead*. Some say, admittedly, that these are small beer, but there is always plenty of it; a friendly critic, J., said that I have strained at a gnat and swallowed the Round Pond; another, mentioning that Hilliot had written a thousand lines, added, "Would he had blotted them all." Undoubtedly these remarks are to some extent justified, and my critics correct, but taking it all in all, by and large, isn't it enough to drive any man into the forecastle, or to drink?'

'You are lying to me,' Popplereuter said, puzzled, leaning over, glass in hand.

'Yes,' I said, 'I am. I'm sorry, you don't know how little. But even if I were to put the case more directly, if I were to make a tactile effort in the direction of clarity, a sober collocation of the news – I know you don't understand me, but I'm getting just drunk enough to be determined to bore you to death – or I can be a tomb! The important point is that the apparent facts are largely imaginary. I assume the guilt of a mother, or of a father, or of a heredity, imagine it completely, to be able on the one hand to give an adequate explanation of my more inexplicable actions, and on the other in order to be clothed in a dark, blood-stained dignity. Some of these points are raised, and you may have read for yourself, in my much maligned and certainly dangerous and misleading work, *Hamlet*. I delight to imagine that my father is mad, when as a matter of fact he is only in a nursing home with a stone in the kidney; I delight to imagine that my mother, who occasionally suffers from conjunctivitis, is going blind. But it is I who am the father, or who would be the father, the mother, and who postulate the responsibility for both; it is young Dana who belongs to the ranks of the blind and the dumb. I grant you, there *is* the business of my aunts, all knocked for a row of milk bottles in the cemetery at Oslo, but that was the consequence not of some terrible physical cataclysm, so far as I can make out, but of frailty unhappily wedded to a titanic strength and an irrefragable stupidity. At least I hope that that's all there is to it. But out of this emerges something simpler. I am sick with love for a girl. She wears a white skirt, and a soft blouse and a school blazer edged with brown.'

'Ah, I love her! You love me! Nicht so besonders schlecht. Ha ha ha!' chuckled Popplereuter.

'My grandfather, on my mother's side, was a sea captain who went down with his ship. He was bringing my mother a cockatoo. Prosit.'

'For the balance of power,' said Popplereuter.

'Consequently I have in me an inborn craving for the unrest of the sea. Meereinsamkeit. Oh, but this craving was not, is not conscious enough, as Petit the poet said, intellectually to be diluted into a mere intangible wanderlust . . . No sir. Well! . . . Good night, Confucius; I envy you your extreme happiness!'

Norddeutscher Lloyd Steamships: Miki Bar – Dancing; Richard Barthelmess in 'The Amateur Gentleman'

We paused, swaying on our heels, before the snowy theatre front. A sailor was reeling round in front of the box office.

'Hullo,' I said, 'that's next week. Look what we've got today, for Christ sake. Olga Tschechowa in *Love's Crucifixion*. What do you make of that, Watson?'

'Olga Tschechowa in *Love's Crucifixion*,' spelt out Popplereuter. 'Richard Barthelmess in *The Amateur Gentleman*. A smashing drama of the good old days of Merrie England! Next week!'

As we approached the box office I saw that the drunk sailor was Norman. He was wearing only a singlet and a pair of dungarees. I thought he was drunker than I was. Norman suddenly put his arm through the woven wire *guichet* of the box office, and thumped his fist.

'I want one third day-return to Birkenhead Central,' he roared.

'Hullo there, Norman,' I said.

He turned round, but spun again on his own volition before recovering his balance. It seemed as though a recognition of myself was slowly filtering through his veins.

'Hullo there, chummy! Are you with me, shipmates? You're with me? Good!' He staggered to the box office again. 'Three, four, five, fifteen day-returns to Birkenhead Central. Do you hear me? Hey, where's Andy, you fellows? I've lost Andy. Where's Andy, do you know?'

'I haven't seen him, Norman,' I said.

'I've lost him. I don't know where I've lost the sod. You seen the sodding sod anywhere?'

'No, I haven't. What about coming into the pictures?'

'Nei, I must find that sod.'

'Oh, let him go to hell!'

'Yes, go to hell,' grunted Norman, forsaking Andy a little at a time.

'Everybody go to hell.'

While we were talking, Popplereuter, who had been sitting on the kerb, suddenly pulled himself together and got up; he walked the length of the step and pushed some money imperiously into the box office.

We were admitted. The cinema glowed with pink light inside. The walls were fairly plain and the concealed red lamps gave it to me the appearance of a tomb or a catacomb burning with fire. To enter it was to enter a mephitic forecastle, for it seemed to me that the place was full of seamen and firemen. The audience moved, smoked, coughed, and murmured as a single mass, colourless and quiet. A long note from the orchestra drew two halves of a gauze curtain lamely across the screen, meeting in the centre. Drunk. We were all drunk.

'Andy said he'd meet me at the Sailors' Home,' babbled Norman, who couldn't find his seat anywhere.

'Well, why not go there?'

'No, let's stay here.'

'Is it the English Sailors' Home?'

'Scandinavian.'

'There's a Norwegian ship in dock, Norman,' I said.

'Let's go there. What ship?'

'T.S. *Martensen.*'

'Let's go there.'

'We'll stay here for the time being and see if there's anything doing.'

'Norway, eh?'

'Yes. It would be all right to be in Norway again,' said Norman.

I buried my face in my hands. What was Norman thinking of? Janet came to me across the snow. The seasons changed quickly: spring plants were staring at the sun in Tvedestrand; there were bare arms among the storm-tossed washing; the soundless black depths of a fjord closed over my head. Home. Yes, everybody wanted to go home. But home to what? A little imagination and *this* was home! One of those Saturday nights with Janet at the Birkenhead Hippodrome. Twice nightly, 6:30, 8:40! Two two-and-fours please! The first house. The orchestra tuning up, like tired men snoring in different keys. The gathering rush of the falling curtain. When there is a fireproof screen to the proscenium opening it must be lowered at least once during every performance to see that it is in proper working order . . .

'Are you asleep?'

'Bitte?'

'Asleep?'

'Nay, nay. Besoffen.'

The curtain parted in two, each half creaking back into the wings. To whom did this island belong? The American Hatoba, the Oriental Hotel, and the Kyo-Bashi . . . Oh these infernal advertisements on the screen! No. 1 quay. No. 2 quay. No. 3 quay. No. 4 quay. O Hiro Bar Yamagata-Dori. Phone number, Sonnomiya 2580. Possibly Aeschylus' geography was not much more chaotic than my own. Janet, writing to the ship agents in Singapore, did not even trouble to find out where the ship was, which she could easily have done, by buying the *Journal of Commerce.* I hadn't read her letter yet. I felt it inside my pocket, warm against my heart. Hilliot invictus, Prometheus absolutus, Dana solutus. The solution on my chest. Not bad geography in the λυόμενος, Desmotes. The tongueless caverns of the craggy hills cried misery then; the hollow heavens replied misery; the ocean's purple waves, climbing the land, howled to the lashing winds, and the pale nations heard it, misery!

Two shillings please. This way, Janet. Clutching the metal disc, then leaning together against the gallery, while all Liverpool coughed below.

'Des flammes déjà!' I screamed, as the theatre suddenly blazed with light for the intermission, and two sailors from the *Oedipus Tyrannus* entered noisily. 'This reminds me of the old Bermondsey Music 'All, Bill.' 'No, boy, you can't beat it.' They started to sing. The audience protested with a thousand hushes; it sounded like a sort of unanimous organ pedalling; I thought, my God, one might as well be back in the Central Cinema, Hobson Street, Cambridge! The whole bloody business is retrogression, anyway. A small boy chased by the Furies. Good God, good God.

Sudoh and Co. – manufacturer and exporter of curios and vases, porcelain and satsuma ware, tea sets, screens, bronze wares, pearls . . . Cloisonné lacquered wares, tortoiseshell wares. 10, 11, and 12 Chickaramachi 4-chome, Nagoya, P.O. Box No. 2 Akatsuka. Tel. 586 Higashi. Factories: Chikusa-cho, Nagoya and Mino, Seto, Owari . . . We deal Production of our Own and all Round value Call and see them Everything so Lovely we'll give you A1 satisfaction Inspection invited call and see them Now is best chance.

I started to clap, and the audience joined in. They clapped and stamped, roared and spat and belched. The stamping was a horrible noise, and again I thought of the pedals of a thousand windless organs being rhythmically tramped upon –

Mano Hotel ideally and beautifully situated by the romantic sea. The house of excellent service. Music and Dancing every evening. The grand ballroom has just been reconstructed. Commands a fine view of the bay overlooked from Verand. Auto service under the same management at any time. Baths always readly. Swimming always readly from directly out pier. Radio has been installed. Serve nothing but best beer and liquor and other refreshments.

'We want the picture,' I roared . . . The lights were slowly liquidating. A captain appeared. Everybody loved Mary Lou, the cutest girl in Oshkosh . . . Mary Lou appeared on a balcony, and put her head on one side; she clapped her hands and jumped about with admiration as a horseman, pursued by a youth in a shining two-seater, approached in a white whirl of grainy dust . . . 'Where did you get the cuddle buggy?' she asked. The audience screamed and trumpeted and hooted. 'How do you get that way? It was not my husband. It's that human balloon over there.' The comedy went on, without aim, without meaning, pathetic images of the perfect absurdity of life. 'Wait a minute, just wait a minute, can't you? Now then, listen everybody, if men were dominoes, why, you'd be the double blank!'

But suddenly the machine gave out with a whirr, the screen grew bright, the lights were turned up. The clapping began again.

'Come on, let's go,' I said impatiently. We edged out into the alley and staggered down the steps into the street.

On – on to the *Martensen*.

'We're going the right way to the wharf,' said Norman. A native passed, clacking on sandals, pulling a carriage by the shafts. 'Rickshaw!' he shouted. 'Rickshaw, rickshaw, rickshaw!' He pranced round us as excitedly as a dog.

'Yes,' I said. 'Drive to the Scandinavian Sailors' Home first –' There was no need to be afraid of Andy now!

'No savee.'

'It's this way, somewhere,' said Norman drunkenly.

'Go on, drive,' I cried.

'Me no speak English.'

'Go on, man. Go straight ahead, for Jesus sake.' Somehow we all squeezed in together. The rickshaw-wallah ran away with us, his sandals padding; the starry night was full of clack-ack-ack, the soft sound of wheels. Not like the Lake Isle of Innisfree, I thought, as we passed an hotel, the Oriental, blazing with light. The wheels made a gentle sound, like stirring leaves. A wealthy Chinaman smoked a cigar. A drift of cold sparks settled on Popplereuter. The driver spat contemptously. On–on–on. Three stokers swayed along the road, singing *Seraphina*. 'Seraphina's got no drawers, I been down and seen her, Seraphina,' they shouted happily.

'Stop!' Norman shouted. 'Here we are.'

Without knowing it we had reached the Sailors' Home. Norman clambered out and reeled along the road to see if it was open and Popplereuter put his arm round my shoulders.

'This is life, eh?' I grinned.

'Mein lieber alter Freund,' Popplereuter chuckled affectionately.

'Is that bloody place open?' I said.

'Nordiskt Lasrum for Sjömaen. Oppnaski . . . Ingang till Lasrummet. Oppet fra KI 5 tell KI 9 1m . . . Lasrum Skandinaviska Sjomans-Hemmet . . . Foreningen for de Skandinaviske Sjømannshjem,' I read.

'I can't find the bloody door,' said Norman.

'To hell with you,' I said. 'Hurry up.'

Popplereuter and I shouted, barracking him. The rickshaw-wallah stood in the shafts watching in silent contempt.

'Here's a church. Gustaf Adolf Kyrkan,' said Norman.

'Come back, you can't go in there.'

Popplereuter and I both laughed. He produced his pipe, and started filling it from a tin of Brinkmann's Standard Mixture.

'You can't go to church, Norman,' I said.

Norman lurched back to us. His features collapsed suddenly.

'I don't know why I'm on this bloody game at all –'

Again the rickshaw started off with us, and now I became conscious for the first time that I was sweating. We stopped at the south station and mobbed the booking office.

'Third return Birkenhead Central,' said Norman.

'Third return Port Sunlight,' I insisted, because I was not going to be beaten tonight.

At last we were forced to leave the station. We paid off the rickshaw-wallah. The streets flowed on like mad canals of light, while cars and trams, like barges of fire, madly sailed them. '*Free Press, Free Press*, Murder of Brother-in-Law's Concubine,' screamed the posters. 'Tennis shoes for the whole family.'

Then we were standing on the wharf, looking up at the soaring stern of the S.S. *Leeway* from Swansea, which had docked forward of the *Martensen*. Two stewards stood up there, high up on the poop, their dishcloths over their arms.

'Have you seen Andy?' I shouted up to them. 'You couldn't mistake him. He's a big guy with no chin, showing the influence of whisky.'

'No. We've just come in. The skipper's having a dinner,' said one of the stewards. He spat; the spittle landed on the 'Y' of *Leeway* and dribbled slowly into the harbour.

'Hey, have you lost a pigeon,' I asked.

'Come off that, anyway,' said Norman. 'I don't want to lose my sodding Mickey.'

'Are there any bumboats,' whimpered Popplereuter.

'Come on, let's all go to the *Martensen*.'

But the *Martensen* still seemed to be deserted. We hauled ourselves, panting, up the gangway, and stole down to the engine room. 'Fuld. Halv. Sagte. Vel. Stop. Klar. Sagte,' we read. But a quartermaster came out of the dark to meet us.

'We only came to see if you'd lost a pigeon.'

'We wanted to see if you'd found Andy.'

'Bumboat.'

The quartermaster gazed at us sleepily, thunderstruck. Suddenly we felt foolish, and turned tail. We tore down the gangway and ran together along the wharf till we were out of breath. We danced down the road. Oh, we felt fit for anything now!

The next thing we knew, a pimp was taking us down a dark side street. Two runnels of urine ran down either side. Women squatted on the steps of the houses, and, as we passed, hoisted up their skirts, as if mechanically. A gramophone was going somewhere, playing *My Sweet Hortense*. The street was mainly unlighted, but there were dim lamps in some of the windows. Girls called to us as we passed by. We were led through a swing door and down a dark passage into a lighted hallway. There was a continual uproar going on in the house – a kind of yapping. Then we saw that the hall was full of cots and the cots were full of puppies, three puppies to each cot. We turned round, to see an old harridan with a shaggy face, evidently a European, shuffling in carpet slippers. Her legs were bare but hairy. She drew back a curtain to the right of the nearest cot. Then we all went into a bedroom. A large bed with a much-haloed Jesus above it intruded on my consciousness, and next to Jesus a meek kitten – a photograph on a calendar – peered innocently from the wall. All around the rest of the room were Biblical mottoes and prints of the Virgin Mary and Mary Magdalene. Next to the large bed, which was covered

102

with a single sheet, stained and splotched by footmarks, was another cotful of dogs.

'Hey, where are you going?' shouted the harridan.

'Out,' I said.

'You're right,' Norman agreed, more sober.

On, more bars, more drinks, more rickshaws.

'Hans very unhappy, very unfortunate. Hans very homesick,' mumbled Popplereuter.

'All right. Come in here and cheer up.'

We pushed through the turnstiles into a small anatomical museum . . .

'This super collection,' we read, 'with all the latest additions, comprising upwards of a hundred models and diagrams, the only one of its kind in Asia . . . *In these models the visitor sees the awful effects of MAN leading a DEPRAVED life visiting the iniquity of the FATHERS upon the CHILDREN and upon the CHILDREN'S children unto the third and fourth GENERATION . . . Model of well-developed CHILD just BORN all its proportions are such as to cause the mother's HEART to throb with THANKFULNESS for so great a blessing . . . Obstetric preparations. The Forceps . . . Phimosis and Paraphimosis . . . The face of an old BACHELOR, he became IDIOTIC and rapidly sank into second CHILDHOOD; what a fearful account he will have to give of himself at the JUDGMENT DAY . . . THIRTY-SEVEN models in EIGHT glass cases portraying secondary symptoms all taken from LIFE. Some of these diseases have been greatly aggravated by the use of MERCURY and also wrong treatment namely ulceration smallpox warts and tumours . . . Supinator-longus; pronator radii teres; flexor carpi radialis . . . fasculi of flexor sublimis digitorum. The HEAD and NECK showing the awful and DEGRADED state in which MEN come when they DISOBEY the laws of GOD; the wages of sin is DEATH.*

'*Extraordinary superfoetation of TWINS, one of the CHILDREN was white, the other black . . . Embryology and foetal development PARENTS frequently live over and over again in their CHILDREN for they certainly resemble them not merely in COUNTENANCE and bodily CONFORMATION but in the general features of their MINDS, and in their virtues and*

VICES . . . If she is disordered and defective its vital function must suffer; or gross food may render it FLABBY. If she does not RESPIRE sufficiently it will be PUNY and BLOODLESS; if she is drugged it will be of BAD habit; if she is mercurialized or antimonialized it will have a predisposition to CONSUMPTION . . . Let the thoughtless man here pause, and read a sentence from the Bible; if any man defile the temple of God, him will God destroy, for the temple of God is holy, WHICH TEMPLE YOU ARE . . .'

We pushed our way out into the street. There was a dead stillness in the air, presaging storm. A shaggy buffalo, head lowered, charged at the moon. We ran until we were out of breath and hiccoughing.

'What a hell of a place!' exploded Norman, and was sick, Popplereuter supporting him.

'It's all nonsense,' I said. 'All out of date; bunk. To tell the truth, I feel just ready for women.'

'You can't go, after seeing that.'

'Yes, I certainly can. That place is all rot!'

'You don't know anything about it. You'll have to have women first.'

'All right. Don't make such a fuss about it,' I said, annoyed.

'No, don't, please. For my sake, sonny,' he went on, growing maudlin. 'For the sake of your shipmate, don't go. Keep yourself decent for your girl.'

'I shouldn't go if I was you,' said Hans sympathetically.

'I'm going,' I said, and strode off. Norman ran after me and caught me by the shoulder.

'Get off, you scared rabbit,' I said, making a wild cut at his arm. 'You're drunk.'

'Do it for my sake!' cried Norman.

But now it was my turn to climb the topmast. I shook Norman off angrily. 'Mind your own bloody business.'

Sailors' Temperance Restaurant . . . Soldiers' Canteen Bar . . . Boston Bar . . . Café Baikine . . . Bar and Cabaret . . . Trocadero . . . Satsuma Wares . . . Richard Barthelmess in 'The Amateur Gentleman' . . . Bar and Cabaret . . . Satsuma Wares . . . Norddeutscher Lloyd Steamship Company . . . Miki Bar . . . Dancing . . .

'Ah!'

'What can I do for you, sir?'

'A drink, please.'

'Certainly, sir. But I think you'll have a bad head tomorrow.'

'No. I've got beyond that stage. But a wet March makes a sad harvest as you suggest.'

'Well, what is it to be?'

'Old squareface, please. Dog's nose. Thanks. I'll take it over here. What sort of a place is this, anyway? I seem to have strayed into a European quarter.'

There was a photograph behind the counter of a Calcutta rowing eight.

'Strayed is right. But European quarter my foot. At least –' A burst of syncopated music came from upstairs, a door banged, and all was as quiet as before.

'At least – what?'

'Well, we get all sorts here, American, English, Norwegian, German. All sorts.'

I sipped my gin.

'Well, you have dancing here, at any rate.'

'Oh yes. Would you like to go up and have a look-see?'

'Yes.'

'Well, go right up.'

I finished my drink and left the room, nearly tripping over a red weighing machine with a glass face which said: 'Try your weight.' I did not think I would, but went on upstairs. Pushing open a door, I entered the dance hall. There were a few patrons and they were not dancing, but drunkenly cuddling their partners at their own tables. They looked like Scandinavian sailors. I waited by the door, sizing up the crowd. The band struck up a tune and dawdled through it haphazardly, without enthusiasm. Most of the women were lolling about, talking to sleepy-eyed waiters. They played again, this time a moderately lively dance piece, but after a dozen bars it deteriorated into a listless, lifeless rattle. 'Tan-tan-taratatan,' whanged the cymbals. The entertainers – if entertainers they were – and harlots paired off with the waiters and hangers-on and began a lifeless, listless dance . . . A girl came across to me and pulled out my tie.

'Hello darling.'

'Hello, love.' I felt gallant. 'Feel like a dance?'

'Sure. Come on.'

She made a curious impression on me, the same way that Janet had done the first time I met her; there was something mysterious about her, like stars. I looked down at her thinking that in appearance also she resembled Janet extraordinarily. I shut my eyes and imagined that this was indeed Janet and I dancing at the New Brighton Palais de Danse. Then I remembered my letter. But the girl was speaking to me.

'Me nice girl; very nice very clean very cheap jig-a-jig very sweet very sanitary.'

I was brought back to earth laughingly.

'Yes I'm sure you are,' I said. 'What's your name? Oh, you've got a card – what a funny place to keep it! Now, let's see – if I can see. "Olga Sologub." Olga Sologub. No relation to Olga Tschechowa? No? Not Olga Sologub – Love's Crucifixion? "Olga Sologub, queen of love. Night work a speciality." Yes, I'm sure you are. But isn't there a novelist? Russian? No relation? Yes, that's very adroit indeed. They allowed you to have these printed, all right. Yes. And how old are you, may I ask?'

'Sixteen. I say!'

'Yes?'

'I kind of – like you!'

'Yes, I like you too. Can you read the name of this tune on the score?'

'*Dead Man Blues.*'

'Well, we're nice and close now. *Dead Man Blues,* a high-flying hit. Good God! I had that tune on the gramophone in my digs at Cambridge – on Parlophone.'

'I say.'

'Yes?'

'You've got nice eyes – sailor boy.'

'No, no. Good God no.'

'Beautiful teeth. I like your teeth – sailor boy.'

'No. Good God, you mustn't say that! You've got nice eyes.'

'You've got nice hands, sailor boy.'

'No, no. I say, nobody's ever said that. Besides, you can only see one, as I've got the other round your waist. As for my eyes, they're green. Green!'

'They're beautiful.'

'Are you Russian?'

'Yes.'

'A refugee?'

'Yes. A Russian refugee.'

'Good God. The only Russian I ever knew was a lady undergraduate at Newnham; she was an awful bitch. But of course you don't understand what I'm talking about. Do you know this lingo?'

'Japanese or Chinese – or what do you mean?'

'Well, er – Japanese is spoken mostly, eh?'

'I can teach you all the Japanese you have to know now. Listen to me. Good morning is Cha-yo. Good day, Konnichiwa. Good evening, Konbanwa. Good-bye, Sayonara. Take me to Katayama store, Katayama e tsure te yu ke. Show me kimono. Kimono wo misete kudasai. How much? Ikura? Show me better one, Motto yoinowo misete. This is very pretty, Korewa taiken kireida –'

'My God, have a heart!'

'Please don't stop me, please!'

'Oh, I see!'

'I *will* take it, Sore ni shimasko. *Too* expensive, Amari takai. Show me some *less* expensive, Motto yasuinowo misete. Give me *change*, Tsuri kudasai. That's all, Shimai –'

The tune suddenly, as if in annoyance, came to an end, with three muffled explosions on the cymbals.

'Let's have this dance over again!'

I turned her round and, placing my two arms on either side of her neck, clapped her hands for her. The sleepy-eyed waiters, the entertainers, and the hangers-on clapped too. The band started in again on the *Dead Man Blues*. The Scandinavian sailors and their women started to sing something. Whatever it was it was out of tune.

'Tan-tan, taratatan; tan-tan-taratatan,' whanged the cymbals, and 'whom wham,' went the drum. Whom wham! 'I've got them! I've got them! I've got those Dead Man Blues, yes sir!' I crooned, looking down at Olga and drowning in her eyes.

Round and round we swung rhythmically, moving our bodies now in little quick nervous vibrations, now in long, sweeping drags.

'You enjoying yourself?'

'Sure.'

'Why "sure"? Why the American stuff?'

'Aw, you're silly, you are, kid!'

'I'm in a silly mood, honey. I don't often get an opportunity of going ashore. My supervisor would strongly object to it. Not to mention the proctors!'

'Well, are you going to come upstairs?'

Again I remembered the letter, and a deep wave of nostalgia and of physical sickness swept over me so that I staggered and almost fell. I felt I was going to pass out.

'You bet your life,' I managed to say. 'But give me half an hour. I want to cool my brain a little and think.'

'Aw, what do you want to go and think for?'

I caught hold of her by the neck.

'Hey, do you love me?'

'Sure I love you. Do you love *me*?'

'Rather. I'll be back in half an hour. I must cool my brain a little and think. But will you wait for me?'

'Yes. I love you.'

'Say 'I promise.''

' "I'm not a fool I've been to school." '

'Say "I promise." '

'I promise.'

'All right then,' I said. I staggered to the door. As it swung to the last chords of the *Dead Man Blues* were truncated. *Try your weight*. I did not think I would, but went on downstairs. 'Gordon's Old Holland Gin.'

'You going out?'

'Yes, I'm all seized up. I must go out and think.'

'You look all corked up to me. But you've got hold of a fine bird up there. Olga, eh?'

'Yes, but let me tell you, we've got a finer bird on the ship. A fine bird. Yes, sir.'

'Yes?'

'Yes. All the seamen and firemen come along and look at her

108

while she's having her bath. I put her to bed too; goes to bed without a murmur.'

'No? You can't fool me. It's the skipper's canary.'

'Ah, you're too clever. It's not. It's a pigeon.'

'Is that so? And where did you get that?'

'It flew aboard. It came from Swansea.'

'Well, I never!'

'Well, I'll be back soon!'

Richard Barthelmess in 'The Amateur Gentleman'; Satsuma Wares; Trocadero; Bar and Cabaret; Café Baikine; Boston Bar; Bar.

The night wind ruffled my hair. It was a tepid wind. I opened my mouth and swallowed it. But the night was dark and the sky tempestuous. Olga liked my hands! Strange ... my all-abiding sense of guilt about my hands! Well, I felt better now, in the air again. But supposing Janet had said – announced one day as if casually: 'What nice hands you have, Dana ...' It would have made all the difference – all the difference.

After I had been sick I entered the Yumato Hotel once more. I looked nervously at three tourists (were they Americans?) arguing in a corner of the lounge. 'Une fantaisie bien américaine.'

'Yes, sir?'

'A starboard light. Savee starboard light?'

'Me savee.'

I lit my pipe and settled myself in the chair. Now I could read Janet's letter in comfort.

Somehow it had gone.

What the hell – what the hell – what the hell! I can't have lost it. I couldn't possibly have lost it, possibly. But it's no good looking, Dana, it isn't there. Oh, Mother, what have I done? My God, is this me? Is it? Oh, forgive, forgive, forgive, Mother and Father forgive. Don't let me die, don't don't.

'– why didn't you stick up for me, then? –'

'– I'm not going to stick up for you –'

'– you're wrong!'

'You're either one way or the other!'

'A quizzy little bitch, anyhow!'

'– that's unfair. You said that before. I simply agree –'

'– she said that, and I agree –'

They were Americans. Passengers? Yes, obviously – off the *Jefferson*. So here was another nightmare of indecision; another dispute about a P. & O. boat; perhaps even another lost letter!

How ridiculous it all was! All truths wait on all things; they neither hasten their delivery nor resist it; they do not need the obstetric forceps of the surgeon; the insignificant is to me as big as any. And so forth, and so forth ... The conservation of the human sub-species. I have lost Janet's letter. Whether life was worth living or not was a matter for an embryo rather than a man. 'Post coitum omne animal triste est. Omne? Supinus pertundo tunicam.' 'For on this my heart is set, when the hour is nigh me, let me in the tavern die, with a tankard by me, while the angels looking down, joyously sing o'er me – "Deus sit propitius huic potiori!"' What was it my supervisor said? 'Dana Hilliot is a tinkling sciolist.'

'She said that, and I agree –'

Suppose I offered to rescue Olga, and she accepted. What then? What, indeed! I could carry her away in a rickshaw to the ship. There might be a little unpleasantness with the quartermaster on the gangway. But let that pass. I would bribe him, with a kiss if necessary. Hide her in my bunk. But how would the others take that? Draw lots for her; quarrel among themselves. Murder! We're going to have our home comforts, the same as any other bloody man. I have lost the letter ...

'You're either one way or the other, Kenneth.'

My mother soaped my face all over; my mother cleaned my ears. My mother separated one from one my inexpressive toes. A daddy-longlegs straggled round the light; the white ceiling sweated; the shadows of the trees shook darkly on the frosted glass of the window. A sudden draught came up the waste pipe. Afterwards, gazing at the picture of my grandfather in the old nursery, I noticed for the first time how infinitely blue his eyes were, and slightly obscene; watery, as though he had never wiped the salt spray from them. 'Why are you so dirty, Dana? My father was always so clean, so spruce. He had his master's certificate before he was twenty-three. When he came ashore he always came in a cab, and wore a top hat. He always wore a

110

deerskin cap; you never see them like that nowadays. He was an angel from heaven. He was bringing me a cockatoo.' And my grandfather's eye would water visibly in the picture and seem to say: 'Don't listen to what she says, son. The sea will get you as it got me.' Lost. Lost. The letter! Searching, groping all the time for things: for facts, for letters, for dates, for beauty, for love. And never knowing when we have found it. If we will ever find it. Absolute beauty, absolute truth, did they exist? Of course they must. Could one be, as it were, within touching distance of the one, the supreme, inerrable truth and yet never realize it, never grasp it? If there was such a truth, had someone ever stumbled on it unawares and been dazzled by the blinding light of absolute and piercing veracity? Had Christ? Had Buddha? Had Confucius? And what then was that truth? Absolute truth, absolute beauty, absolute good, absolute everything – were they all one? What the hell! Did they all converge to one mainmasthead finial of absolution? One simply did not know. But there was always that faint hope, that shadowy expectation that some day – when one was chipping a deck, or splicing wire, or reading *The Blue Peter* – there would come on one out of the nothing of nescience, this conscious knowledge of the one truth which would mean absolute power, absolute happiness.

But that being so, what was there to be done about it? Nothing. Nothing at all. Take refuge in the comic strip, then associate the mackerel with the goose, the gooseberry with the swan; dream of lutes, laurels, seas of milk, and ships of amber; observe that the 'hopeless flux and the temporal order of things belong merely to the material occasions upon which essences recur, or to the flutterings of attention, hovering like moths about lights which are eternal.' Consult the midbrain, the misencephalon. Port and starboard – the misencephalonic lights. To your post, lamptrimmer! Proceed, Phlebas, to the forecastle head, binoculars in hand! You, carpenter, to the windlass to await orders! Lookout reports a large sea moth, two points on the starboard bow, proceeding in an easterly direction! Bosun, see that all hands are on deck in ten minutes with their oilskins, sea boots and butterfly nets ... Away. Away. I shall bend my sail when the great day comes; thy kisses on my face – and anger and regret shall fade, and in thy salt embrace all that I knew in all my mind shall no more have a place; the weary ways of men and one woman I shall forget . . .

Janet Rohtraut. Beauty Rohtraut, listen to me. I am so tired of holly sprays and weary of the bright box tree. As for you, Andy; as for your weary ways, I shall prepare for them a bath of steaming hornets, while through the attic window must be blown the scent of stock-gillyflower; I shall read for the last time, the hundred and first, reading the story, the only story, of Apuleius, while, from afar, Mikhail Kuzmin's flute is heard, playing softly –

Soldiers' Canteen.

Heres to Pa nds Pen Da Soci alho uR
InHa RmlE ssmiR THan
Dfunl Etfrie ENDshiprEi
GnbeJ Ustand
Kin DanDevils Peakof None.

Hey, buddy, come and sit down. There's room for you here . . . Certainly I'll sit down. Here, there's no room here. Then move your big knees, Alf. Here, your nose is bleeding, buddy, who've you been leaning against? What've you been doing, crying or something? Oh you're the gear, the proper ruddy masterpiece, you are. I don't know. I must have banged it against something. I lost a letter from my girl. Come here, that's right. Let me wipe your face. He's lost a letter from his girl. Why, he's only a kid. How's that? That's fine, thanks awfully. Would you like a drink? . . . Like a game of darts, son? Aw, you can't hear yourself speak in this sodding place. Can't bloody breathe neither. Can't bloody move and that's a fact. Ha ha ha ha! Ha ha ha ha! Were you at the cricket match? No, I didn't know there was one, see? Would you like to buy a concertina? Would you like to buy a cockatoo? No, our galley boy's got a pigeon . . . Well, what of it; what've you been doing with your bloody self, eh? Getting drunk, now? I am drunk. No you're not, certainly you're not. Say Lake Chagogawogmanchogomog-chawgohuatungamog. If you can say that you're not drunk. Well, I'm defeated. I plead guilty. Three months' C.B. for you, my son, drunk and disorderly. We'll put you in the Chinese Labour Corps. The order of the rising sun – tee hee! – for pro-miscuous gallantry. What was that you said? Don't send my boy to prison, it's the first crime wot he done ... There ain't enough glasses to go round. No? Oh well, you have mine, sonny. What are you, you talk like a colonel. No, I'm a quartermaster. Not a quartermaster on the *Oedipus Tyrannus* are you? Do let's get this straight. Are you a soldier or a sailor? Well some say soldier-sailor but we say sailor-soldier. Of his Majesty the King? Yes – of his Majesty the King. And fighting against whom? Fighting against whom? We ain't fighting for any bloody body. We're fighting against China. With bamboo guns. You're plastered! We're in Japan. Well, what if we are? It's on the China coast. You're not drunk. Say perturbatantus Constantinopolitani innumerabilibus solicitudinibus. If you can say that you're not drunk ... Come again, have you any more of those? You bet ... Think about this. The English say *ivory*; the French say *ivoire*; but the Germans say *Elephantumbeinstein!* I've just been with one so I know. The débris, rather than the fruits of my knowledge. It's the heat, it often makes me feel that way. Well, where've you sprung from anyway? I've sprung from a ship. What – a football boat? No, a coffee pot. Fore and aft and six standing derricks. So you're just Jack ashore for tonight, eh? Yes, we're homeward bound after Manila. You ought to go and see our museum. It's one of the seven wonders of the world. I've been to *a* museum. It's the damndest place I ever saw. Our galley boy was sick when he came out – sicker than when he found the miscarriage down the number seven hold. Hell – are you a pilgrim ship, then? We were last voyage and this got left there some way. Well that's the place. It's a rare spot. That's there for your benefit. You're in it. Ha ha ha ha. Here's looking at you! Where are you out of? Liverpool. Liverpool; did you say Liverpool? That's my home town, or nearly. Yours; my gosh where do you come from? Where? New Brighton. Do you know it? That's where my girl lives. I'm a Port Sunlight man ... There's a museum in Liverpool too; did you know that? No – where? In Paradise Street. *As I was walking down Paradise Street* ... Well this godforsaken place has got about three names and we can't pronounce one of them. But we must have another drink on that. Pass the jug. Well, here's to Port Sunlight! Here's to New Brighton! ... Hey, get out of there, Gandhi! 'Listen to me, I tell your fortune.' We

don't want our fortune told. Get out! ... No, here's a Port
Sunlight man wants his fortune told. Go on, sailor, and he'll
tell you what the Tranmere Rovers are doing this season. All
right. 'Listen, I tell your fortune. No, how much. Anything you
like. Thank you very much. I talkee English a little. You are
interesting, very interesting, study. Let me see your hands. Your
hands – oh, poor, poor hands – have not been used to the hard
work; not till now, but now you work hard. You get home and
then you get rich – oooh very rich, richer and richer, day in by
day out, little by little, slowly by slowly. You play well on the
instrument. What are you – American?'

'English,' I said, interested. It was a good word to say when
drunk.

'Now! Shuffle the cards. That's right, now cut with the left
hand, so. Three times ... No! Like this, good, good, *now*; you
know a club man, when I say a club man I mean a *dark* man ...
he thinks nothing of you; avoid him. He gives for you not one
Jesus Christ goddam. You know him?'

'I don't know,' I said. 'It might be nobody.'

'But he is not so important. You have a club girl! when I
say a club girl I mean a dark girl. She thinks everything of you.
She gives for you a Jesus Christ goddam. You know her?'

'I suppose there's nothing for it, sweet hour.'

'She has a club man whom she thinks of a little too ... But
you are a musician. Velly, velly good – everybody like you
when you play. How do you play?'

'Badly.'

'Ah, no savee sing Tipperlairley, hey?'

'Come again, brother.'

'No savee sing Tipperlairley?'

'Oh, *Tipperary*. Yes, yes.'

'Your father is a club and your mother is a heart. They would
like to do everything for you, but they do not know how to do
it. Your mother loves you when you are a baby boy, but not so
much now. They would like to see you better. You are not a
good man.'

'Mucho bueno. I defy you!'

'You will soon be on board a ship. I see a friend on board the
ship, a real friend. He is neither a club man nor a heart man.

114

He has a funny face. You do not know him very well. But he is your father too. And I see another, a taller man, a big man, a friend on board the ship. And a friend of other friend. You do not know him very well. You will cross deep waters together.'

'I hope I don't stay in this hole all my life, anyhow,' I said with a laugh. 'God!'

'You will cross deep waters. You are tender man. You have tender heart. You are gentle. You are *good* man. *Good* boy.'

'I am not a good man.'

'You are a *good* man, *good* boy.'

'I am a good man . . . good boy.'

'You are a good bloody rich man. You get rich little by little, day in by day out, slowly by slowly.'

'Does anyone really love me at all, for heaven's sake?'

'Two men on the ship, I see, will be your faithful friends. The girl she think about you all the time and fret about you. But you are good man, good boy –'

Yumato Hotel. Yumato Hotel. Bar. Bar. Bar. Bar and Cabaret. Café Baikine. Boston Bar. Richard Barthelmess in 'The Amateur Gentleman', Richard Barthelmess in 'The Amateur Gentleman'.

'Rickshaw! Rickshaw! Rickshaw! Hi tiddy wing tilly willy wong! Rickshaw! Hi tiddy wing tilly willy wong –'

'Hi! Are you a proctor? If you're not a proctor, have you lost a pigeon?'

'Hi tiddy wing tilly willy wong.'

'You look as if you've lost a pigeon. You look like a proctor. Must be proctor.'

'Rickshaw! Rickshaw!'

'Here, give me that thing. I'm going to take you for a ride!'

'No, please, please!'

'Get in!'

Richard Barthelmess in *The Amateur Gentleman* . . .

The wind came slowly at first, like my own intermittent breath, as I ran down the Yamagata-dori in the shafts of the jinrickshaw. Like the beginning of Debussy's *Hommage à Rameau*. Then it came in quicker puffs; finally it bellowed as if ejected from the maw of some dragon; it blew in the teeth of rickshaw-wallahs and in my teeth, and I braced myself against it in the shafts like a shying horse. It snatched at the bottom of lampposts whirling old copies of the *Singapore Free Press* across the road. Stones blew across the road. The holy chorus swept down the burning streets, the swinging signs stood high against it, and groaned. The posters shouted: *Free Press, Free Press,* murder of brother-in-law's concubine. Shrill light flickered behind glimmering panes, where kimonos and soft fabrics slept. The wind flung down the streets and crumpled the waters of the street. The night, pocked with bright stars, twitched its face and drew black blankets over it. Ah, mother, mother, what is this man thy darling kissed and cuffed thou lustingly engenderest to make his brag and rot crowned with all honour and all shamefulness? The Amateur Gentleman? The Yumato Hotel, nine million two hundred and fourteen bathrooms, H. & C.? Me nice girl very nice very clean very sweet very sanitary? I don't want my son coarsened by a lot of hooligans? My son whom thou lustingly engenderest? Ah, sorrow, who dost borrow the lustrous passion from a falcon's eye, but you cannot borrow your son because he is being coarsened by a lot of hooligans. Ah, Zeus, hear me now. Zeus. Zeus. Dis. Dios. Dii. Deorum. Deis or dis. Dais. I. S. R. Miles, the mathematics master, sitting at the head of the hall, presiding over preparation, his eyes lecherous and rolling, the eyes of a ferret. One had always suspected his homosexuality. Herod, he looked like. Herod, watching Salome. Among them you will seem like a moon moving in a white cloud, but do not ask the head of this man! Male Salome. Satsuma wares. Salome wears – what? And they pierced his hands his side his feet, and dey heard dat noise in Jerusalem street ... My missus's tightly bound, she's all tightly bound. Harry Weldon in 1925 singing that at the Derby Castle, Douglas, his audience bringing him back for his curtain over and over again.

Twice nightly 6.30 – 8.40 ... The rooty drip of manly blood, the surging sea outweighs; the world uncertain comes and goes, the lover rooty stays. Beware the pretty face, my son, and shun the scrumptious chatterbox. Still, we're gaily yet, and sweetly tooly for a kiss.

An electric train, friendly, swayed past, blue lightnings in its wake. Yes, yes, yes, it said, as it clattered over the points, return to the wedding night, behold the bridegroom cometh!

116

Behold the bridegroom cometh! Post coitum omni animal triste est . . .

Hoo-ah-hooooo, wailed a siren from the river. But why all the bother? Do this thing. Laugh about it, because it is funny; cry, for it is beautiful; smile, because it is inevitable. Hold it ever in your heart for its preciousness; be proud of it, boast of it to Janet. Well, it *was* Janet, wasn't it? But if I could only be purged before doing it, were I only cleaner, more beautiful, how much more lovely would it be! How appealing the simple sadness of the scene could only the soiled Narcissus that was Hilliot be washed by rain from heaven . . . Hearts that should be white turned red . . . And all the sorrow of her labouring hips. North wind blow south over my vineyards, north wind brings the snow; I do not think that this is the north wind. Snow on the high pitched minster roof and spire; snow on the boughs of leafless linden trees; snow on the silent streets and squares that freeze. Under night's wing, down drooping nigh and nigher. To be plunged in snow; immersed soundlessly and without pain in a substance as cold as Janet's cheeks were in November; cold as the dawn; or as a dry bath of sheets. As cold as green grass, early, on a March morning, or sea under a momentarily cloud-veiled sun, as oilcloth to bared feet; to be morally refrigerated and lastly to be eaten, without equivocation, by a lustless Eskimo. Inside the church within the shadowy choir dim burn the lamps like lights on vaporous seas. Drowsed are the voices of droned litanies. Blurred as in dreams the voice of priest and friar. Cold hath numbed sense to slumber here!

No – no – no, said a train empty, the conductor talking to the driver from behind, leaning over his shoulder, clattering downwards towards the Yumato.

I ran along the streets with the rickshaw-wallah. Snow fell softly across my dream and old bells chimed dully. The cold wind of which I thought chilled me to the bone and blew in my teeth; there was a procession of horsemen in high white hats; my heart rhythmically beat with the rhythm of the horsemen; πολλὰ δ' ἄναντα κάταντα πάραντά τε δόχμιά τ' ἦλθον; my heart swayed and bounced to the motion of the horse, my heart bounced downhill like a stone! Αὖτις ἐπεῖτα πέδονδε κυλίνδετο λᾶας ἀναιδής.

117

It was afterwards, though, in the stable, in the dreaming warm stable afterwards, that I saw her alone. Over the white familiar fields to happy go. Is that spring where you are, Olga darling, spring with the music of melting snow, spring on the Russian steppes, and spring in your heart? Spring on the West Cheshire Golf Links, with its background of cylindrical brick-red gas works, the daisies blowing (innocently!) in the wind behind the freehold land for sale, behind the chain factory. I dreamed back along a chain of days. Olga's shadow ran before her along the snow. I saw her stir the samovar and sweep the kitchen and break the ice to get more water. I saw how in the deep dark cold winter her mother put more wood in the central stove and threw her wolfskin coat on her daughter's bunk to keep her warm. I heard her brother's merry shout, as he chopped wood, and saw him blow on his hands. I heard the tinkle of sleigh bells, and saw snow, light as wool, falling from the eaves. Cold hath numbed sense to slumber here! Then hark, one swift soprano, soaring like a lark, beats around arch and aisle, echoing dark with exquisite aspiration; throbs that soul of fire, higher, higher yearning with sharp anguish of untold desire; *Café Baikine. Richard Barthelmess in 'The Amateur Gentleman'; Bar and Cabaret; Satsuma Wares; Norddeutscher Lloyd Steamships; Miki Bar – Dancing.*

'Hullo there!'

'Hullo. So you've come back after your think, eh? Well, there's plenty of fun going on upstairs. You trot up.'

Try your weight? No. I ascended the stairs unsteadily and pushed open the swing door. I saw that all the girls were taken, dancing with soldiers or sailors. Soon Olga swept past; a sailor, a bad dancer, whose features were indistinguishable in the gloom, was bending over her.

'You've got nice hands, sailor boy,' I heard her say to the man. 'You've got nice hands, sailor boy.'

They are dancing wildly tonight, wildly in the village of Czernoff – a Negro fireman had taken his shoes off and did a crazy dance upon his enormous bare feet, a coconut in each hand and a cigar behind each ear. The music rose to a scream of dreadful pain. Another Negro joined the first in his dance. Modo and Maha. Olga came round again with her sailor, and as they passed they chasséed crudely under a light while I recognized the sailor with whom she was dancing. Andy.

Arrow points to your correct weight only if you stand still on the platform until red hand stops before dropping coin. Patent No. 1,546,553. Peerless Weighing Machine Co., Detroit, Mich. 186 lbs. You are of a simple disposition, quiet and home-loving.

Tin. The sailors' kindled watch lamps burning; the harbour lit up like a town ...

4

'I ain't telling you the word of a lie but this Yankee fellow came up to me and 'e sez steyord 'e sez fond of cigars so I sez yes I am fond of cigars – like who wouldn't be on this here fore-and-aft sea crane. Waal 'e says ketch hold of these – plenty of these where they come from. And he give me a great box of cigars. Yes.'

'Yes, but that's only cigars. This bird was a journalist or something of that on a paper in Australia. He's travelling round the world for it and singing songs at the piano. He says if you talk to me –'

'Lor lumme days. *Talk* to you. Do you mean he stood you that feed just for talking to him?'

'*Certainly* he did. He kept saying, now say that again. And all the while he was writing in a little black notebook.'

'Well, what did you tell him?'

' 'Ave you heard about Hilliot, chaps? Andy nearly crowned 'im this morning with a frying pan. The seven bell dinner watch sent 'im up to the galley to tell him the sea pie was lousy.'

'– guano –'

'Well, so it was, lousy.'

'– Pass –'

'I don't like 'im; serves 'im right; he's what you call a no-classer, that feller.'

'Where is he now?'

'– one no trump –'

'Oh, dreaming about on the poop, he always gets up there during the lunch hour.'

'– Gang –'

'He's probably listening at the skylight to all we say.'

'Three hearts.'

'Probably –'

'Romeo; wherefore art thou Romey bloody O –'

'But I didn't know there was a seven bell dinner today – not on Sunday.'

'That's not your ruddy heart! It's my ruddy heart!'

'Yes. We're sailing this evening. The mate came down and served out a lot of bull about getting in more mail. So Mister Hilliot had to get a seven bell dinner in.'

'And Andy nearly crowned him for telling 'im it was lousy. Well let me tell you that that's the lad's job. The sailors' peggy always has orders from the bosun to complain about the food; you know, if it's rotten –'

'Yes. But the silly devil went about it in the wrong way. You know the way he'd go up. Not going straight to the point, like. You know the way 'e does ... Well, it's no business of mine sort of thing but these fellers – these *damned sailormen* say your food's rotten. No wonder that Andy got on his ear.'

'Well, for God sake. But Andy's all right, eh?'

'Yes, Andy's all right, fellers.'

'Guano gang –'

'Well, wot did Hilliot do?'

'Hey, you don't shuffle up these cards right and all.'

'Damn all. He didn't do a darn thing. A good thing for Andy, I reckon, but any way Hilliot just said well, just as long as you know, Andy. And walked out.'

'Oh, wot a twirp!'

'Hullo, 'ere's the second steward.'

''Ow go, second?'

'*My* trick –'

'Second, while you're about it, you might give this godawful peggy of ours a clean dishcloth. He never washes the thing he's got: and it's about as white as a gyppo's –'

'Are you still abusing that boy? I like him for myself like. He's got pluck that Hilliot. I seen him aloft too, right on the foretopmast there, swinging on the ladder and laughing like a son of a bitch.'

'And the bosun bawling him out from below.'

'Guano –'

'Yes, mister!'

'One club –'

'Well, what about that dishcloth, second?'

'Pass.'

'Reminds me of the story of the nigger fireman on one of

Lamport and Holt's. Ah doan' min' dirty hands: Ah doan' min' dirty face: but ah du like clean *food*!'

'Ha ha ha!'

'Pass –'

'Well, well, so do we –'

'But Andy doesn't like 'im, second. '

'Gang, guano –'

'No, my gosh.'

'Andy crowned 'im this morning with a frying pan. Or would have done if Hilliot hadn't got out of the road.'

'So I heard.'

'It was pretty good, I thought. It'll teach 'im that not every little Christ Jesus in the temple can come running round cargo steamers.'

'*My* trick!'

'*Well*, no. But what he done in coming to sea at all shows the right spirit.'

'*My* trick! –'

'He came up to the ship in a car didn't he? – no – I dunno – but the Chinese storekeeper tell me.'

'Well, boys, he didn't come up to the ship in any car last night; as a matter of fact, he got on to the *wrong* ship.'

'The wrong ship? Second, how come?'

'The *Hyannis*. Sister ship to this one came in late last night. He was tight as a tick so couldn't tell the difference.'

'– *my* trick –'

'But the *Hyannis*, her fo'c'sle's forward, ain't it? Like it should be on any ruddy boat, instead of being stuck under here like a lot of bloody ventilator covers.'

'Yes. That was the joke. He went right down aft looking for the forecastle and, of course, couldn't find it; so being very drunk he slept on the *poop*.'

'Well, wot did he do in the morning?'

'– *my* trick –'

'He just got up and walked off. Nobody said a word to him.'

'– for Jesus sake –'

'– for Jesus sake –'

'– told me so himself this morning when he came aboard. I was standing on the gangway –'

'The damn fool – eh? That's why he's on the poop now. Afraid the Captain'll tell his mama.'

(But, tut-tut, a pipe must be filled to contemplate this scene with more penetrating intelligence, and a thick dirty hand inserted into my right dungaree pocket in search of the tobacco pouch, the last birthday present you gave me, Janet ... do you remember? It was in the Central Park, a year ago tomorrow, when we paused to watch the children playing on the swings, and then, 'Look, would that be any good to you, dear? Many happy returns of the day ...' Loew's Orpheum. Ruby fisheries. Do you remember going there to get the cod steaks for your mother? Well, I have my pouch now, which I have drawn out, crackling and yellow, sprinkling crumbs of tobacco around me. And now I have my pipe well alight. The day? What of the day? Well, the sky has that sort of blackness which in February, in England, would presage thunder. There was wind last night; and moreover I slept on the wrong ship. But there is a feeling of approaching disaster, of terrible storm, and my own mood, one of hilarious morbidity, conceals also just such a thing. It is useless of me to tell you about it. Instead – what shall I tell you? Of the junk that is standing out to sea? Of the Japanese destroyer that came in the morning? Of your letter, which I lost, leaving it in the hands of a drunken German wireless operator, and how I wept all night thinking of it, peering at Liverpool through a telescope, counting the waves? Or shall I make the tactile effort, surprise my mind in a state of dishevelment, and give you a sober collocation of the news? No. Let me tell you of the fortune-teller then, who said 'Everybody like you when you play instrument, nobody like you when you not play ...' The Taropatch? Tarot Pack. Or, as a last resort, merely of the crew or of those at any rate whom I can see through the skylight. Mcgoff, for instance, down there, filling his pipe too, the old devil, with hasty trembling fingers; Ted, taking the scurf out of his fingernails: ha, a touch, a visible touch! Horsey: lying across the table with his face on his arm. The second steward's broad back and the patch on his trousers; Andy, too, has a patch on his trousers ... But the joke's on me. I have to admit that of these men who become day by day more intricately and more intensely part of me I know nothing.

Nothing at all! Even of Andy, the great Tattoo, who is not present, but who is more a part of me than the rest, I know nothing. That awful incident in the galley – everybody is talking about it. Why do I not fight Andy then? To know a thing is to kill it, a postmortem process! Why won't I? Undignified? Too Richard Barthelmess? . . . Perhaps, but I might have lost, and I know less than nothing. But there is no reason to fight, even about last night! Bad, dreadfully bad, as that was. My fault. But how can I stand for it, how can I suffer on top of last night's usurpation when I was beaten out by that simpering chinless applesquire, this further petty insult added, in the galley, to an injury of which he was not aware? I won't stand for it, by God. Jimminy Christmas no, as Taff would say! But perhaps Andy won't want to fight, even if he has invited it plainly enough. Then this is not heroic, and there's the humour of it. To fear the foe, since fear oppresseth strength, gives in his weakness, strength unto his foe, and so his follies fight against himself. Argal. Let us take refuge in the sailor's coil, contemplate a world of winches as a world of machine guns: let there be a sabbath of earthworms, a symphony of scorpions, a procession of flying grand pianos and cathedrals, and the idea, the absolute, is fly-blown. Tucket within, and a flourish of strumpets. Beware Andy! I move like a ghost towards my design, with Tarquin's ravishing strides . . . Nevertheless, I fear too greatly decisive action in an emotional crisis of calibre; nor do I wish to admit to myself that I consider Andy sufficiently important; but this, as you say, is clearly enough a case of self-defence –)

'– one club –'

'– one heart –'

'– one diamond –'

'– one no trump –'

'Well . . .!'

'Lor lumme bloody days eh.'

'I don't care if he do, mate.'

'Lor lumme bloody days eh.'

'This first mate's a man; he's got me weighed up; like *that*.'

'– *dishcloth* –'

'– here, you're cheating! –'

'No, I'm not.'

'Yes, you are.'

'Yes, I am too.'

'He had the ace in his shanghai jacket.'

'No, I tell you, the poor twot didn't say a thing. He just said well as long as you know, Andy.'

'All these bloody no-classers are the same.'

'You can bet your boots. We had a feller once – been in the Royal Air Force he says during the war as a capting. Capting hell. First time he goes aloft he nearly throws a fit.'

'I wonder wot made that bird 'Illiot come to sea; doing a good lad out of 'is job, that's wot I say –'

'That's what Andy says.'

'That's what we all says, I reckon.'

'No. You've got the lad in wrong there. You can't get him on that at all. It's up to the man himself to get the job. If he don't, why then, I guess he don't.'

'That sucker's got influence at the office.'

'He came to the ship in a car. Do you know that?'

'Oh, watch it! Let's talk of something else.'

'– and listen here, this mate, he, he, says – Air Force officer or no perishing Air Force officer, you're not nut –'

'Go on, you ain't got hiccups, 'ave you, mate?'

'Not going up to that nest again or I'll lose my bonus. So no more painting for you, Mister Officer, he says; the next job of painting you'll do will be –'

'Aw shag off, second, you'll be in the boy's *bunk* next.'

'This Air Force officer I was telling you about was always falling off derricks. *Hullo,* Andy.'

'Hullo, there.'

'I ain't telling you the word of a lie but this Yankee feller come up to me and 'e sez steyord 'e sez fond of cigars so I sez yes I am fond of cigars – like who wouldn't be on this fore-and-aft sea crane. Waal he says ketch hold of these – plenty where these come from –'

'Hullo, Andy. 'Ow go?'

'All right. But do you know what? We're taking a cargo of lions and bloody tigers and elephants to London. Then we're going to New York and nobody's to be allowed to pay off. But elephants – Christ, what's the ship coming to. I know because I was told the cook's to feed the bloody things.'

'Well, it doesn't interfere with us much. There's nothing like that in the articles. No bloody fear!'

'Well, the skipper reckons he's getting the Greek to lend a hand to the keeper.'

'Well, he's got a way with animals. I suppose Spanish Pedro will go with him. But I don't reckon it matters much to the crowd.'

'Hullo there ... hullo, second; hullo Mcgoff.'

'What about last night, Andy. *We* saw you.'

'Oh, you did. You may've seen me at half-past nine – but you didn't see me at 'arf-past two this morning. Or if you did you oughtn't to have done.'

'No – nor me.'

'Nor me.'

'Nor my ruddy self.'

'Well, what were *you* doing, Lofty?'

'What do you think? I didn't go ashore at all. I'm a God-fearing man and I don't go running after women.'

'Aw, watch it. Well anyhow, it's Sunday today.'

'I don't care if he do, mate. That's wot I always says. I'm a feller like this, I don't *mind* ... Always willing to do a good turn for anybody, that's me. I don't care if he do.'

'Russian, eh?'

'Second – can we have another pack of cards – the King, Queen and Ace are all bollocksed up in this pack and you can spot 'em, you know.'

'A change for last night, eh? Won't your usual Jane get jealous?'

'Sure. There's a pack in the linen locker. Here are the keys.'

'A fine woman.'

'Well, before I was in the guano gang, I was only an apprentice lad for myself like, apprentice, and we was going out to Walfish Bay, the whole gang of us, with a cargo of lighters in sections, although at Cape Cross they had to lead from surf boats because the lighters all got all broke up –'

'Six pounds a month, mate, and all found.'

'Well, I can't rightly say as I've ever been on a ship with

126

animals before but this much I will say, and I ain't tellin' you the word of a lie, that I was on a bloody ship once that was carrying a stuffed *hippopotamus*, for Christ sake! She was called Huberta or something of that and she'd been shot in Cape Province, you know, King William's Town. This hippo'd been the bloody masterpiece in South Africa, see? They reckoned she'd walked ten thousand miles and the natives thought she was a goddess or something and sacrificed oxen to her. And I ain't telling you the word of a bloody lie but a special law was passed – nobody could shoot her, see? She walked all the way down from Vongolosi and Lake St Lucia to Durban where she walked into a concert just as they were starting Tchaikovsky's 1812 or something of that and she walked through the main street of sodding Durban too, only in the end four bastards of farmers shot her –'

'Is that so –'

'– is that so –'

'Carbeerian sea, a guinea note –'

'Well, I don't care if 'e do, mate –'

'Six months or so I suppose we was there under canvas like and I'll tell you it was a rum shop. There was one chap we had and we called him *Deaffy* –'

'Wot do you think of that for a cockroach?'

'– this is better, eh? You shuffle them –'

'– king of the steamflies, eh –'

'Everything in white, you know, lovely buildings, very nice indeed.'

'And one night this chap Deaffy come into wot you might call the messroom, you know. And 'e sez, look 'ere fellers come along with me there's a bloody big *barrel of wine* oooooh eh. Just been washed up on the shore. So we got our cups and a corkscrew and followed him along – it was pitch dark outside – and we came to where the barrel was – and one chap had brought a *basin* –'

'– your deal –'

'Can't you see the water biling, I sez; and this bloody old skipper turns round to me and 'e says, Lamptrimmer, 'e says, we always speak the King's English on this ship –'

'And it wasn't wine at all but Cape Dopp, wot we call Cape

Dopp – raw spirit gawd blimey. Why, do you know, we all went mad, *mad*, and they had to tie Deaffy up to the bullock post.'

' – two diamonds my bloody foot! –'

' – two diamonds my bloody foot! –'

'Yes. And the joke about it all was that it hadn't been washed up on the shore at all, but Deaffy had pinched it, see, from the store.'

'Good God!'

'And there we all bloody were doing time and building breakwaters round the magistrate's house.'

'See in the *Free Press* here two freighters collided in the fog, not a hundred miles from here . . . Not so bloody funny eh, if we've got these bloody animals on board if we get fog.'

'Oh stop growling, for gosh sake!'

'Yes, round the magistrate's house.'

'Fancy that, now.'

'That reminds me of the time in –'

'Chameleons. Fellers used to keep 'em as pets and make 'em drunk on Cape Dopp. They were as long as that, you know. Beautiful pretty things. They used to roll about and change into all sorts of colours: it was like being at Masculine and Debutante, you know, and then I had a pet one and one day a silly bastard fed it on nuts and bolts. Nuts and bolts, yes. Oh, we had a rare time there, I can tell you . . . didn't wear no shoes! Oh no, no shoes, walking on the salt plain, we wore what we called veldshols. One day coming back from the West Indie feller's tent – I'd had one or two, you know – I got lost in the salt plains all night and there were jackals and scorpions, bags of the bounders –'

'Scorpions. You ain't heard nothing yet. Let me tell you this, when I was in Belawandelli, it was on a Norwegian bastard out of Trondheim, the *Hilda* –'

'– herons, vodka distillery –'

'Your trick, Ted.'

'We had one fellow there in the guano gang, not a surf boat man, but loading the bags. He used to work from five in the morning till about nine, he was a sneak, a proper sneak, and a religious bounder too, you know . . . and he was always going to the boss with complaints! We got no money ourselves, we used to gamble with sticks of tobacco, and you know how expensive clothes are out there – well he used to get clothes sent from home and sell them to us at a much increased price like, the bounder. So one day we kidded him along that there was going to be an attack by the Vompas – a tribe – wot we call the *Vompas,* yes – they come from Vompaland, and we kidded him along and kidded him along and one night, see, he was in his tent –'

'– she's only got one titty but she's all the world to me –'

'One titty –'

'But she's all the world to me.'

'– one heart! –'

'– two diamonds! –'

'And you know how cold it is at night there and the tents were stretched tight as a drum; and there we all were outside firing off rifles into the air; and throwing haricot beans into the tent, and of course he thought they were *bullets* and then we went into the tent with assegais – there were always plenty of those knocking about – and some of us pretended to be wounded and one thing and the other, and there this bounder was all the time underneath the bed, praying for Christ sake!'

'– fer Christ sake –'

'– praying!'

'Niggers. Yes. Fuzzy-wuzzy niggers there used to be there, curly-headed. Dirty? My God, I've seen them cooking the entrails of a sheep and squeezing the stuff out of them like putting your mouth under a tap and eating it, and if you asked them they say Wo! auh! Wolla wolla! Very good! Very good!'

'– 'yes? –'

''yes? –'

'But in the end Deaffy went mad with the loneliness; and it took nine or ten strong men to hold him; and he used to lie down on the ground with his eyes wide open and let the flies crawl over his eyeballs . . . yes, and one day he was in charge of a donkey-wagon with guano; and the donkey died; and he lay down beside the donkey and died too; and so in the morning when we found them, the jackals *had scooped them both out –*'

'Gawd blimey eh!'

'Well, talking of niggers, there was two whacking bull niggers in the Miki too, last night; firemen they were, and when I told Olga –'

'No, you don't say for gosh sake, Andy.'

'For gosh sake.'

> (ἐπι δὲ τῷ τεθυμένῳ
> τόδε μέλος παρακοπὰ,
> παραφορά, φρεναδολὴς
> ὕμνος ἐξ Ἐρινύων.)

'And do you know what she said? He he!'

(ἐπὶ δὲ τῷ τεθυμένῳ ... If I could only shut my ears to this, and my eyes, and not have the whole sordid matter set forth in all its startling vividness; if I could drown or fly away; if I could only be walking again down Bateman Street, Cambridge, Eng., that day in late February with spring approaching and the grey birds sweeping and dipping in curves and spirals about the singing telegraph wires – or weren't there any? – and later the two undergraduates fighting outside 'The Red Cow'. And the green buses. Station – Post Office – Chesterton, which always swirled so surprisingly from behind corners as though they had some important message to deliver! ... The same in Tokio as in Leicester Square. New Brighton. Half-past five, on a wet changeable evening in May, three months ago ... The sun has just come out. The two figures, the girl with the brown eyes in the school blazer and a white skirt. Janet Travena and her lover walk slowly through the afternoon sunlight. Halfway down the Town Gardens, he pauses to light his pipe. An eddy of smoke pours on the damp air. The warped match drops in a puddle. The two figures, now triumphantly arm in arm, pass out through the open gate to the left of the deserted turnstiles. They stroll slowly in the direction of Egremont Ferry, along the desolate promenade, and past soaking walls where sodden advertisements are clinging like wet rags. The sun disappears behind a cathedral-shaped cloud, gliding solemnly, but reappears and what a warmth of friendship and light is then showered upon them, and upon the two saxophonists of the Palais de Danse, Zez and Mas, whom they know, who are squelching back to their lodgings along the shore, capering and laughing among the spinach-green rocks . . . The sky has been quite emptied of its colour. 'Mas, Mas, Zez!' they shout. 'We must get them to play *Chloe* – but no, they can't hear. It's against the wind.'

With bodies braced and motionless the two figures look high up into the watery sunlight where white sea gulls are drifting backwards complainingly, they laugh up at them, and then look down at the tide, which is coming in against the wind, crumbling weakly on the black beach. A dirty Belfast fishing smack, very low in this tide and under a modest spread of brown sail, suddenly careens as she slips through the lapping choppiness of the viscous Mersey, her patched brown sail bellying slightly out to leeward, leaning, leaning, till her curved gunwale is almost under. 'Oh, look, Dana, look, it's going right over, it's going to capsize, look!' 'Good lord, no,' he gently reassures her with the pressure of his arm. 'It's intended to do that . . .' But what does anything matter except their love? The fishing smack continues merrily and confidently upon her course down the Mersey. Later, however, avoiding Egremont Ferry as they ascend a street of houses built on an incline to Brighton Road, which runs parallel to the promenade, as they waver at the King's picture-house, with its peeling stucco, where they are showing on Thursday, Friday, Saturday, *Love's Crucifixion,* with Olga Tschechowa, and mingle and flow with the crowd, they realize with a slow, dark horror that, even had Mas heard, it would have been all to no purpose, they would never have been able to dance to Janet's favourite tune – *Chloe, the Song of the Swamp* – for this is the last day. They are parting, perhaps forever . . .

At half-past seven, by the clock on the Liver Building, he returns on the ferry from Liverpool.

Sitting in a friendless saloon, semicircular, and bare of furniture, on a hard striped bench, he smokes his pipe in silence, raising his head only once to the multi-coloured chart of mercantile marine flags on the *Journal of Commerce* flagsheet. Outside it has started to rain again, a colourless dusty rain, and through the windows he sees two sailors in shining oilskins loitering under the gangway. Liverpool sweeps away from him in a great arc. Through the rain-scarred windows he watches Liverpool become rain . . .

131

At a quarter to eight, descending from his train at Queen's Park, where, to please her mother, he has once seen Janet safely into a tin church for a prayer meeting, the one figure now drifts slowly under the grainy sky past Morgan Roberts' Osteopathy and Manipulative Treatment and the children's playground on the left into Brighton Road again. Thence down the very street built on an incline he had ascended two hours before, a street of 'by the yard' houses, he sees the Mersey slipping by like, he thinks, an enormous open drain . . . He notices two children playing at the top of the steps, and remarks what they say: 'Oi'm not going down there!' says one. 'Oi am, Jim,' says the other.

It seems to him then that the Mersey is like a vast camera film, slowly and inexorably winding. Soon he will be entangled in her celluloid meshes, and wound out to the open sea. The *Oxenstjerna*, of which he knows, will be wound out again, away from her home port. 'I have the sympathetic instinct, *simpático;* swordfish swim in me. I bear, not without murmuring, the burden of a thousand ships. But do you think I'm playing this game for nothing?' the sea seems to be saying. Simpático, simpático, it laps, sadly bantering him.

And now that lonely figure, a century or two older, lives in a decaying excavated world, with only a few white flowers of memory left, until they too crumble to dust and corruption. If he could only unlive the past two months, back to her, never to be separated from her!

Now he can only wonder whether she has forgotten the things he told her; that story, for instance, poor Harry Crosby's story, so incredible and delightful, of the man who invited the seamstress, the little seamstress with the cross eyes, to take her thread and needle and sew his mouth on to his lover's – who asked the village blacksmith (in the bar of the Pip and Bellyache) to forge golden chains to tie their ankles together, and who arranged with the coiffeur for his hair to grow into hers and hers into his – yet with what result in the end? The scissors of the Fates were brought and severed them apart. A sad story, he reflects, especially when he thinks of Crosby's own fate. But those lovers are you and I. It is spring again, the sun is on the lake, the daffodils are nodding and blowing. There are toy boats sailing, dipping their tiny prows into the cool water. The puddles are lying at the foot of the Wallasey sandhills after the rain, the groundsel is growing on the vacant lot by the County Inn. At eleven-thirty Samuel Broster comes smiling out of the bar parlour, tying his apron. The very same day. The same men have walked foolishly round the ferry boats on their way to business in the morning, smoking their pipes and reading the morning papers; tonight there will be the same hangers-on at the marketplaces, guiltily watching the naphtha flares.

Nothing has changed. Nothing. Only that the lonely figure, the lover, myself, Dana Hilliot – none of them are with you to see these things. The Yellow Sea, the Black Sea, the Dead Sea, the Red Sea and all of the seventy-seven seas, and more than seas, lie between us. Or is it only a nightmare? . . . I am not on a ship. I wish I were, since I don't know what it's like. I wish I were. I wish. I were – what? A pair of ragged clauses scuttling between two dark parentheses? Possibly I am. Anyhow I am not a seaman. No. The ship is not alongside the wharf in Tsjang-Tsjang. I am not on a ship's poop, listening at a skylight. More likely I lie in my bed at home – a cold, dry bath of sheets! Beside me, the reading lamp with the scarlet shade. The cold marble mantelpiece with the gas fire beneath, the mysterious, quivering green curtains! Golf clubs in the corner, tennis racket on top of the wardrobe, toothbrush, sponge and soap. The copy of the *Blue Peter* on top of my heaped clothes. Bar-bells and a rifle. For a moment I think of the book I have been reading – Kipling's *Captains Courageous* – and fall asleep, easy as a child, gliding down a steep incline into slumber. For a moment, like Proust, I listen to the noise of my own weeping; then I dream a dream. In this dream there is Andy – but who is Andy? – singing as he rolls aimfully down the Kuan Tsien road; Andy fumbling with his entrance ticket to the Miki dancing saloon; Andy dancing lumberingly and possessively with Olga – but who is Olga? – like a chinless orang-outang in the forest with his human captive; Andy leaving his shoes outside the door. And later, after the second bottle, shifting his shoes outside the second door. There is Andy leaning out of the window in his shirt sleeves, singing to the moon –)

'I don't care if 'e do, mate.'

'No. Well, that's what I sez anyhow, Andy; I see a look in his eye which means trouble.'

'Trouble. Yes. It will be trouble too if I have anything to do with it. Trouble! You're right!'

'– *three* no trumps, Jesus Christ Almighty!'

'I'm damned if I see what you've got against the boy all the same.'

'Well, you'll see right enough, once the fun begins. What you do with a chap like him, stamp on his foot, and – whup! – like that. Uppercut. That's what he wants, the Glasgow punch.'

'Ah, that's a deadly one that is –'

'Shut up, for Christ sake, we're playing bridge.'

'He pinches my steam covers, too.'

'Ah, come now, what would he want to do that for anyway?'

'Gawd knows, I don't. But I saw him with my own eyes, or rather, no I didn't, but the chief steward did, and he says he took it to keep extra soda for scrubbing out! . . . And he pinches soft soap off me. He'd pinch the milk out of my tea, that boy, and that's the sort of thing that comes out of your public bloody schools. Well, I don't really know. I don't really. Honest.'

'What Hilliot wants is a good strong woman!'

'Ha ha ha!'

'He went ashore last night.'

'Yes, and you all know what happened, don't you?'

'He went and slept on the *Hyannis*.'

'Because he couldn't find his way here.'

'– is that so? –'

'– is that so? –'

'What was the name of the place?'

'Sapporo Café and Bar. Here, I've got the card. Listen to this. Nice and clean accommodation. Quick service. Sapporo Café and Bar, No. 157, Yamagata-Dori, Tel. No. 6705. Soft and hard drinks. Mariners are all welcome. Here is a place you must not fail to visit, everything at very moderate charges.'

'Hello, Sculls.'

' 'Ow go?'

'All right.'

'All right.'

134

'I ain't telling you the word of a lie but this Yankee feller came up to me and 'e sez steyord 'e sez fond of cigars so I sez yes I am fond of cigars – like who wouldn't be on this here fore-and-aft dunbarge. Waal, he sez, ketch hold of these – plenty of these where they come from. And he gave me a *great* box of cigars. Yes.'

'I had an experience like that on the *Plato* – in Manila – last voyage ...'

'Last game –'

'Listen to this, just *listen* to this. Here you will find every comfort and equipment that is sure to please you. Here you will find also best foreign wines and liquors of well-known brands only. Sold by retail or bottle. *He he,* just *listen to this little lot.* A variety of magazines and newspapers are kept in our hall for your free inspection.'

'Ha ha ha ha.'

'Hullo, Lamps, boy. How are yer doing?'

'Hullo, Jim boy.'

'All right there, Jock.'

'All right.'

'That's right.'

'Me nice girl, very nice, very clean, very sweet ...'

(Why not, Janet? I put it to you; I mean *really* kill Andy. Everybody knows he can't swim. And we're going to sea tonight. That habit he has of sitting on the starboard rail behind the galley! It will be dark before he has knocked off, which makes it all the simpler. Yesterday, a little way up the coast, two freighters collided in the fog. At sea tonight. Murder at sea. A murderer in thought, a murderer indeed. Now I see it plainly. Listen. All is set. Andy sits on the rail. No fog yet – but a ship has signalled 'fog ahead'. All clear for the moment, dangerously clear. The starlight's cold. Wait your moment. The lookout changes, but the watch below still lie in their absolute slumber; high up above me the topmast trembles in a gust of wind and the aerial aloft sheaths a gentle threnody; the watch on deck lean idly against the bunker hatch until, a spatter of rain coming, one moves aft to turn the ventilators. This is the hour of consciousness, the hour of blood, dedicated to the sea tiger. My mind is brilliantly clear; every seam in the ship, every nut and bolt, every steamfly, every thought and dream of every member of the crew is there minutely drawn and of extraordinary importance. The ventilators themselves, yellow-throated, moan and hush like cowrie shells, echoing the surge of the water. The bosun snores as he has never snored before, within his narrow bunk, his white cap neatly folded under his slim white pillow; the carpenter lies on his side, counting, through the brass-rimmed porthole, the reeling stars; now the stars are numbers of hammers he has in his shop, now the digits of the tank sounding on the blackboard in the engine-room entrance, the number of steps from the galley to the clusterlocker, the number of taps under the steam piping, flakes, flakes, flakes, flakes of shavings ceaselessly tumbling and fluttering. Cloom-cloom. Andy sitting on the rail. Cloom. Wait your moment . . . The door of the lamptrimmer's cabin, white-silled, windily creaks and strains softly on the taut hook; a shaft of wild moonlight turns to silver the dull yellow curtain rail of his bunk, the carafe of cloudy water clicks in its hole, glock-glut, and the kerosene lamp is moving slowly over in its chain with the long roll of the ship; the photograph of his wife has come adrift from the bulkhead and hangs, limply flapping, on one nail. Norman is asleep, and in his dream he sees a procession of policemen, bandy-legged and smiling, twirling batons absurdly as they pass down Scotland Yard on the night of Bank Holiday, the last policeman being actually Norman himself. Steamflies are creeping among the tarred seams in the blackness beneath the lamptrimmer's bunk, narrow as a baby's coffin, making a tiny noise in the stillness like the pattering of rain outside as they are stealthily prowling over the dirty discarded chain-breaker singlet, underneath the maul and the heavy-smelling sea boots, and the limp bags of caustic soda – lunar caustic – and soogie. Outside all is silence. It is the silence of the jungle, roaring with a noise worse than death. Cloom-cloom-cloom-cloom-cloom . . . suddenly the telegraph rings, the silence changes its note. Fog! It rolls up in scurrying wisps, a phalanx of ghosts which fills the alleyways with white breath. The siren sputters, blasts a terrible warning over the grey wilderness. Fog banks to left of us, fog banks to right of us. Every two minutes the foghorn must go, according to Board of Trade rules; wait two minutes,

Andy – sitting on the rail. Now I can do it pat. Now. Oh, oh, oh . . .

Once again, but now with what satisfaction, I move into the forecastle and light the hurricane lamp against the darkness. How the solitude of the friendly lamp penetrates me now! Perfect, just as I thought. Nothing could have been better than the way his death-cry had been strangled by the siren! All just as I thought! I light the hurricane lamp in the darkness and it fills the darkness of the messroom with a solitude which becomes my own. I become a part of the sea – solitude of the hurricane lamp and of the sea-darkness and spray flowing over the ship and into it, a part of the messroom itself – six feet by six – of the oilstove, and of the fly-blown light which is never used, and the strip of oilcloth on the deck, and of the pink-patterned cotton clothes; for now in the light of my ghastly deed all these respond as they have never done before; and, as never before, I feel my mood communicable to the imponderable alley outside, and to the sea-breathing of mariners, to the remote sea-sobbing and the beating heart of the ship.

Outside on deck where I must go to dance my wild delight I feel the mood of the special night coming to take its place; the mood of time dripping its rain through the fog vanishes, and the mood of the roaring lion and tiger, the mood of the murderer, is resumed. The ropes are pearled with fog; the iron bows rise slowly to the rain-white swell; the siren diapasons *AAAAAndy! AAAAAndy!* And other voices, now near, now far and falling, call in reply: *Aaaaaandy! Aaaaaandy!* The *Oedipus Tyrannus* is feeling her way along now, shrouded for the grave. Amidships the friendly cabin and ceiling lights, seen dimly from the well decks, suddenly plunge, with a sickeningly accelerated motion, into the infinite; there is the crash and clatter of shovels in the stokehold, and the ship, thrusting at my unsteady feet, soars upward – always upward, quiveringly into the darkness. The siren roars up after it on a note that Roland might have blown on the last fissure of the Malebolge; then there is silence again, the faint silence of waters.

No one has seen him go . . .

In the morning Norman, whose duty it is to arouse Andy, upon being called by the quartermaster at four bells, slides his hands with their broken, blackened nails under his slim pillow-case to bring out half a crumpled cigarette, Gold Flake, charred and uneven at the end where it has been smoked before turning in. He jumps up and sits on the edge of his bunk, the lower one, with his legs swinging and his feet poised to drop into size seven unlaced sandshoes; he looks around the room, noticing particularly Ginger, the pantry boy, lying on his bunk with his mouth open, and his underpants, which are all he wears at night, vibrating with the thrumming of the engine.

He will remark for the hundredth time the pictures on the wall. Tallulah Bulkhead – or is it Bankhead? Ginger's mother taken with an armful of horrible children. Joe Ward taken at the Police House. Flint with his twin brother. Monozygotic twins. Taff standing on Bull Bay sands, Amlwch, swinging a mashie niblick. He wishes profoundly and for the hundred-thousandth time that he may grow that extra inch, praying softly: 'Our Father which art in heaven may I grow another inch and become a policeman of the Lord.' He pulls his check trousers on over his sandshoes and pays attention to his chain-breaker singlet. He brushes his hair – and oh, how yellow it is! – and cleans his teeth, spitting into a bucket. Now he is walking along the well deck, his bucket on his arm, scarcely pausing as he spits resonantly into the scuppers; now he is hoisting himself up the galley companion-steps. He enters the galley (where a quartermaster's singlet is drying) and rakes out the fires. Four bells strike, he throws his cigarette to leeward, and goes to call Andy. The white cabin door, brass-silled, windily creaking on the prehensile hook. Everything the same as the chief cook left it when he turned in, according to his custom, just as eight bells all-hands-pipe-down had finished striking. The chief cook snores peacefully – let him lie till a quarter of six. Andy – where is Andy? His razor strop is stirring in a breath of wind through the open port; the canary in its brightly bordered cage is already chirruping with joy, its little heart almost breaking with anxiety to see the blue morning. The slim parcel of blan-kets, embroidered with the Company's crests – 1840 Steam and Sail – undisturbed. Andy! Andy! Anybody seen Andy! Was he sleeping out on deck, do you know? No, not bloody likely, too damp, not a worthwhile thing to do when the tropics was

138

lousy with malaria! Too damp, Norman, that's it, too damp. No good worrying any more about Andy, think of yourself, of your mickey, take the cover off his cage as though you should hope to find Andy there, and see – how knowingly and sagaciously the pigeon eyes you! He knows. Mark well the calmness of the sea, the clear sky of the summer sky engulfed by the porthole, and the new horizon which slowly diameters it and sinks again; mark well the kindly shadows swimming on the deck; hear, more acutely than ever before, the tramp of feet overhead, the bosun's orders, and the insistent, dominant hiss of the hose; fill your lungs more gratefully than you ever remember, with the pleasant smell of the coffee being made by Dana Hilliot. For no – not an infinitude of despairing blasts can bring back Andy – and what, indeed, if they could? For tattoo marks, like the faces of the dead, tell us nothing. The peacock on his right bicep now, the eagle, the snake and the bathing girl remember nothing. Where are the Stars and Stripes now, the Norwegian flag, the crucifix, the barque in full sail! The hands have clasped another cross, and the flowers are drowned in salt; the heart remembers nothing. Think then, Norman, always of that extra inch, get the potatoes from the potato locker and proceed with your work as scullion. For the sea is picking Andy's bones in whispers. Pedro, the Spaniard, will help you in the galley now. Yes, yes, yes, Sculls. Oh you who throw the peel and look to starboard, 'acuérdate de Flebas, que una vez fué bello y robusto como tú' –)

'Hullo, Joe.'

'How go?'

'Not bad.'

'Not bad.'

'How are you doing, Mcgoff?'

'Ah, Jock, I've got a little story to tell you. Now I ain't telling the word of a lie, mind you, but this Yankee feller, you know that chap, you was there – you saw him, didn't you? – well he comes right up to me and he says: Stey-ord, fond of see-gars. Straight he did. So I sez yes sir, I am right fond of cigars –'

'Skipper, old feller. I knew years and years ago it will be now –'

'Well of course it was his business to find faults. When he

139

does that he's pleased and lights a cigar. When he ain't got no faults to find no cigars for the skipper that day, savvy? Well, I reckon it's the same on this goddam dugout –'

'Plenty of these where they come from, ha ha!'

'Well, I always believe in writing so's a chap can read, he might owe me something –'

'Ha ha ha.'

'– naval relics –'

'Chatham –'

'Heard the bosun getting at Hilliot the first day. Well, he was only telling him what to do like –'

'– one more game, come on now, boys –'

'What's that, Andy?'

'Bosun, the first day, telling Hilliot what to do. "I expect this room to be speckless," he said. Well, look at it. I bet the bilges are kept cleaner than this and he pinches enough soft soap off me to keep the whole ship clean, gawd blimey – and that ain't all. "You've got my room, the carpenter's, and the lamptrimmer's rooms to do," 'e said, "and our washbasins to clean – and the brass to do in there as well and everything to be scrubbed out every day. If you don't do it, I'll hit you till you do. You've got all the meals to get in, and you've got your own washing to do as well as the washing-up, and you've got to keep yourself clean. It's my business to see you do that. Sailors aren't dirty. You ruddy farmers think they are. But they're not. Muck in ..." Well, look at the boy now, he never washes himself, this room's like a pigsty, gawd blimey, eh –'

Oedipus Tyrannus – Liverpool.
Seamen. Boddy-Finch Life Jacket. Matroser.
Utdrag av Kostreglement for den Norske handelsflaate.
Certified for use as sailors' messroom. Tin.

'Murder with his silent bloody feet –'

'Why, here he is!'

'Hullo, lovey, what've you been doing?'

'How go, Hilliot?'

'Andy, I'm going to speak to you. Listen, everybody, while I speak to Andy. It's for you too. Now then, it's about time I had this out with you. I don't deny I've been listening to what you've been saying from the poop. And you can't –'

'Well, for –'

'– deny that you've been doing your level best to make life a misery for me since we left home. And what's more, you've been telling a lot of damned lies about me! You say I pinch your steam covers, and your soft soap – well, let me tell you I don't! I've never –'

'Well, for Christ –'

'– pinched anything of anybody's. You said that I've made a mess of my job. Well, I don't think that's true – this room's not too bad. It's as good as you could make it yourself. Anyone could see that. And I'd like to know how you make it out that I'm doing another lad out of his job. God damn it, man, it's surely up to the lad himself to get the job. But wait a minute, I've got something more to say; I haven't wanted to fight before; but to be frank with you that wasn't because I'm afraid of you and your Glasgow punches – no, simply because I didn't want to hurt you.'

'Well, for . . . Christ –'

'You weak-chinned son of a Singapore sea lion! you cringing cowardly bloody skulker! You've got a face just like a filthy jackal, all nose and no chin . . . What a spiteful, cunning, dirty wreck of the *Hesperus* you are! That's just it, your face. Your measly, weak face. I've just been afraid *for* you, that's all! Why, by Christ, if you'd got a chin, you little bastard, I'd hit you on it!'

'For Christ sake go easy, Hilliot.'

'Why should I go easy? Come on, you ship's cook, you chin-less wonder, you – put them up. Up, I say.'

Tin.

'Here . . . go easy, Hilliot.'

'Why should I go easy?'

'Sit *down*, Andy; don't be a bloody fool. Sit down! Sit down!'

'What the hell? What've I got to go easy for?'

'Well – listen – it's like this –'

'Like what? What's wrong with you all? You know I'm in the right.'

'Now then, Hilliot, don't be a bloody fool either and go shooting your face off about Andy. He's an older and better man than you.'

'Yis. He's knocked seven bells out of harder cases than you in his time.'

'Yes, go easy, boy . . . We all know, you see, that Andy lost his chin in the War, and he's had plates in it, and all, and if you hit him on it, he might croak. You mustn't talk like that. We know it's your first voyage and you get just the same as any of us got on his first voyage. Andy and I've been shipmates for ten years. You mustn't talk like that. Go easy, man.'

'Three times torpedoed!'

Tin.

'So it's that way, Andy.'

'– well, I'm going to work in a bathing costume and a sweat rag this afternoon.'

'Me too.'

'Where was it you bought those bloody things – Cebu?'

'Yes, that's right. Well, I dunno what sort of a ship this is at all!'

Do you know what the Board of Trade man said – wouldn't go across the dock in her.'

'Aw, she's just a laundry boat, that's what, going round picking up washing.'

'Laundry boat, eh? Huh. She's an orange box, a balloon boat, a haystack –'

'A Dutch bomb.'

'– Mate says we're getting a lot of animals in this afternoon: elephants, tigers, leopards and I dunno what all. I suppose that'll mean the watch on deck. I suppose that's what he meant by *more mail*, gawd blimey. I dunno when we'll be away tonight, I don't really. One of the elephants for Rome, we get her off at Port Said; oh, they've all sorts of bloody things all going to the Dublin Zoo, eh, and a special keeper fellow's coming aboard with them, prize snakes and Java sparrows, for gosh sake – I suppose to feed the snakes. I dunno what sort of ship this is at all with a lot of pouncing serpints aboard her –'

'Three white leopards –'

'Well, certainly I don't know when we'll be away tonight.'

'Yes, I says, I certainly am fond of cigars.'

'– pass –'

'– pass –'

'– pass –'
' – one *spade* –'
(*And Samson tol' her cut off-a ma hair*
If yo' shave ma hade
Jes as clean as yo' hair
Ma strength-a will become-a like a natch-erl man,
For Gawd's agwine t'move all de troubles away,
For Gawd's agwine t'move all de troubles away . . .)

Hilliot stood by the rail amidships looking down on the quay.
He had some time off before turning to again. The noise of the
winches rattled in his eardrums. The sense of the impending-
ness of departure seemed even to have pervaded the stevedores
working there; when a couple of special messengers arrived
there was a kind of fever on the dock; but on the boat there
was a feeling of furious haste – get things squared off. But
would the *Oedipus Tyrannus* never sail after all? All the animals were by now safely on the foredeck, which was chirruping
and champing like a jungle and Horsey had been sent forward,
grumbling, to scrub the elephant.

Hilliot started to wander round the ship, hoping to find Andy
alone. Mosquitoes had driven him out of the forecastle; elsewhere flies seemed to have penetrated every cranny. The air was
full of them. There was not a breath of wind, and the sparkling
sky roared with heat, like a cauldron. He could not distinguish
the sun in the tingling ether; the whole vast blue seemed to be
a catherine wheel, gigantic and invisible, whirling and blinking
and spinning above the *Oedipus Tyrannus*. Hilliot longed for
the open sea.

'Hullo, Norman,' he said. 'Where's Andy?'

Norman was standing in the galley ankle-deep in buffalo
blood, doing something to a butcher's hook. A score of flies were
drowning in the blood, buzzing and scrambling on top of each
other.

'Somewhere with the chief steward,' panted Norman. 'What
do you think of this, eh? Nothing but a bloody zoo ship. And
the cooks have got to feed the tiger and all . . . Well, I have
got to go to the frige now.'

Hilliot leaned on the rail and looked out to sea. Suddenly he
put his hands over his ears to shut out the frantic din of the
winches. He felt as though he were lost in a dark tunnel, and
all at once he saw light at the end of it; and the light was sun-
shine in a quiet garden, with wind-blown roses and peonies;

and Janet was there and stroked his forehead with her cool hands, while they listened to the singing of a tap; and the flower bed was all runnelled with the water.

Oh Jesus! he was on a ship; he was just a dirty sailor looking out to sea, nothing more. A dirty sailor not listening to a running, hissing tap in a garden but to dirty bilgewater pouring senselessly out of a ship's side.

But his heart was full of remorse for what he had said to Andy, and out of this remorse came a strange, wistful tenderness for everybody, for the ship, and even for his home. He would work hard for Janet when he got back. Melancholy-eyed he continued to gaze out to sea. But what a dismal prospect it all was! How alike all these harbours were! Even the ferry boat which was gliding smoothly across the water, edging sideways like a crab from the scend and sway of the stream, struck some reminiscent pang in his heart. Of course, he was only thinking of the ferry boats on the Mersey.

And as he watched, she obscured momentarily from him a small Chinese tramp steamer, which lay anchored between two reefs. How meagre and old and battered she was! Waiting for the shore gang, lingering till she became scrap iron. But once even as the *Oedipus Tyrannus* she had been quivering for life and the open sea, and the shouts of stevedores had echoed in her iron sides.

Ah well, that was the way of things!

But beyond, far out at sea, a ship was making for harbour. The funnel was well aft and Hilliot made out that she was probably an oil tanker . . . Yet how senseless these entrances and exits had become to him! Now all that was left was a desire to get away from this seaport town whose name had once attracted him so much, and to return ridiculously to the starting point! So this was the East, the East which he had longed for. And now he had had his fill of it, and longed to breathe normal air again, to climb out into the great day. Now all the ports were the same to him; they were not towns, but congested, weedy rivers in which lifeless men flowed together and apart and together again like battling torrents. What was left, now the sense of discovery and with it all else of value had departed? It meant just dust, the torrid brightness of roads, the everlasting swinging of the double doors of taverns, dodging bicycles and rick-shaws.

He would no longer see things for the first time. Each port had roared its smutty laugh at him, bringing him nearer and nearer to his own little destruction.

Yet he knew that he was not really being honest with him-self – if he could only make friends with Andy perhaps things would be very different; it would possibly not be such a destruc-tion after all.

Anyhow, even if it were, it would not be so much as the disso-lution of an electron, the bursting of a soap bubble in the dark.

He readjusted his sweat rag round his neck and wiped his brow with his forearm. He started to fill a pipe . . . Yes, Andy was in the galley this time, but he was not alone. The chief cook was with him, chopping up meat on the meat board.

He put the filled pipe in his pocket; he would smoke it after tea. Then he helped himself to a drink of tepid water from the boiler dipper. He kept his eye on Andy, who did not look up.

It was one bell, a quarter to four, time to make tea for the crew . . . Perhaps he would be able to speak to Andy when he gave him the tabnabs. But no, on second thoughts, Andy's atti-tude did not somehow suggest a desire for conversation. Was it his imagination, or did Andy himself, of all people, seem a little ashamed?

The tabnabs were already cut, on a plate by the boiler, and Hilliot felt that he must speak to Andy alone.

He filled the teapot which he had left in the galley since dawn, and took it with the tabnabs down aft to the forecastle. He must wait his opportunity, that was all he could do . . .

The sailors crowded round with their cups. The skylight which opened on the poop was wide, showing a triangle of blue sky. Hilliot sat watching it, drinking his tea, from which he was continually having to pick flies. Occasionally a hurrying shadow passed over the skylight – a sailor or a stevedore.

He did not wash up the teacups but left them as they were for supper. He got up restlessly and went out on deck again to smoke. Everywhere was hurry. There was still a fearful noise of winches and screeching coolies, and the shriek of a ship in the harbour letting off steam forward . . . The cargo, chests of tea, was hoisted in slingloads of ten from the piles waiting on the wharf; the leading winchman, who at one moment was hanging over the bulwarks, and the next rushing to the brink of the well, admonished, with an imperious forefinger, the winchman seated on his straw mat. The slings of ten poised themselves over the gaping hold, and then plunged into it. For a moment the work of the derrick was suspended to allow the purser to climb up the sheer ladder from the depths. 'When will we be away, sir?' Hilliot asked him. But the purser disregarded the question and spat reflectively. 'No cop, eh?' he complained. 'Twelve hundred perishing bills of lading, eh; and they say that seafaring men are grousers. Christ, eh, it's a dead loss. Each bill may represent god knows how many packages. Well! A lot they care in the office, is what I say.'

Hilliot was going to say something sympathetic, but the purser had to go on. 'And all these damned animals and a keeper fellow on board and all.' He sniffed reflectively. 'God, man, it's a dead loss. It's all right if you're not a married man, but I am, it's not healthy, that's what I say.'

But Hilliot had lost interest now. What did the purser know of his troubles? . . . He watched him, as, finding no sympathy, he splashed away through a pool of coal dust and water, scattering cigarette ash. Then, feeling curiously lonely, he turned into the galley. The chief steward was in there, still talking to Andy. Damn it, had he missed another opportunity while he had been drinking his tea? He felt that he could not now wait much longer, something was – something was –

He went out on deck and found a coil of rope, and sat there brooding for he did not know how long. The sun slanted down on his head. Suddenly he realized with a shock that the ship had been cleared for sea. From along the steam piping jets of steam were rising. The winches had stopped, the stevedores gone. An apprentice was dodging about, looking in a lifeboat beside him.

'What are you looking for?'

'– stowaways –'

Then the boatswain came up to him, rolling a cigarette. 'Oh, you're the boy, Hilliot,' he said briskly. 'I just promised Andy to give Norman's mickey a drink of water. Norman's down the refrigerator, you see, and I've got a job of work to do. Give the little bugger a drink for Norman, will you, there's a boy.'

Hilliot watched the boatswain disappear hurriedly into the petty officers' washhouse, then he came to give the mickey a drink.

But the mickey was not in its cage, which was open.

He looked on the number four hatch. It was not there. Above him, on a line strung between the rail aft of the wireless room and the bottom of the galley chimney a quartermaster's dungarees flapped themselves dry, but there was no mickey. Hilliot called Andy, who was sweeping up the galley, but still talking, and the chief steward. They searched everywhere, on the boat deck, in the galley, down the boatswain's alley: the mickey had disappeared.

'The bastard couldn't have flown, though,' said Andy, bewildered. 'Norman clipped its wings.'

'We must find it all the same, or it'll break his ruddy heart,' said the chief steward.

In a few moments they looked over the side. There, not six fathoms from the boat, the mickey was swimming. Its clipped wings beat the water pathetically. It was gradually sinking as it became more and more sodden. Andy and Hilliot looked at each other. For a second their quarrels and all else were forgotten.

But Hilliot's mind was made up. 'I'm going in after it,' he said resolutely. Andy caught him by the shoulder.

'Don't be a bloody fool, man. Stay where you are. This harbour's a death trap ... You don't know what things are in the damn place, crocodiles, sharks, and I don't know what kind of bloody things at all.'

The boatswain and the carpenter came up. 'What's this, eh?' said the boatswain. 'Hilliot want a swim? Well, he can't go, because I don't want to lose my bonus.'

'It's Norman's mickey,' said Andy.

'Gawd blimey, eh,' said the boatswain reflectively. 'Has that bloody pigeon got loose? Well, I always said it would. I always said Sculls didn't know how to look after it. By crimes, the bastard's swimming, ain't it, Chips?'

'Well, it's the last time that bird ever will swim,' said Chips.

'Yes. All Lombard Street to a Tahiti orange on that, mate,' said the boatswain, as he started to roll a cigarette. 'I'm afraid he'll make a nice little bit of supper for one of them sharks, eh?'

'Thirsty, I suppose,' said Andy moodily. 'It's this lousy heat, you see –'

'Well, I was only telling young Hilliot a moment ago to give it a drink – no, not five minutes ago it will be. I had to do a bit of sooging in the petty officers' washhouse, thirsty it must have been, you know, and seeing the water like –'

'Ah yes,' they nodded their heads. 'Thirsty, that's what it was.'

Andy's grip relaxed. Now it was Hilliot's chance.

'Well, I'm going in after it anyhow,' he said, but still hesitated on account of Andy, looking round for support.

'Look here,' Andy burst out, 'you've been a bloody nuisance on this packet already, without us having to put a boat out for you into the bargain and go sculling round picking up the bloody pieces.'

The word nuisance halted Hilliot. At this moment, of all moments, he did not want to appear braver or wiser than Andy, and made no move, and said nothing. Andy was an old seaman, *homo sapiens*. Andy knew a thing or two. And now, relenting from his fury a little, he was shaking his head and murmuring: 'Crocodiles, sharks, voyage before last I remember Norman, yes, I tell you it would be suicide to go in.'

Instead, a mean feeling swept over Hilliot. This serves Norman right for going up that mast, he was telling himself, against his will; that'll teach him. Anyhow, the bird was happier dead. He felt both sick and astonishingly elated, watching intently – his bowels melted, but nothing must be missed.

Tin-tin; tin-tin; tin-tin; tin-tin; eight bells were struck on a ship out in the harbour, followed by a silence. Only the water and the refuse pouring ceaselessly out of the *Oedipus Tyrannus's* side could be heard, and that was part of the silence. Two quartermasters shuffled up, and one of the A.B.'s from the forecastle with a bucket full of his Sunday's washing, and two ordinary seamen in the Cebu bathing costumes.

'Wot's to do, boss?' they asked. 'Is there a Jane in the water or summat?'

'Damn all Janes here,' answered the boatswain. 'It's Norman's mickey.'

'Aw, wot a ruddy shame,' the men murmured. 'But sheer killing yourself it could be to go in after it in this place.'

'Here!' cried the chief steward. 'Christ! We must get a sampan. We can't let the bloody bird drown like that.'

Then all eyes were looking where a little white motor boat was skidding along the water coquettishly and then turning almost in its own length and retracting its course looking more foolish than ever. The crowd yelled at it, all hooting and trumpeting at once, but its engine was making too much noise, and its only occupant dividing his attention between the wheel and the spurting exhaust, which he seemed to be admiring from time to time by looking over the side at it.

The chief steward spread his hands helplessly. 'We can't let the bloody bird drown like that . . .'

The mate and an agent were talking near by. They had not seen the mickey. The men shouted desperately at the motor boat. Hilliot thought, but said nothing. Then he drew Andy aside. 'Andy, before I do it,' he said quietly, 'will you forgive me for what I said to you in the fo'c'sle this morning? I didn't mean it, Andy, on my word of honour; your chin's fine. And now I'm going in.'

'No, you're not to!' Andy cursed. 'You must be crazy. Here, hold him, somebody.'

'Yes, don't be a fool,' the men growled, holding him. 'There isn't time.'

'Besides,' Andy added, 'the bastard in the motor boat may hear us yet.'

Suddenly the mickey could struggle no longer. Then it was gone. The motor boat was still playing about; it was as carefree and as jolly as a frisky terrier. Quickly its occupant was spinning the easy wheel while it circled around gaily and with incredible speed, then turned on itself and rolled in its own swell.

It was a nightmare, a whole eternity of horror. Hilliot was in bed at home, but he knew he would wake up soon in the kind sunlight. 'I'm sorry, Andy,' he repeated. But what did it mean, what good was there in being sorry now?

The motor boat was away as inconsequentially as it arrived, keeping a straight course for the estuary and leaving a glaring white scar of foam behind it. Its white segment of stern – *Mabel – Tsintao* – soon dissolved into the blue of the harbour.

Norman was coming out of the refrigerator. He was smiling as he slipped off his extra jacket. The boatswain told him what had happened. 'Well, you see, it was like this, Norman –'

'And what's the big idea not telling me before?' Norman said at last, bewildered. 'What's the big idea, I'd like to know. You knew I was down the refrigerator, Andy. What's the big idea? You mean you stood there and watched that poor bloody mickey drown?'

'Why, hell's bells, man, there wasn't time,' said the quartermaster, who had been gangway quartermaster that first night alongside. 'Why, we have to stand by. We can't go jumping into the ditch after canaries, for Christ sake –'

'You shut your bloody face,' cried Hilliot, surprised at his own anger.

And Horsey said: 'Yes, Hilliot's right, shut your bloody face, you nancy quartermaster . . . But it wasn't anybody's fault just the same, Norman,' he added, turning to him.

'What?' cried Norman. 'Well, time wouldn't have mattered if any of you'd been a bloody man.'

And Hilliot thought, agreeing with him, no, time wouldn't have mattered.

'Well, you couldn't go in, Norman, really,' he tried to explain, distressed for him. 'This harbour's full of sharks and crocodiles.'

'Yes, and I'll tell you something,' snarled Norman. 'You're full of prunes, that's what you're full of.' But his anger suddenly collapsed. His face went white as chalk, and he went slowly down to the forecastle.

The crowd remained for some time talking, and, after a few moments the agent, whom the first mate by now had left, came over to them. He was a jolly agent, familiar and affable with all men, whatever their station, that was obvious. He removed his cigar, and mopped his face. He remarked on the ordinary seamen's bathing costumes. 'They're very nice, very nice texture,' he said, spitting a brown stream.

He replaced his cigar. 'And if any of you boys want a bathe,' he puffed, 'it's all right just about here this time of year. No sharks have been seen within three or four miles. They just won't come in now. I've been in myself several times; it's the only thing in this weather. It's really quite safe. You could get the pilot ladder put down, chief, or the boys could go off the wharf ... Perhaps you've been in already though.' He looked at his watch. 'Well, I must be off. No, you really haven't got time for a bathe now.'

Hilliot watched him cross the wharf. He had seen a shark lately, but that was over five miles away, and there was no danger. A dock train started its racket again ... Then he was left alone. Oh God, oh God, why hast Thou forsaken me? He saw, in a blurred fog, that the oil tanker was now considerably nearer in, and this for some reason or other seemed of extraordinary importance to him. She blew her whistle cautiously and shyly, as though she were an intruder to the port, and Hilliot knew that he could always remember that she had blown her whistle just in that way. There was a sustained bass roar in reply, and the *Wölfsburg*, with her black hull and one large black smokestack, glided by, butting the translucent silver of the bay. There went Popplereuter – and his letter. Gulls, motionless and uncomplaining, floated over her as she disappeared round the corner of the breakwater. He watched the oil tanker come right in – she was an American – *West Hardaway*, *Portland*, *Ore*. – before the boatswain shouted his 'All hands fore and aft!'

The cry was passed on, from mouth to mouth: Stand by, all hands fore and aft. Ah yes, they knew how to make you work on this dugout all right, spoiling a man's Sunday afternoon, they grumbled.

Hilliot was working at getting in the derricks. The yellow booms were lowered cautiously in their horizontal berths and the tackle squared up neatly around them. He helped the carpenter and an apprentice to straighten out the tarpaulins on the hatches with an enthusiasm which was part of his misery, and to knock wedges into the cleats. The second mate, walking reflectively and with a measured tread, appeared on the poop and mounted to the docking bridge. Then he made a decision.

'Get up steam in those after winches. They haven't been used for working the cargo, eh?'

'Aye aye, sir!'

If he had only known! ... But Hilliot obediently set the port and starboard poop winches going, accelerated and reversed them. They hissed and clanked, pouring out billows of steam; hot oil dripped from their undersides on to their unchipped, uncleaned beds which were inch-thick in hot flaky paint and rust.

'That'll do. Stand by.'

On the *Oedipus Tyrannus* there was the most extraordinary complete stillness. The gangways had gone in, an officer on the bridge was looking down, even the animals were quiet; everywhere was a feeling of poised suspension; there seemed to be no valid reason for not sailing. What were those devils on the bridge thinking of? Hadn't something arrived yet? Jesus, won't she ever sail, wondered Hilliot – won't this ever stop?

Suddenly the siren boomed, swallowing all the other harbour noises with its terrific volume; it echoed back and forth across the harbour; it was the cry of an imprisoned animal thrilling to the prospect of release.

'All right, eh. Stand by,' said the mate again.

Again the siren lanyard was jerked and the noise rang forth this time even more devastating, till all the *Oedipus Tyrannus*'s old plates were dithering and quivering with the delight of it.

Its echoes hovered uncertainly in the air, mingled with strange alien sounds which it seemed to have aroused, and the resumed cries of the animals themselves.

'Let go!' The skipper's voice could be heard dimly coming from the bridge.

'Let go,' echoed an apprentice who was standing on the boat deck with a megaphone. 'Hold her with the spring.'

The second mate yelled back to the apprentice, repeating the captain's command.

'Let go aft, sir. Hold her with the spring.'

The telegraphs jangled with an angry sound, and as below the engines began to pound rhythmically, the *Oedipus Tyrannus* stealthily moved, the hawsers dripped and writhed as she backed out slowly from the wharf. Native coal-humpers and stevedores on the wharf gazed up with absurd seriousness at the great ship's fouled iron sides, as if it were surprising to them that the *Oedipus Tyrannus* should ever be able to sail at all. Hilliot thought he detected a vague, unexpected disappointment in their looks, as though they had lost something.

Other natives, obeying unseen instructions from forward, dodged along the quay casting away the ropes from the dolphins. A little boy followed them, dragging a wooden fender at which a suet-coloured dog was barking. Somebody off watch in the firemen's fo'c'sle had started to play a Chinese fiddle.

'Starboard a bit.' The captain's bass voice, far away, drifted to Hilliot's ears just as the ship's bows were getting clear of the wharf.

'Slack away aft!'

The lamptrimmer approached Hilliot at the winch. 'Go forward and see if the bosun wants any help in his port watch – we've got too many here on the poop already without you stewing about them winches.'

Hilliot ran forward, but when he reached the saloon deck he stopped. No, such things couldn't happen really. But Norman's words made a sort of incantation in his brain. 'Time! Of course there would have been time. Time wouldn't have mattered if you'd been a man.'

'Heave away, Chips!'

The first mate's voice from the prow intruded on his consciousness, and he watched the drum-ends of the red-leaded windlass clanking and racing around gladly; little by little the dripping hawser came up through the fairleads; then it was taken off the impetuous drum-ends and coiled down. Beyond, the hawser was falling into the harbour. 'Let go ashore, and mind the bull rope,' shouted someone. The elephants trumpeted in reply, and Hilliot heard the tiger make a rhythmic thud; and he could almost feel how he was moulding his body to the shape of his cage.

'All gone forward, sir!'

'Aye aye, sir!'

Just then the lamptrimmer came up beside Hilliot. 'I thought I told you to go and help the bosun,' he said angrily. 'Well, never mind now. Go and get the keys of the hospital from the chief

154

steward. We're going to coil down a rope in there. Look sharp!'

Hilliot obeyed the order, and the hush of the saloon passage suddenly and completely shut out the sea sounds and polyphonous rumbling of the winches. A white coolness, out of the dark, swooped at him, bringing with it a heavy smell of damp biscuits, condensed milk and carbolic soap.

'Here, take the lot,' said the chief steward irritably. 'The long one's the one, and don't forget to bring them back.'

The noise of the winches, long-tentacled, was swimming in through the door at the farther end of the saloon passage. As Hilliot hurried aft, taking the keys, the noise and heat swam about him.

'Let go aft!'

'Let go aft!'

'Here, hold this!' somebody shouted to Hilliot.

'Here, for Christ sake, what do you think you're doing there? Let go, there! Let go there! Didn't you hear me say "Let go"?'

Hilliot was holding a double wire round the drum-end of the port winch; it snaked away from him, kinking and writhing. The lamptrimmer cleared it. Hilliot could hear below him the propeller thrashing out furiously. The stevedore threw the bight of the hawser clear. The boy with the suet-coloured dog waved his hand. Soon they were well out in the harbour, abeam of the disused junk. Then the *Oedipus Tyrannus* swung round and steamed ahead for the open sea.

The *Martensen* was following close astern. They followed the land where there were more wharves, and many ships were docked all along the line. The hospital door opened, revealing a dingy apartment where the rope was to be coiled down. The port watch set about coiling it. Soon the wharf and the junk were fading in the distance.

The *Martensen* changed her course eastward; their firemen were now dumping ashes overside.

The second mate was still directing the winches. 'Heave away, oh,' he said to Hilliot, who put his hand on the hot lever to increase the steam. 'Give her a little more steam, eh?'

'End oh!' shouted the lamptrimmer at last.

The second mate descended from the docking bridge, gravely

and slowly. 'Get all your ropes coiled down,' he mildly suggested to the lamptrimmer.

'Aye aye, sir.'

'That'll be all, men. Good night,' he said abruptly.

'You can go below now, you fellows,' the lamptrimmer said soon.

'Well, when we've coiled this little lot down.'

A fresh breeze came up from the southwest, and the *Oedipus Tyrannus* rolled a little to port, and it seemed as though a spasm of satisfaction once more ran through the plates of the ship as she recovered and rolled over again, this time to the starboard side. Down below a shovel clanged. All hands found themselves at the windward side, watching the sunset. Andy was looking at it from the buttertub where he had been sitting yawning at a three-weeks-old *Singapore Free Press*. Norman watched from his stool outside the galley where he had been peeling onions. The ship is turning homeward. We're homeward bound now, seemed to be the thought in the heart of every man – that was what the engine was saying. Homeward bound for Gallion's Reach, although we can't pay off.

Behind them the town sparkled, with its myriad lights; huts straggled up the rolling hills, like the vanguard of a weary army, marching with flickering torches. Farewell, Olga, farewell, farewell – beat the engines.

After all, perhaps his quarrel with Andy would be made up tonight. He would tell Andy all his troubles. He would tell Andy all about Janet; he would understand, and they would become good friends; he would even get him a job ashore, but sometime they would be old salts again, and tell each other sea stories. What was that business, you know, about Norman's pigeon: and they had just stood there and watched it drown!

On the number four hatch Hilliot found a long piece of string, part of an old heaving line, attached to a cleat ... The boatswain and the carpenter padded up and down the deck in carpet slippers. Amidships shadows stole silently around the bulkheads – quartermasters returning their messkits to the galley. The bars of the galley were like the bars of a penitentiary and the quartermasters' hands moved slowly and remorselessly behind them. Let me get out!

156

But on the ship now there was a feeling of peace and slow-ness and languid discussion; he could feel that the *Oedipus Tyrannus* had settled down to be a ship once more, instead of the mere appurtenance of a wharf. The watches were set, the third officer was pacing the bridge, the lamptrimmer came staggering down a companion-ladder carrying the anchor light, the lookout man was on the forecastle head listening to the sobbing of the prow; while below them all the engines pounded steadily, the pumps were pulsating and throbbing with their muffled beat, the blood of their hearts.

Once more Hilliot came to the engine-room entrance, stepped over the fiddley and looked down into the very heart of the ship, where now, instead of desolation and silence, four stokers, foreshortened by the height, were dancing in front of four blazing chasms, driving in their slice bars. Shouts and cries floated vaguely up to him . . .

He gazed round the engine room. Ah, there at least no inter-ruption entered. It was a wonderland, a laboratory of laborato-ries, a twilight island of mysteries.

Why was it his brain could not accept the dissonance as simply as a harmony, could not make order emerge from this chaos? Surely God had made man free from the first, tossing confusion of slime, the spewings of that chaos, from the region beast. Chaos and disunion, then, he told himself, not law and order, were the principles of life which sustained all things, in the mind of man as well as on the ship.

Suddenly his heart leapt. Andy was standing by the opposite entrance. The blackened trimmer to whom he was talking de-scended the ladders rapidly, his hands slipping on the glistening emery-papered rails. Hilliot went over to Andy.

'Look here,' he said immediately. 'I'm damned sorry for what I said about your chin. Will you forgive me? It doesn't show anyway. Nobody could tell it wasn't a bloody good chin.'

'There's nothing to forgive, for Christ sake,' Andy said slowly. 'I've treated you badly all right. I suppose it's because I'm get-ting an old man. And I was wrong this afternoon. Oh, well, there's enough bloody trouble aboard this packet, what with firemen going sick and animals, and this afternoon, without the cook and the deck boys always wanting to knock seven bells out of each other. That mickey, eh? Christ!'

Peace was made.

'Well, I must be getting,' Andy said. 'Come into the round-house later, son.'

He shuffled off and Hilliot felt light-headed and infinitely happy at that moment.

The tragedy of the afternoon, the horrors of the voyage were forgotten; all at once he had a perfectly clear vision of himself, as if a red leaf should fall on a white torrent. Instantly there was no lack of order in his life, no factors wrongly co-ordinated, no loose tangled ends. It was he and no other who brushed disarray with his pinions.

And all at once the maelstrom of noise, of tangled motion, of shining steel in his mind was succeeded by a clear perception of the meaning of the pitiless regularity of those moving bars; the jiggering levers began to keep time to a queer tune Hilliot had unconsciously fitted to their chanting, and he saw that at last the interdependence of rod grasping rod, of shooting straight line seizing curved arms, of links limping backward and wriggling forward on their queer pivots, had become related to his own meaning and his own struggles. At last there dawned upon him a reason for his voyage, and it was the strong, generous ship he knew he must thank for giving it to him.

Those enormous cones of light flooding some places, and leaving others in broken masses of shadow – they were the lanterns of his mind swinging in a house of darkness: but sometimes the very lamps themselves were quenched by roaring day, and the house of darkness itself blossomed into a tree of light!

Cloom – cloom – cloom – cloom. Looking down he could see through the bulkhead doors where the red and gold of the furnaces mottled the reeking deck, and the tremulous roar of the cages' fires dominated a sibilant, continual splutter of steam. The *Oedipus Tyrannus*'s firemen, among whom he again recognized Nikolai, half naked, gritty and black with coal, and pasty with ashes, came and went in the blazing light, and in the gloom; flaming nightmares, firelit demons. The furnace doors opened, and scorpions leapt out; spirals of gas spun and reeled over the bubbling mass of fuel, and sheets of violet flame sucked half-burned carbon over the quivering firewall into the flues. With averted head and smoking body Nikolai shot a slice bar through the melting hillocks, and twisted and turned them. The iron tools blistered his hands, his chest heaved like a spent swimmer's, his eyes tingled in parched sockets, but still he worked on, he would never stop – this was what it was to exist –

He remembered that time in the Red Sea, when Nikolai had rushed up the iron steps, and collapsed on deck, blood pouring out of his mouth. They had rubbed him down with ice and laid him out on the poop to cool. 'Hot,' was all he said. 'Hot,' to the English second engineer. Two days later he was on duty again as No. 8 fireman, and Hilliot had seen him once or twice up for a spell from the stokehold, his hair blowing in the fresh wind that had come after they passed Perim.

Ah, God might count all his children, but he didn't count firemen, he left that to the Board of Trade.

He pulled himself up with a jerk. What could he be thinking of? He couldn't stay there all night, that was plain.

A ceiling light shone on the tarred seams where Hilliot found himself again out on deck. The great ship slowly sank beneath him into an avalanche of sea, above him the stars reeled, but the *Oedipus Tyrannus* was like a wild animal in a pitfall. She quivered powerfully as she beat against the dark wall of sea.

Behind the galley he found Norman crying.

'Come on, Norman, for God sake.'

'Sorry I'm making such a twit of myself.'

'You're not. Only cheer up. It's all in a lifetime.'

'It's all in a lifetime.'

Then Hilliot saw that Andy was sitting on the rail outside the galley. He approached him and stood by him in silence, craning over the rail, listening to the water bubbling and hissing down the leeward side. Then they went to the roundhouse, and Andy opened a bottle of whisky. They were knocked off till next morning.

He loved the ship – he loved life.

Presently Norman joined them.

'Well, how go there, Norman?'

'How go there, Hilliot?'

'How go.'

'How go.'

They sat quenching their thirst in whisky. They drank it half and half, smiling as they gulped down its throat-smarting fire, which the rust-brown water from the galley tank could never extinguish.

'Soon be home,' sighed Andy, and the others agreed, laughing, not knowing what they meant.

Eight bells rang, sank in the blast, in a distant, metallic measure. Somewhere a lantern clanged with eternal, pitiless movement. A verse of idiotic clang reeled dully in his brain. But there was a cosy glow in the cabin, and it was good to sit there discussing the affairs of the *Oedipus Tyrannus,* as the steaming lamp moved slowly over on its chain.

Down below the engine hammered out the revolutions with its slow persistency, but now every stroke was taking them westward, always westward! You'll soon be home again, the engines seemed to be saying.

You'll soon be home – the lights out in the night smile like old friends for you, and the air is full of secrets you know. So you will stand again on the familiar platform, lost in the dark sounds which grow everywhere about you; the river's soft tones, people down on the road, singing fir-tops, and air which nourishes earth with the trembling rapture of a mother. Here is your place on earth! Listen to my song, you are at home!

Oh, journey up to the gate along the only way in the world. The night wind whispers 'I remember you.' The birch trees up there, and the house, two lovers cheek to cheek nod in the murmuring of the west wind: 'Our son, he is yours and mine.'

'Soon we'll be home again,' Andy repeated. 'New York or no New York.'

'Yes, that's sure,' agreed Norman, and then all of them were silent.

Outside was the roar of the sea and the darkness.

'Well, Hilliot, we'll be in Dairen this time next week.'

'That's an important place, that is, important in the war. You want to have a good look at that place if you want to tell your mother anything. It was the first place to be attacked by –'

'Aw, you mean Tsintao, boy.'

'No, I do not mean Tsintao.'

' 'E means Tsintao all the bloody same.'

'No I do *not*.'

'Yes he does, yes he does.'

'It's snowed up in the winter, like Montreal. And you want to have a good look at the tugboats there.'

'You bet your life. Got icebreakers on them.'

'Icebreakers my arse.'

'Whew, just smell at this heat. My singlet's wet through.'

'God damn you I mean it! I'm not joking.'

'– don't jolly us up. 'Ow many did you have?'

'About fifteen.'

'Gee whiz, where do you put it all?'

'Ahm a long long girl, she said, ahm a long long girl.'

'*Can I have a wine card?* Waiter, have you got a wine card? That's what she was asking. The bosun got mad at her.'

'Me no drinkee for drinkee me drinkee for drunkee, eh, as the Chinaman said.'

'– trotting, they used to have, trotting, but they don't any longer. A pack of crooks that's what they are.'

'I seen a man running; his chin was stuck out like that, *you* know –'

'That's my old army knife, that is, mate. It's opened many a tin of bully beef, that knife, so I know it's all right.'

'Ha ha ha!'

'– you know the way they do. He just sort of *squoze* the rabbit. You know the style.'

'No, no. Just – you know.'

'Prohibition! that's what's done it. America's all shot to hell now and it was a goddam Dutch bastard who came over and suggested it; now I'll tell you I'm this sort of fellow ... I speak straight. I'm this sort of chap, you know, when somebody does me once, he doesn't do me again; I always sez right out straight, who the bloody hell do you think you're talking to –?'

'Good boy – good old Lofty.'

'Now I tell you straight if I had my way I'd hang the whole god-damned lot of them, the sons of bitches. I wish I had him here – this is the sort of chap I am I tell you straight. He'd get out. Yes, ha, ha, he'd get out. But he'd have to be carried out! No feeling with me.'

'Hullo there!'

'Hullo, I can't get to sleep. It's too hot.'

'What's the temperature?'

'Hundred and two in the galley. Only one fire in there too.'

'I'm sweating so much I could go through the chief steward's mangle.'

'Oh, go jump in the ditch.'

'The mozzies are awful; they won't let you sleep.'

'That's the worst of being stuck under a poop like a lot of godblarsted ventilator covers.'

'Look at Mr Bloody Mcgoff there, kneeling on his bunk with a magazine, killing the bastards on the deckhead – there he goes! Oo – slap! That's the way to treat 'em.'

'Hey, Mcgoff, how many have you killed?'

'Ssssh! the watch below's asleep.'

'How many have you killed, Mcgoff?'

'I can't get one of the bastards. They're a funny sort of mozzie. They sort of slide away when you're going to hit them. I do believe the little bastards *think*.'

'Yes, you're right, they *do* think. I don't know how they managed to stay on board after we left port. The wind generally blows most of them overside. Bad enough with the steamflies – never mind mozzies. I'll say this is a little different from Liverpool, eh, Hilliot?'

'Oh, I'll say so.'

'Oh Cape Cod, Hilliot, yes. That's where they *eat* swordfish. Delicious, oh boy, yes, betcher life it is. What? *No, certainly* they do.'

162

'Certainly it is.'

'– in Funchal, yes. In the market there porpoises – are they? – porpoise steaks? Damn – big – red – things –'

'– likee Margarita? Not today, I said, not today.'

'I've been all down the West Indies there. That Funchal ain't in the West Indies, it's in Madeira.'

'I know it, man. I know Portuguese I do.'

'*E prohibido affixar Anuncios,* eh – gawd blimey, eh.'

> '*And Jack went aloft for to hand the top-ga't sail.*
> *A spray washed him off and we ne'er saw him no more.*
> *But grieving's a folly,*
> *Come, let us be jolly,*
> *If we've troubles at sea, boys, we've pleasures ashore.*'

'Ssssh, the watch below's asleep.'

'Now come on, let's have a song.'

'Agencia dos bloody vapores. I was in Funchal once in an old collier out of Cardiff and we spent three weeks there coaling. It was pretty awful, as they didn't know anything about coaling and took a long time. We didn't have any clean food for three weeks – there was coal dust everywhere – and there we all were going ashore and buying basket chairs –'

'I know it, man, I know it. And let me tell you, that's nothing. Gawd blimey, boys –'

'I should say we *did* get ashore. We spent all we bloody had on chairs and vino. I got two fine chairs for the missus. Gawd blimey there was a Portuguese warship there; you should have just heard the row when the admiral fellow went on board. Cannons and guns, gawd blimey. Funchal *shook,* I tell you –'

'Like the story of the nigger. Ah doan' min' dirty hands, an' ah doan' min' dirty face, but ah du like clean food!'

'Ha ha – you want to tell that to Andy.'

'Hilliot, lad, you tell that to Andy and he'll crown you again.'

'No, he wouldn't crown me again, not even if I did tell it.'

'– in little toboggans drawn by bullocks, you know, Cinderella goin' to the ball.'

'– found 'im in the Quinta das Cruzes Hotel there, raising hell.'

163

'I stayed on board last night on that damn –'

'Ciné Jardin.'

'– and Salsichas e pure de batata. It's a good place for stewards that.'

'Yes, that's the sort of bloody chap he is.'

'All hands pipe down now, eh?'

> *'Longside of a Don, in the terrible frigate,*
> *As yardarm to yardarm we lay off the shore,*
> *In and out Whiffling Tom did so caper and jig it,*
> *That his head was shot off, and we ne'er saw him more.*
> *But grieving's a folly,*
> *Come, let us be jolly,*
> *If we've troubles at sea, boys, we've pleasures ashore.'*

'– all hands pipe down now, eh –'

'Ssssssh, for Jesus sake!'

'– for Jesus sake –'

'It's no good all hands piping down with these mozzies about. Hilliot, did *you* bring all these mozzies aboard with you ... dead loss. There! Got you – fair ruined that one anyhow.'

'Hullo Mcgoff, what's that you got there? A magazine, eh? Any nice tarts in it?'

'Not much –'

'Of course, Hilliot, you've got eddication and I ain't. I want to tell you that I'm just a plain British working man ... And I'll tell you another author I like – G. Bernard Shaw. He speaks right out, that fellow, wot he thinks. He's set agin' the whole of 'em, the whole lot of 'em, yis. Wot I mean to say, intellect, you know.'

'Dialect, sez he, 'ave you ever seen a dialect?'

''E meant derelict, he he –'

'Ha ha –'

'Ah, yis, yis – I don't mean from a literature point of view, I mean from a reading point of view. I dunno how to explain – like. You see, he's always got a message for the proletariat – like. You see us working men ain't the sort of bastards that the moneyed class think us, lying in all morning smoking cigarettes and then telling the tale to the Labour Exchange in the afternoon. No, we work all according to secedule-time –'

'Well, the-ere, that's a difficult question to answer like. I mean you've got all his plays like ... and all his *satire*.'

'Cabara –'

'When I was in the Gall-eye Pole-eye peninsuala –'

'– what you might call a jamboroo, scouts' jamboroo –'

> *I had fed the skipper's cat,*
> *I had washed the bosun's room,*
> *I had spliced the main-s'l slat,*
> *I had painted the jibboom.*
> *When sail-ho! came the cry from the man on the lookout*
> *Sail-ho was the cry from the crew ...*
> *And sail-ho was the yell from the prisoner in his cell,*
> *As the Spaniard hove in view ...*

'Sssssssh!'

'Ssssh, the watch below's asleep.'

'Now then, you look what you've done, you've woken Matt.'

'Yes, you're right, boys, you *have* woken Matt. And Matt's bitten all over. Here, who are these rich bastards in the fo'c'sle with mosquito nets? ... Dizzy? Hilliot? You've got a mosquito net haven't you? Well lend it me, for Jesus sake. You don't sound as if you wanted to go to sleep over there talking and singing with the lot of them –'

'Well, you can sleep in my bunk if you like. It's lousy anyway.'

'Aw Christ! What do you call that. An invitation? No thanks!'

'Well, you can take it or leave it. I'm not going to sleep in it.'

'Aw, put a sock in it. Well, I'm going to sleep, chaps, and if you wake me again, the fellow that does it I'll slip him thirteen inches of saltpetre –'

'We weren't making a noise, Matt –'

'No, like hell you weren't! Good night, everybody.'

'Good night, Matt. Sweet dreams.'

'In Brindisi – mosquito net – they call it zanzaziere or something of that –'

'Well, well, well ... We'll be in Dairen this time next week.'

'The English papers call it Dalny.'

'I've heard it called Dair*een*, boy. But I don't think the place 'as got a proper name.'

'Well, it don't deserve none. It's a *god*-awful place.'

'– I suppose that means a wash-down tomorrow and a skipper's inspection. Well, I'll have to *try* and get some sleep – even if I don't succeed. Hell, isn't it hot!'

'Hot as the hinges. Thank Christ some of those flies have blown away anyhow. They were crying like babies all last night on the flypapers.'

'You want to stop talking, you do.'

'Aw, shut up! I'm going to try and do some dhoby in the washhouse. The trouble is I'm not sleepy. But you can't go to sleep with all these mozzies ... *Ooooo,* you little bastard!'

'Good night.'

'Happy dreams.'

'... better take your magazine with you.'

'Oh well, thanks. Good night.'

'Good night.'

'It *is* hot. Damned hot. Reminds me of the Congo.'

'The Congo, eh? Don't talk about the Belgian Congo to me. Belgian ruddy Congo. Christ aye.'

'Where were you?'

'I made two trips – and we lost four men the first trip and three men the second. I don't want to think about it. It makes me ill to think about it. Where were you?'

'Me? Oh, I only been there once, and quite enough too. Bakana we were. Boy, but it was hot all right. Where were you when you croaked all your men?'

'Well, we lost one at Bakana. Died of malaria. And we had another chap took ill in Bakana and another in Nogi, and, let me see, another in Boma; and the whole three of them died in hospital at Matadi.'

'Fer Christ sake –'

'– fer Christ sake –'

'Second trip it was bloody worse ... we went upriver to Leverville. Everything was all right till then. Then three chaps – all firemen they were – got blackwater and croaked. Yes sir. I came home d.b.s. me ruddy self.'

'And what had you got?'

'A dose of syphilis.'

'Well, you don't need to go to Congo to get *that*.'

'I don't reckon the Belgians got any right to have a state of their own. They have enough trouble looking after themselves. Poor little defenceless Belgium – all that bull.'

'No, but their King, King Bert – he's –'

'On the level.'

'– five thousand feet above sea level.'

> *'One day with a davit to weigh the kedge anchor,*
> *Ben went in a boat on a bold craggy shore.*
> *He overboard tipped, when a shark, and a spanker,*
> *Soon tripped him in two –'*

'Matadi –'

Tin-tin; tin-tin; tin-tin; tin-tin.

'No, sorry, boys, I've got it wrong. Now all together!'

> *'But 'tis always the way on't: one scarce finds a brother,*
> *Fond as pitch, honest, hearty, and true to the core,*
> *But by battle, or storm, or some damned thing or other,*
> *He's popped off the hooks, and we ne'er see him more.*
> *But grieving's a folly,*
> *Come, let us be jolly,*
> *If we've troubles at sea, boys, we've pleasures ashore!'*

'Aw yes, I mean Matadi's a railway connection, the end of the trading ports – like. That was a well-laid-out place, you know. Oh yis, a very very well-laid-out place. After that it's all swamp; malaria and blackwater.'

'I knew a chap, a missionary 'e was –'

'I suppose that was back in the old slave days like they did all them atrocities. Old King Leopold, eh? Ears cut off and wrists cut off ... native gin. Boy you should just see those niggers there drinking quinine. They start standing up all right, but finish right down on their knees, ha-ha, like this. And the funny thing is – or perhaps it isn't so funny – they always *must* have a whisky chaser. Some of 'em would throw the quinine behind their backs and drink just the whisky chaser.'

'Ha ha ha ha!'

167

'Shut up. Don't make such a bloody noise.'

'I knew a chap, a missionary 'e was. Aw but they're all the same these goddam missionaries. They come on board just before the ship sails and invite you to a prayer meeting the next night.'

'Hullo, Pateman, what's it like on the lookout?'

'How go, Cock.'

'All right, how are yer doin'?'

'Phew, it's hot in here, for Christ sake. What, mosquitoes still? Oh boy, how I wish I was back in Liverpool.'

'Well, mustn't grumble. We're going that way.'

' 'Oo's relieved you, Cock, boy?'

'Paddy there. Paddy there. It's no fun I can tell you with all those animals growling ... the elephant was being sick just before I struck eight bells ... Got any cigarette papers anyone? Hilliot? No, you always smoke that basting pipe ... Anyone seen the Greek, the keeper wants him. Oh, by the way, here's a letter for you, the first mate give me. Came aboard yesterday afternoon.'

'What, a letter –!'

'He's amidships with the Spaniard –'

'– from Dublin to Holyhead you can get it very, very severe. During the war it was, full of troops an' all –'

'All 'ands, crew and everybody.'

'Newfoundland's where I want to go again, boy –'

'Tor Bay, eh, and eat codfish tongues up there, eh?'

'Codfish tongues my foot. We want Liverpool.'

'– bacon and eggs, you know, and one bloody little piece of toast.'

('Prosit! Gesundheit! Hoch! Good luck with the girls! Auf Wiedersehen. Hans Popplereuter, ordinary seaman. E. D. Hilliot, S.S. *Oedipus Tyrannus*, c/o Butterfield and Swire, Singapore. Please forward ... S.S. *Oedipus Tyrannus,* Tsjang-Tsjang. 26 Dornberg Road, New Brighton, Cheshire, England.

'Dana dear, I love you such a terrific lot, and I want you to be happy always. I loved our talk our last Sunday evening just before you went home, because you were so manly, and you put things so simply and without making excuse for them, and I understood and felt proud of you. Please always tell me things

168

in that way. I shall always understand if you do! Oh, Dana, the sun is shining ever so brightly and the grass in the cricket field looks wonderfully fresh after the rain – will you tell me that you love me always? A gipsy has called and told my fortune. She says I will cross deep waters: and won't be lucky while I'm in this house ... It was terrible leaving you and going on that ferry boat. Liverpool went into the fog and Seacombe came out of it like a sort of evil spirit. I went to watch your ship sail next day but there was mist and two other ships with red funnels: and was that yours on the far side? It seemed to fade into the dock wall and the funnel wanted painting anyhow and I felt lonely and wet. I played golf on Friday by myself on the shore. I was quite thrilled with some of my shots. I arrived home soaked but happy – the dye of my mackintosh had run into the collar of my blouse! On Saturday I went into the Winter Gardens alone and saw – what do you think? *So This Is London!* ... I tried to pretend you were there and you almost seemed to be; perhaps you were thinking of me then; even your old guitar seems to miss you and listens with all its strings for your heavy step. But I must ask you – how do you like being a sailor? Is it very hard work? I just live for the day when you come back. Heaps and heaps of love, Your own Janet ...'

'Miss Janet Travena, 26 Dornberg Road, New Brighton, Cheshire, England. Via Siberia ... Seamen's Forecastle, S.S. *Oedipus Tyrannus*. Eight hours out of Tsjang-Tsjang ...

'My own Janet: If you were one with Charcot, Bernheim – I would try to tell you – if I could only tell you – if it would be worth your while to understand.

'Darling ... darling ... darling ... I love you, but all I can think of is that I have changed. Would you really be amused to hear how I like being a sailor? and do you really imagine that I know? At any rate I can tell you more plainly now that to begin with it was all *misery:* first, the misery of parting from you: then the misery in adjusting myself to the ship, and my failures in the process of adjustment; then the misery of my all-consuming envy of Andy: I told you about him, and the misery involved in his persecution of me. Then, just before we sailed this afternoon, a tragedy occurred, a failure, a culminating frustration which has been the worst in my life: from which the greatest of good, absurdly enough, seems to have arisen. It doesn't matter what the frustration was – what would interest you is the result – I have made it up with Andy! Early this evening, over a bottle of whisky, I told him of my love for you – and what do you think he replied? He replied that this love business fair used to make him tremble at the knees! but that he'd had it all knocked out of him now; it didn't mean a damn thing to him: when he got back home, which possibly was for a fortnight a year, sometimes only for a day, they would get a sort of hip bath down and get into it together in front of the fire: then after a day or two, "finish" – he went on the booze then until he joined his ship. That hip bath, and going from one woman to another in port, were all that had been left to him by "love": as for myself I'd get out of it soon enough. So now I have a perfectly clear vision of myself: I find myself as a creature of luck: I have something Andy, really, except perhaps, as a fantasy in youth, has never thought of; a promontory from which I look incredibly down on the insignificant race of womanizers. Divided between what might be called a promiscuous stallion instinct and desire to be like Andy and the others I have to some extent obeyed that instinct, but there is the very different thing of yourself. Seeing all that, my initial inferiority towards Andy has fallen away, and suddenly I have a fondness for Andy! I actually hope Andy acquitted himself well with Olga, but then I can't very well tell you about her: any more than I can post this letter. I have identification with Andy: I *am* Andy. I regard it all now with sanity and detachment. But I have outgrown Andy. Mentally, I have surrounded Andy's position, instead of being baffled and hurt by it ... And to continue, in this crude jargon, the "débris rather than the fruits of my education", the relative ease and quickness with which I have shifted my balance towards Andy, after the interrogative stage of things, is partly occasioned by the fact that yourself acting as an inhibiting factor are at the same time a sublimatory factor. Although Andy beat me out in port, it ceases to bother me because first, there is yourself; secondly, being in love with you I have the universal experience of sublimated all-embracing love for mankind. There is no further need to invent a venereal lineage for myself; it is no longer amusing; my innocent little aunts, and their equally innocent parents may rest in peace in Oslo cemetery. Put a flower on their graves for me – a rose instead of a lobelia syphilitica.Purveyors to His Majesty the King: as for my father we shall exhume him from his imaginary madhouse, reinstating him to his normal position of tutor, to his liver trouble, his pipe, his dog and his games of chess; my mother may return fearlessly to her eyebaths and her Sanatogen – she may even learn to be proud of her wandering son and I foolish to deny my love for her; my guardian becomes miraculously what he has always been – the family chauffeur. But here's the rub, Janet. Having accepted Andy, must I also, since I am a sailor, accept the component parts of Andy, the fulsome fleshpots and the woman-scented evenings, the rough red drawers, and the bawd and lodging? Yes, within limits, of course, I mean that I must no longer confuse moral courage with physical courage; it's time enough for a little common sense. I have to accept Andy and that is no more dangerous than accepting life. But in future I shall be more interested in biceps than forceps; I shall lift weights rather than pints. As for my books, I shall throw them overboard and buy new ones ... Let their writers sign on troismâts and learn how to swarm up a rope with passion! My writing? You or any woman can do that for me. I don't know a damn thing yet. But one day I shall find a land corrupted and depressed beyond all knowledge, where the children are starving for lack of milk, a land unhappy, although unenlightened, and cry, "I shall stay here until I have made this place good." Oh, it is not enough to say, "I have a stir of fellowship with all disastrous fight", or "I am alive, can't you see the love of life in my face?" or "I am tired of this music and those paving stones, tired of the street-lamps and cobwebs, tired of the dust, so I shall be a man, I am going to sea again"; nor is it enough to do these things in order to load oneself with finer mountains, to identify a finer scene; better to whip the sea or deface one's mother's house – fathom the shallows. So the question at once arises – where is a workable object? where is something to change for the better, to transform from wasting into growth – something that I can cope with? Where are the slaves that must be freed, the children who must have milk? I shall find them. I must find them. When my

171

duty is done I shall sail out to get you; we shall return to the land and find it blessed. Meantime I shall never go down with a ship, unless necessary, because my duty will have been done to her; and although it seems cruel to us, although I may never come back, and though I admit all this is ridiculous, this is the only way to make our love our own in the eyes of God, the only manner in which I may learn to pity others without pitying myself, to laugh without self-contempt, and to weep without excess of joy.')

'– pulled the railroad up –'

'– *counteract* –'

'– Engine room in Nantucket; sand, as nice a little engine room as you would want to find.'

'– and the Jews went round, you know, gathering scrap stuff. And they lost everything. They bought a factory and I'm not telling you the word of a lie they gave the factories a bloody price for it, and scrapped roads, wire, rails, New Bedford –'

'beniculars, he had too, strapped on his back: he was – bit of wot you might call a ventroloquist, you know –'

'– going down to Halifax –'

'– What did you say? Engine room! ... Well, let me tell you something. I was in a bloody ship once that really did have an engine room to write bloody home about. It had triple-expansion bloody engines but the funny thing about it was that the steam –'

'Hey, no stewards in here!'

'No stewards in here –'

'This mate's a bloody man; he's got me weighed up, like *that*.'

'– went through the bloody high pressure cylinder, and then went through a bloody sort of electrical superheater bloody fancy thing before it went to the intermediate bloody cylinder; I was down below on her, so I know, and what's more we only had one fireman every bleeding watch, eh –'

'Well, by Christ, you must have worked yourself to death on that little lot, eh?'

'Going through the Red Sea, you should have been there, my Christ, eh –'

'Going through the Red Sea. I'll tell you something, mate: it was last voyage. I was thirsty, and I see the mate's door open and the water glass there and now don't you ever do what I done without thinking! I drank up the water and by Christ the syphilis thing was full of mozzies –'

'It was a bloody funny engine and all. A ship of 1,600 tons gross and 2,850 tons deadweight, I ain't telling you the word of a lie ... And then the bloody steam went into what you might call its second stage with a re-bloody-generated heat less than 500 degrees superheat of the boiler bloody steam –'

'– then I gets malaria bad and we had a lot of pilgrims on deck we was taking from Singapore to Jeddah and they was all dying and having children all over the bloody place, eh; well, one chap, a young chap with a beard, had malaria too, bad, and slept on deck just outside my –'

'– saturated bloody steam with no super bloody heat in the bloody boiler, taken on the first and on the second bloody expansion, think of that, well she would have needed from thirteen tons to –'

'– put some gin in my quinine, this mate, eh. Well one day this Hadji outside gets very bad and he was groaning and that I couldn't get to sleep and I thought I was dying and this chap carries on with his groaning and cursing and that till just as I thought I was going to kick the bucket myself I shouted –'

'– exhaust steam drove a low power engine –'

'– die, you bastard, with all my strength, and *by Christ he did*!'

'– generate the bloody electricity which operates the regenerating super –'

'Christ, he did. I'm not telling you the word of a bloody lie either.'

'Soft runt, don't you see that the bloody electricity –'

'Oh, put a sock in it. We all know that you're the bloody man who stoked the ship all by himself.'

'Chinky firemen are the best anyway, cheap labour, you know. Those Annamite fellows are all right – give you all the samshaw you want for a little soap. Spit, my golly! Oh well, I reckon all rice-eating people are great spitters –'

'– story about a Chink fireman I heard and the English sailor at the Christian cemetery in Hong Kong. "Hey – you pig-tailed bastard," the Englishman says, "wot time your fliend comee up eatee chow chow, hey?" Chink replied, "Allee same time as your fliend comee up smellee bloody flowers." '

'Ha ha, well I reckon they're cute little fellers them Chinks, all the bloody same.'

'Nothing to touch white firemen. Look at our Skowegians.'

'Ah well. Ten months more of it boys – first hundred bloody years are the worst they say.'

Tin-tin.

'Boat to starboard, eh?'

'Yes, lots of boats in the coast, like this. Probably an old junk or something of that.'

'They're good sea boats, them China junks. Yis, I was in a typhoon once, in an empty ship, the *Peleus* it was. She was a proper old bastard, the *Peleus,* and no frige on her: an icebox, you know. And roll – by crimes we nearly rolled the sticks out of her going across the Western Ocean. The chief steward kept his room like a pigsty and smoked a tin of cigarettes a day – the dirty 'og! Well, we were in the Yeller Sea and a typhoon comes on and we was an empty ship and suddenly we see this old cow of a junk.'

'Well, that wot I said, wasn't it? you big twat.'

'If a cow had a wooden tit it would be funny, wouldn't it?'

'He he.'

'– a laundry boat, going round, picking up washing –'

'Talking about cows, all round the West Indies I been, Barbados, Bridgetown, that's hot stuff . . . All the grape trees coming down to the water's edge, you want to stay at the Colonial in the Milk Market there – nigger orchestra. The Marine's no good – that is, if you got money. I had. That was during the war. I tried the Marine, and the Balmoral. And then I went to the Colonial. I lived there for three weeks with a black cow . . . fighting drunk I was all the time and all the niggers playing "I'm forever blowing Bubbles" on their bloody banjos –'

'What's them red trees they 'ave there, flamboyant?'

'Flamboyant that's right, all those islands. Montserrat. There's a god-damned place for you, Plymouth Montserrat, a lot of niggers with Irish accents there and a hurricane blows the whole damn place down every year! Yes, I'm telling you the truth. I saw wot was left of their school – just the black-board, that's all –'

'– is that so? –'

'– is that so? –'

'Not much to look at Montserrat, black sand, eh?

'Yes, and there's a mountain there, a ruddy great mountain, and I climbed it and I had a guide who went up in bare feet, eh. It was the *hell* of a climb, like climbing up a tree all the way – ink trees and wild cabbages they were – and we kept stopping and his nigger guide'd say, "Catch yo' breeze, man! catch yo' breeze!"'

'Catch yo' *breeze*, man. Ha ha!'

'Oooooooo, eh?'

'Wild cabbage, yis! There was, growing at the top. And all the niggers go and throw pennies in the pond up there on Easter morning –'

'Niggers, caw they're funny blighters, aren't they? A rum lot.'

'– nigger I saw doing a shimmy dance once, singing! Ah'll shake ma shoulders, an' ah'll shake my *knees,* ah'm a free-born American an' ah'll shake what ah *please*!'

'– free-born American, eh? Ha ha ha ha.'

'Yes, ah'll shake what ah please is –'

'Perim in the Red Sea, they have red-headed niggers. I don't know if any of you fellers ever been ashore there. There's one pub, the Red Lion . . . And it's as flat as a flipper and bloody hot. We took a chap out there once to be a signalman. A funny chap he was and always trembling, dithering he was all the time, reckon he'd 'ad shell-shock or something of that . . . Lloyd's paid his first-class passage out, but he looked so damned awful they put 'im in a spare bunk in the fo'c'sle with the stewards and made 'im eat standing up, in the pantry. We called 'im Perim –'

'– lef' foot follow right foot and right foot follow lef' foot: remember, feet, when I was a chile yer promised to be kind to me!'

'He he he he . . .'

'Ssssh!'

> *'And if the river were whisky*
> *And ah was a duck,*
> *Ah'd go down to the* BOTTERN
> *An ah'd never come up. No sir,*
> *Ah'd never come up.'*

'Fer Christ sake don't make such a –'

'Wash, his name was. I dunno why we called him Wash. Well, he must be sixty-five now. He'd been a slave. Yes, he'd been a slave. Well, this nigger called Wash was sitting on this First Mate, Dickinson his name was, a hot-tempered kind of man, sitting on him. Gawd, you can't 'elp but laugh. And Dickinson was shouting, trying to get up, you see, while Wash was carrying on with his work. Wash kept shouting down at Dickinson – he he – *hush yo' man, hush yo' man* . . . You can't help but laugh at these niggers!'

'That reminds me of the one about the –'

'Condensed milk? Where's the condensed milk, Hilliot? Oh, here it is. By gosh, the bosun'll chase you when he finds out you keep your hammer and scraper in –'

'Beaumont, yes. We tied up to the trees in the park there, why, it's only a spindle-head, that place, that's all it is, just a spindle-head. It was a bit of an event too, a ship coming there. And all the girls from the park came and dabbled their feet in the water. We had 'em up on the ship afterwards for a dance. We put an officer ashore there with rheumatism.'

'*Rheumatism*, ha ha, yes, you're right.'

'Oh well, malish, as the Arabians say –'

'– of the one about the two nigger winchmen in New Orleans, "Ah wish ah was rich." "An' why you wish yuh was rich?" – "Ah'd buy you." – "And what would yuh do with me?" "Ah'd put yuh in the *privy*." He he he, he'd have put 'im in the privy. You can't help but laugh, you can't help but laugh! –'

'Hot! My God, this is the hottest night this voyage –'

'Do you remember York? Six weeks we were there. Ruddy murder it was too. Had an AB spent all his port's draw buying a wireless –'

'Waal, he says ketch 'old of these – plenty of these where they come from –'

'Oor, you can buy cigars dirty cheap in Manila, boy.'

'Oorgawdblimey you should have seen him. Ruddy bull rope broke on the fo'c'sle head and – *he he* – he got it right here. Ruddy bosun gave 'im a dog's life.'

'Both mates were tight fore and aft. The lines were no damn good and they wouldn't hold over the dolphins. The second mate nearly *fell* off the ruddy docking bridge.'

'This feller I'm tellin' you about spent all his watch below fishing down one of the after ventilators with a heaving line. Well, you can't rightly blame him. My gawd, but it was a hungry ship. Vegetables mashed up with a lot of ship's biscuit for breakfast, a cupful of scouse for dinner, and a slab of Harriet Lane for tea –'

'The skipper was dancing up and down on the bridge shouting like hell. They tell me he lost his bonus.'

'Serve him bloody well right.'

'That's wot I says.'

'Manila, eh, reminds me of Cebu. That's the place for you, Hilliot, the town of ukeleles. We had a feller flogged his go-ashore suit for one. Why he never even learnt to *tune* the damn thing.'

'We went to Cebu on the *Plato*. We tied up to buoys just alongside the maternity hospital. The mozzies was awful –'

'Yes, and Swettenham was the hell of a place for the mozzies too. We 'ad a galley boy once, on the *Rhadamanthus* this was. Nancy little chip he was too and –'

'They say they dump the miscarriages in the ditch. Anyway, none of the crew would go swimming.'

'Now, as I was telling you about this hungry ship. We were carrying a cargo of Crosse and bloody Blackwell's plum puddings and tinned chickens and all sorts out East for the Christmas season. Ruddy murder it was to think of all that food under hatches and us poor twats forward eating Harriet Lane all the time –'

'Well, it's better being forward, mate, and have a proper fo'c'sle.'

'Yes, my ruddy oath.'

'Well, one night this fellow got a catch on the end of his heaving line and we helped him haul it up to the fo'c'sle. And it was a damned great box of – what do you think? Crosse and Blackwell's tin openers.'

'Cook'd 'ave a fine chance of me if he tried to get a steam cover off me – there I'm telling you!'

'Oh, you're all away to hell –'

'This mate's a bloody *man,* he's got me weighed up, like *that.*'

'I was on a ship once where they didn't have a fo'c'sle at all. Every man had a cabin to himself and hot and cold water. That was on a Russian windjammer. That was all right.'

'– I've been jewed up myself like that trying to get things out of the hold. I once pinched a five-pound packet of what I thought was Formosa tea from Kelung, only it turned out to be camphor!'

'– hottest day I've ever known, mate.'

'– the 'ottest day I've ever known, anywhere in the world, was in England, in Liverpool, on Queen Victoria's diamond jubilee. Jesus, it was hot. I lived in Cheapside then –'

'Basra's hotter than Dalny. I'm telling you that *Basra's – hotter – than – Dalny.*'

'But they're all hot, for Christ sake, these god-damned oil ports.'

'I suppose that's why Dalny's snowed up in the winter and I wouldn't call Baku hot, my ruddy oath.'

'Well, who the hell's ever been to Baku –'

'– climbed up the drainpipe, you know, when I got to the top I was in the *hell* of a state –'

'– sailor and fireman standing outside skunk's ruddy cage at ruddy zoo. Sailor sez he bets he can stand smell longer than fireman. Fireman sez, all right, then, bet you can't. We'll get in the cage and try, 'e sez –'

'Oh, I've heard that one, for Christ sake. And after a bit the skunk comes out.'

'Well, the chief steward says –'

'In the Black Sea, you twat –'

'Yes?'

'– well I'm telling you –'

'This other galley boy I'm telling you about fell down the bunker hatch. Yes, the potato locker was down there and

the third mate took the ladder away, God knows why! He fell
clean down all the way and burst open at the bottom like a
tomato!'

'– I remember I was on a boat once, an old Russian bastard
she was, never 'ad a coat of paint on 'er and she was carrying
a cargo of potted meats – *oh boy* – and tins of peas and things,
for Jesus sake. And the boat was as hungry as hell. Worse than
this packet she was giving us Harriet Lane.'

'I was on a mail boat last voyage.'

'– last voyage.'

'– mail boat –'

'– so I told 'im the truth like that the cat 'ad 'ad kittens in
the maid's bed so 'e said that looks bad, don't it. I was polishing
a tankard at the time.'

'Well the doc was going down at first in this bosun's chair
after this galley boy, so the lamptrimmer, a damn great Welsh
fellow he was, rises up and sez, doctor if you won't go down,
look you, I'll throw you down, whatever. He went down all right
after and was hauled up standing astride of the poor twat's
body. There was bowels all over the place.'

'– mickey –'

'– Norman –'

'– next job I had was a taxi driver down Barry way. That
was better than being behind the bar, oh yes, no good being a
bartender. And one day I saw an old woman, across the road,
vibratin' her umbrella at me.'

'Whew! Did you feel that? She's beginning to roll a bit.
Wallop! Did you hear that?'

'Let's go for a swim on the well deck afterwards.'

'Run up on the poop and close that skylight, Hilliot. We'll
have a sea through here in a minute.'

'Yes, it's going to be rough, tonight. Thank God, some of
these mozzies will go, anyhow.'

'– story feller told me. So rough – that the log carried over
the aerial.'

'Yes, we've heard that one before.'

'Will you take down my washing, mate? It's on the docking
bridge.'

'This other Welshman I was tellin' you about he was a

tommy, this was in the war, and he was court-martialled for coming on parade without his rifle, and he says – speaking in a funny sort of accent, you know some fellers can do it but I can't – "It was not my fault the rifle got lost," 'e says. "I took it into the hut and left it in the corner and then the bugle went," he says, "and I left it there sure enough standing in the corner. The Sergeant told me to get into line to go on fatigue and just before he numbered us off I said, Sergeant, I have left my rifle in the hut and the Sergeant said, Go and get it man! So I went into the hut and there sure enough was my rifle standing in the corner – gone!"'

'Ha ha ha ha ha!'

'Oorgawdblimey, eh –'

'Gawdblimey, eh!'

'Now see what you've done, you've gone and woken up Matt. How are you doing there, Matt?'

'Well, you are a lot of poor fools, waking me up, but I reckon I would have woke up anyway, I've just had a bloody funny dream –'

'I knew a feller once had a dream –'

'– well, and then I got a job as a bartender again, and the next time I went in I says, " 'Ow do, 'ow are we, pleased to meet you, what's yours?" and she replies, "Well the old man doesn't let me drink behind the bar, you ought to know that," and soon after I meets her old man, and, of course, he offers me a cigarette –'

'I knew a feller –'

'Well, I said something of the same thing, you know, that time I was telling you about. "Hullo, Harold," I says. "I thought this was another pub, but I see now that it's only that I've come in by another door. I'm another customer now. This is the jug and bottle department."'

'*Ha ha ha ha ha!*'

'I'll tell you –'

'I'll tell you what this feller said to me.'

'*Hullo* – Taff, what are you doing here? This isn't the stewards' department –'

'He said to me, now listen, if this doesn't prove the ruddy world's wrong I'm a Dutchman. This chap says to me, *and lis-*

ten to this, I don't look crippled do I? No. But I'm more crippled than you think. I was discharged from the army a cripple,
yes, my right foot turned in, this here left arm useless, paralytic
– you've seen 'em mate, men like I was hanging round every
street corner, and you say poor devil to them –'

'Now I'll have to tell you the whole story again. First of all
'e says half of old milk, miss, and just put a little brandy in this
medicine bottle, will yer? Then –'

'I knew a feller who had a dream once –'

'Whew! this place smells of stewards!'

'Now, I could do that, see, and earn everybody's sympafy,
the sympafy of the world at large like. But I ain't never gone
round looking for sympafy. Not in the whole of my bloomin'
natural I ain't. I tell you it was by sheer, you know, strength of
will and the massagin' of my own brother –'

'I knew a feller –'

'Hello, we shouts, wot's that you got in that big basket,
Rufus? Shrimps, eh? Prawns? Scotch Leghorns! Scotch Leghorns, he shouts, penny a bang –'

'– and I say the army masseuses couldn't cure me. Couldn't
do *damn* all. But by my own strength of will and my brother's
massagin' I cured *myself,* see. Then they certified me as fit, and
stopped my pension, the bastards –'

'And all they did was to open the jails and say you're the
fourteenth ruddy regiment!'

'She couldn't breathe; couldn't do nothing. Musselled, she
was, proper –'

'Get out of here, she sez. You see it's like this. I've got a
lot of hungry footballers in the next saloon –'

'It's not often I have dreams, but I had a very funny one
this time. I suppose it must have been you fellows talking –'

'I knew a chap who had a dream –'

'Have you bloody well got to tell this bloody dream?'

'Shut up, what the hell?'

'Here, who threw that bloody shoe –?'

'Shut up. Matt's going to tell his dream.'

'What the hell, Matt.'

'Carry on, sergeant-major!'

'Well, it's nothing much, but I just dreamed I was living in

181

a house in Dale Street, Liverpool, forty bloody years ago, and everything was – you know – realistic like – Victorian, dress, walk, cabs, growlers – everything you could think on. Well, there were three rooms in this house: up – bedroom, middle – living room, bottom – kitchen. This house was haunted by somebody and I lived in it with my sister. Well one day we thought, my sister and I, that we'd lay this bloody ghost like, and on the stairs we met Lofty, the carpenter, the third engineer and young Hilliot here . . . When I saw him I smashed up a table with a kitchen chopper, and splintering off the wood, you know, went into Dale Street. There I met the ghost feller, you know, a chap that looked like a Solomon Islander. In one hand he held a bunch of wire and a pair of scales, in the other a belt, and despite the fact that his hands were pretty full – he was a head shorter than me – he held me in the hell of a bloody grip so that I couldn't move. I am not evil, he said several times, I am the god of seeing that things are done well. There is something wrong on the other –'

(Eyes I dare not meet in dreams, in death in dreams, in dreams in death, how the hell does it go? . . . Dream interpretations. Philosophers maintain that two and two make four. But every little doggie knows more. So-and-so said it was a mechanism, to keep you asleep. What the hell, anyway. Dreaming, when reading psychology, of climbing the Jungfrau. Getting lost in tunnels, tube stations, caves; many thousands. Coal mines with their wheels revolving; but no shafting, no mine, nothing to be mined; stigmata; eyes and exploding gas lamps, a fungus that sang, very sweetly, in a wood; pimps with silver in their wings. Never again. But what has this bloody sailor really got up his sleeve? . . . Nothing. It's a bore. Hell, I could make up a dream as good as this, couldn't I? Yes, but what? Jesus, what *can* I make up? But wait a minute. If those animals got loose, yes, just supposing, if the elephant got out he'd naturally smash all the other cages! Then they'd all be out. Then hell would be popping. God, how funny! How insupportably funny! Monkeys aft and amidships and up aloft. Tigers. The crew eaten. The mandrill at the wheel. When the pilot came on board he was surprised to find an elephant behind the dodger –)

'– so I took out my jackknife and cut the belt into four pieces.

All right, the ghost says then, let me cross the Dale Street tramlines. I won't haunt your house any more –'

'Wouldn't haunt your house any more, eh?'

'Well, I had a dream that knocks the bloody hell out of that. I dreamed that we got the tail end of a typhoon, and we were shipping seas fore and aft, and one bloody great sea came over and smashed the elephant's cage to smithereens. Well, you can imagine what happened. The elephant got out and took a bit of a turn on the deck –'

'What was that, Hilliot?'

'The elephant got out and took a bit of a turn on deck. And that put the breeze up the goddam skipper, because the keeper was sick. But that was nothing – when the skipper came up on the bridge again after seeing the keeper he found that the elephant was going round smashing up the cages; he'd already let out the lions and the tigers, and was beginning on the snakes –'

'Ha ha ha ha!'

'Ha ha –'

'But that was nothing to what happened then. The chief steward had lost the keys of the armoury, and when the skipper came on the bridge again, he found a lion just finishing off the quartermaster at the wheel. He looked round for some way of escape, saw the mate and two AB's being chased up the foremast by a lemur, and then jumped overboard, the stupid runt. For all we knew he was eaten by a bloody shark –'

'For God sake, it might happen too, we've only got to get a typhoon –'

'And then hell was let loose properly, and suddenly my dream switched on to the next morning. I was there somehow, but not another soul was. They'd all been eaten, sailors, firemen, officers, stewards, all the bloody crowd of you! There was a tiger on the bridge, anacondas spiralling down the ventilators, a hyena on the breadlocker –'

'Ha ha ha ha –'

'Ha ha ha ha – for God sake!'

'But that was nothing to the mess. You never saw such a bloody mess in your life – never. The remains of the crew were nothing to what the animals had done themselves. Well, you know what monkeys are. But imagine the lions' lordly leavings –'

'Hee hee hee!'

'And the parrot's household pigment strewn along the deck, or rather –'

'– for gosh sake –'

'Hell, I'll be sick laughing in a minute.'

'Who threw that shoe? Who threw that shoe?'

'Ha ha, for gosh sake –'

'And the walruses –'

'Shut up, for Christ sake! Shut up shut up!'

'– who threw –'

'The walrus's warm waffle –'

'Who threw that bloody shoe? I'll have your bloody life!'

'Bombs from bison's dung, eh? Ha ha ha!'

'– well, that's fair got me beat, I admit –'

'Come on, all right – if you're throwing shoes then –'

'– knew a chap who dreamed he saw the results of a race with jockeys of second and third. He backed and rightly, you know, as an unknown stable boy was the winning jockey. The jockeys two and three were put in the paper too. He won fifty pounds.'

'Christ, damn a man who throws bloody slippers –'

'– reminds me of a chap who fell down in New York on Forty-seventh Street. Afterwards they found out he was a famous jockey. Everybody thought he was proper stupefied drunk. Policeman picks him up! This man's not drunk, he says. What's your name? My name is Christopher Christ, the chap says. And I'm starving –'

'– who used to dream and he always knew he was going to have a fit when he heard in his ears, you know, the roaring of a train and a whistle. One day he disappeared and about three months later he was found drowned gripping tightly a silver-mounted walking stick given him by his lodge –'

'– paper boy, little chap. And he run with his bundle of papers all the way up this bloody great hill and when he got to the top he fell dead. Hymorrage. Blood came slowly out of his mouth, then quicker, then it slivered out like liver –'

'All right, he says. It's my own fault. I'm dead all right now.'

'Well, boys, who's going out on deck for a breather? There's a big freighter coming along to port. Anyone coming? It's cooler now. Roughening up a bit, too.'

'I'll come out later.'

(There is, as it were, a storm flood within, as my heart beats with the beating of the engine, as I go out with the ship towards the eternal summers. A storm is thundering out there, there is the glow of tropical fire! Bad, or good, as it happens to be, that is what it is to exist! . . . It is as though I have been silent and fuddled with sleep all my life. In spite of all, I know now that at least it is better to go always towards the summer, towards those burning seas of light; to sit at night in the forecastle lost in an unfamiliar dream, when the spirit becomes filled with stars, instead of wounds, and good and compassionate and tender. To sail into an unknown spring, or receive one's baptism on storm's promontory, where the solitary albatross heels over in the gale, and at last to come to land. To know the earth under one's foot and go, in wild delight, ways where there is water. Or a radiant, happy intoxication of fields and men and flowers and trees and horses . . . to return again over the ocean . . . The Suez Canal! All around is the desert save where a cluster of palms struggles in the noonday fire; the external stream, which once was lost but lived always in the dream of man. The anchor weighed, to be released, to glide slowly through the grey, sun-bleached land where the desert men kneel in still, confident peace, where the darkness draws in in a moment. Where the wild mysteries of the desert nights gleam in everything, in the sand garden's waste, in the palm's breath, in the starlight's cold, and in stars in motion on the dark stream. Then at last again to be outward bound, always outward, always onward, to be fighting always for the dreamt-of harbour, when the sea thunders on board in a cataract, and the ship rolls and wallows in the track of the frozen sea's storm –)

'Here; out of this! No firemen here!'

'I'm looking for Hilliot.'

'There he is.'

'Oh, hello, Nikolai!'

'Hello. Look here. Two of our crowd have gone sick. You've got to turn down below with the boys tomorrow – skipper's

185

orders! He said you were the only strong man on this side – but anyway, you're the youngest. The donkeyman's off too, so we're properly shorthanded.'

'What! In the stokehold!'

'Yes: you'll be a coaltrimmer now, a proper *limper* –'

'What! You don't mean that really, do you?'

'Sure enough, sonny. It's down the little hell for you. Plenty hard work –'

'Yes; but shall I be able to do it?'

'Sure: my God yes, you'll be all right. You're a high big plump peoples you knaw. And look here, if you talk to the chief, you may keep the job, because we're putting two of the boys ashore. You'll be in my watch for the time being – the eight to twelve.'

'That's great, Nikolai, that's great! My God, that's wonderful! Well: will you come and take a turn out on deck?'

'Sure. But don't be saying it's great till you've tried it.'

– courage: I'll help you where I can. It's your chance. The ship will only get you if you deserve it. Learn the meaning of the words, 'Blessed are the poor in spirit' –

'Hullo! Let's go then, Hilliot.'

– but fight! Nobody will see you when you are really brave. Remember –

'Hullo, let's go then, Hilliot! Aren't you coming?'

– Come unto me all ye that are heavy laden and I will give you rest. Take my yoke upon you and learn of me; for I am meek and lowly in heart; and ye shall find rest unto your souls. For my yoke is easy and my burden is light –

Utdrag av Kostreglement for den Norske handelsflaate. Anvisning for skibbrudne til bruken av livredningsrakatet appar Oedipus Tyrannus – Liverpool.

Tin.

'. . . here's a big cow coming along.'

'Foreigner of some sort, eh.'

'Foreigner yourself. She's a Norwegian, I'll bet.'

'Oh I didn't see you, Nicky; how are the girls?'

'You better ask the donkeyman that.'

'There she goes, she's morseing her name; *O, -x, -e, –*'

'*N, -s, -t, -j*, square-head name all right.'

'*E, -r*; fancy having to paint that fancy name on the life-belts, eh?'

'What's the matter with you, he sez, you looks as though you swallowed Pat Murphy's goat and the horns were sticking out of your arse.'

'It's the *Oxenstjerna*!'

'What, have you seen her before, eh Hilliot?'

'Yes; once or twice.'

'She's a cow, that ship. I was down below in her.'

But oh, Janet, no sorrow is so bad as that which quite goes by.

MORE ABOUT PENGUINS
AND PELICANS

Penguinews, which appears every month, contains details of all the new books issued by Penguins as they are published. From time to time it is supplemented by *Penguins in Print*, which is a complete list of all titles available. (There are some five thousand of these.)

A specimen copy of *Penguinews* will be sent to you free on request. For a year's issues (including the complete lists) please send 50p if you live in the British Isles, or 75p if you live elsewhere. Just write to Dept EP, Penguin Books Ltd, Harmondsworth, Middlesex, enclosing a cheque or postal order, and your name will be added to the mailing list.

In the U.S.A.: For a complete list of books available from Penguin in the United States write to Dept CS, Penguin Books Inc., 7110 Ambassador Road, Baltimore, Maryland 21207.

In Canada: For a complete list of books available from Penguin in Canada write to Penguin Books Canada Ltd, 41 Steelcase Road West, Markham, Ontario.

UNDER THE VOLCANO

Malcolm Lowry

It is the Day of Death, and a fiesta is in full swing. In the shadow of Popocatepetl ragged children beg coins to buy skulls made of chocolate ... and the ugly pariah dogs roam the streets. Geoffrey Firmin, H.M. ex-consul, is drowning himself in liquor and mescal, while his ex-wife and half-brother look on, powerless to help him. As the day wears on, it becomes apparent that Geoffrey must die. It is his only escape from a world he cannot understand.

'If there is morbidity here, it is akin to that of Elizabethan tragedy ... he has created a character in whose individual struggle is reflected something of the larger agony of the human spirit' – *The Times Literary Supplement*

'Mr Lowry ... has written a genuinely tragic novel of great concentration and power' – *New Statesman*

Like most of the work of Lowry, who died in 1957 and has since become a literary legend, this book is in the main autobiographical.

JOSEPH CONRAD

'Conrad is among the very greatest novelists in the language – or any language' – F. R. Leavis in *The Great Tradition*

LORD JIM

The novel by which Conrad is most often remembered by perhaps a majority of readers, and the first considerable novel he wrote.

THE SECRET AGENT: *A Simple Tale*

Based on anarchist and terrorist activities in London, this novel has been described by Dr Leavis as 'indubitably a classic and a masterpiece'.

VICTORY: *An Island Tale*

In his critical biography of the author, Jocelyn Baines places this tragic story of the Malay Archipelago 'among Conrad's best novels'.

THE NIGGER OF THE NARCISSUS, TYPHOON *and Other Stories*

Conrad's first sea novel, together with 'Typhoon', 'Falk', 'Amy Foster', and 'Tomorrow'.

NOSTROMO: *A Tale of the Seaboard*

His story of revolution in South America, which Arnold Bennett regarded 'as one of the greatest novels of any age'.

UNDER WESTERN EYES

An atmosphere of ominous suspense hangs over this story of revolutionaries, set in Switzerland and Russia.

Not for sale in the U.S.A.